"Why don't we play rock, paper, scissors to decide if you stay or not? If I win, you have to leave."

"And if I win, you'll quit telling me to go." Keith's smile broadened. "If that's what you want, darlin', let's play."

Keith had been throwing rock, paper, scissors with Tillie since they were study buddies in high school. They'd played the game for a variety of reasons, whether they'd been friends or something more—for the last bar of chocolate in the school vending machine, for the last bronc ride of the day at rodeo camp or for one last dance before leaving the Buckboard, Clementine's one and only honky-tonk.

And almost every time they threw, the outcome went Tillie's way. Why? Because Tillie had a habit of closing her eyes when they played, while Keith kept his eyes open. That way, he had a split second to make a gesture guaranteed to please her.

And if he wanted to win, well...

"Game on," he said.

Dear Reader,

Weddings are supposed to be fairy tales come true. But most weddings I've been in or helped plan have been a behind-the-scenes hot mess. What better place to set a romance!

Keith is the best man in this wedding. But the groom—his foster brother—forced him out of their business, and they have yet to mend fences. Maid of honor Tillie used to be in love with Keith but hasn't talked to him since she rejected his unexpected marriage proposal. Can this destination wedding be a fairy tale with an unwelcome best man, a missing wedding dress and a bride having second thoughts?

I hope you come to love the cowboys and cowgirls of The Cowboy Academy series as much as I do. Happy reading!

Melinda

THE COWBOY'S
WEDDING PROPOSAL

MELINDA CURTIS

HEARTWARMING

ISBN-13: 978-1-335-05151-6

The Cowboy's Wedding Proposal

Copyright © 2025 by Melinda Wooten

Harlequin Enterprises ULC
22 Adelaide St. West, 41st Floor
Toronto, Ontario M5H 4E3, Canada
www.Harlequin.com

Printed in Lithuania

MIX
Paper | Supporting responsible forestry
FSC® C021394

Award-winning *USA TODAY* bestselling author **Melinda Curtis**, when not writing romance, can be found working on a fixer-upper she and her husband purchased in Oregon's Willamette Valley. Although this is the third home they've lived in and renovated (in three different states), it's not a job for the faint of heart. But it's been a good metaphor for book writing, as sometimes you have to tear things down to the bare bones to find the core beauty and potential. In between—and during—renovations, Melinda has written over forty books for Harlequin, including her Heartwarming book *Dandelion Wishes*, which is now a TV movie, *Love in Harmony Valley*, starring Amber Marshall.

Brenda Novak says *Season of Change* "found a place on my keeper shelf."

Books by Melinda Curtis

Harlequin Heartwarming

The Cowboy Academy

A Cowboy Worth Waiting For
A Cowboy's Fourth of July
A Cowboy Christmas Carol
A Cowboy for the Twins
The Rodeo Star's Reunion

The Blackwell Belles

A Cowboy Never Forgets

Visit the Author Profile page
at Harlequin.com for more titles.

To those who help make weddings come off—seemingly—without a hitch. I hope that afterward you can laugh about the mishaps and hijinks.

PROLOGUE

Friday, two weeks before the wedding

"YOU TOLD HIM you'd be his best man, Keith. You can't back out now."

At his foster mother's words, Keith Morgan removed his black cowboy hat and rubbed a hand over his aching head. It was nearly Valentine's Day, the date of the upcoming wedding where he'd promised to be best man, and it seemed like his head had been pounding since Christmas.

That's what betrayal did to a fella, he supposed. It left its mark.

In his case, a perpetual headache.

"You made Carter a promise, son. And he hasn't released you from it." His foster father was wise but also the king of understatement. "You can't back out as best man over one disagreement."

"One disagreement?" Keith blurted. "You make it sound like a trivial thing. Carter and Brad forced me out of our company!" Sunny Y'all, a venture they'd formed six years ago to bring to

market ranching inventions Keith imagined, Brad built and Carter sold. "They waited until a buyout offer came in and then…"

His head pounded harder and his throat clogged with emotion.

Keith put his hat back on and glanced around the Buffalo Diner in Clementine, Oklahoma, unable to summon even a hint of his characteristic easy-going smile. He took bittersweet note of the empty counter seats. Then his gaze shifted to the worn vinyl booths beneath the front windows, and the scarred white Formica tables. It was the same old Buffalo Diner…minus the one person he was used to being here with. The smattering of current customers had their heads bent over plates of food or inclined forward to hear what their dining companions had to say about the latest gossip, weather forecast or rodeo news.

This used to be Keith's hometown, but he didn't recognize many faces in the weekday breakfast crowd.

Maybe that's a good thing.

All of Clementine had probably heard the news of his business partners driving him out. They probably assumed Keith had done something wrong—lied, cheated, absconded with funds, sloppily crossed a much-needed *i* or dotted a deal-breaking *t*.

Whatever scale of error they attributed to him, Keith resented it.

It wasn't just his foster brothers' treachery that stung or that he'd not received an adequate reason for them to have forced him out. It was concern over how the rest of the world saw him.

Of course, that cowboy no one wanted would screw it up.

Keith returned his gaze to his foster parents—Frank and Mary Harrison, owners of the Done Roamin' Ranch. They were his only parents since he'd been orphaned over two decades ago. Now they were mostly retired. And mostly done fostering.

In their lifetimes, they'd built a successful rodeo stock company and put their positive imprint on dozens of unwanted teenage boys. Their faces bore the stamp of lives spent striving and thriving—laugh lines, frown lines, worry lines, love lines. The love lines were most apparent when they looked at one another.

A bit enviable, that.

They'd probably assumed that the hardest part about raising foster teens was a trifecta of making sure they were in school, channeling their energy in a positive direction and keeping them out of fights—including with each other. They probably hadn't known back then that parenting didn't end when the last of their foster sons received their high school diplomas.

Because here Keith was—*thirty-five*—and checking in with his parents when something wasn't right between him and his foster brothers, wanting the Harrisons to *hear* his side and *be on* his side, so that he'd feel justified in backing out as Carter's best man.

I should have remembered Mom and Dad don't take sides. Or hold grudges. Or often get annoyed with people...unlike me.

People could be a downright nuisance sometimes.

His gaze strayed toward the seats he'd used to occupy at the end of the counter before he caught himself.

That cowboy no one wanted...

Keith released a too-long-held breath. "So, what you're saying is that I should let bygones be bygones, no matter how deep the wound or financial cost. Just go to the wedding, stand next to Carter as his best man and alongside Brad as another groomsman, as if their poison-tipped knives weren't still in my back."

Knives he hadn't seen coming. Knives that cut deeper because he still didn't completely understand why he'd been targeted. Was it greed? Was it jealousy? He didn't know. He could only assume.

And he assumed the worst.

Keith stared at his parents, working hard to keep sarcasm from coloring his next words, "Oh... and you want me to smile the whole time."

His parents nodded. Granted, they looked sympathetic. But what they were asking...

I don't want to be the bigger man.

"It's how we raised you," Mom reminded him.

"It's the honorable thing to do," Dad said emphatically.

Keith nodded slowly. "And sometimes, the hardest thing to do is the most honorable."

How often did I hear those words growing up?

He blew out another breath.

Too many times to count.

Along with his parents' follow-up statement, "But if you can smile through it, you can face any hardship." Keith made a weak attempt at a smile.

I'm gonna need to work on that smile for the wedding.

His parents looked pleased with him. Proud even.

That's something, I suppose.

"We'll be at the wedding to support you," Dad promised. "All you boys."

"You, Carter and Brad," Mom clarified, reaching across the table to give Keith's hand a compassionate squeeze. "We're a family. Granted, some of us are stronger than others."

"And more honorable," Keith muttered, unable to blot out his bitterness completely.

Dad laid his hand over Mom's and Keith's joined ones. "But it's the strong, honorable folks who triumph in the end."

If only that were true.

CHAPTER ONE

Monday, five days before the wedding

"Hello and goodbye, Keith Morgan." Matilda Powell took the arm of her ex-boyfriend's jean jacket and hauled all six feet of brown-haired, blue-eyed cowboy away from the check-in desk at the Ambling Horse Prairie Resort.

The high-end dude ranch was an hour's drive west of Dallas, Texas, in the blustery prairie. But with its timber beams, shiny hardwood floors and twelve-foot wide, two-story tall, rock fireplace, it looked as if it had been plucked from an extravagant mountain ski resort in Colorado.

"Well, hello, darlin'." Keith planted his cowboy boots on those fancy wood planks and tipped back his black cowboy hat, taking in Tillie with tempting blue eyes while flashing that captivating smile of his.

To which I'm immune.

Or, perhaps, not totally…

A flutter in Tillie's stomach contradicted her

so-called immunity, the same way an occasional, nostalgic memory of Keith contradicted Tillie's statement to her friends that—*as a couple*—they were done and dusted.

And why wouldn't they be through? It had been six years since Tillie had turned down Keith's proposal of marriage. Six years since he'd walked out without hearing why she'd said no. And since that small word she'd uttered, he'd ghosted her.

That man and his foolish pride don't deserve to make my heart flutter.

Not even if his dark brown hair curled temptingly at the base of his neck.

Or if his smile had a mesmerizing, easy-going quality to it.

Or if his bright-eyed gaze held hers intensely, the way it used to before they kissed.

Tillie ground her boot heel into the hardwood.

No fluttering allowed!

As the maid of honor, it was Tillie's duty to make sure her cousin Reese's Valentine's Day wedding went off without a hitch. Growing up, she and Reese had been as close as sisters.

However, there was more at stake for Tillie at this wedding than just honor.

Last month, the father of the bride, Tillie's paternal uncle, had promised Tillie a job as his ranch manager if his daughter was happy by week's end. Included in his generous offer was a rent-free home located on his mega-producing cattle ranch. It meant more financial security for Tillie's small family than her grocery store manager job provided.

Coming from a less prosperous branch of the Powell family and now raising a daughter alone, Tillie valued financial security over all else.

Keith's smile flickered into her consciousness. Tillie looked away—*Immune!*

Two weeks ago, it had seemed as if the job Uncle Boone offered was hers. But the closer the wedding came, the more Reese's moods swung from ecstatic bride to frantic bridezilla.

Pleasing Reese and landing that job were the reasons Tillie had arrived a day before the rest of the wedding party. Nothing—*not even the man who'd refused to listen before walking out of her life six years ago*—was going to keep this wedding week from rolling smoothly toward the finish line.

Outside, a brown draft horse with a bell-studded harness pulled a black buggy with yellow wheels from beneath the timber-beamed portico. The covered carriage was filled with hotel guests and their luggage. Cars weren't allowed beyond the main lodge valet station. Guests were transported to the far-flung web of luxury cabins via a fleet of horses and buggies driven by cowboys wearing what looked like their Sunday best—brown checked shirt, black string tie and jeans, tan cowboy hat and silver-tipped brown boots.

Inside the main lodge, cowboys and cowgirls greeted guests in their matching Sunday best. In the plush bar to the left of the check-in desk, they made visitors fancy coffee and fancier adult beverages. They served guests meals in the restaurant to the right of the check-in desk and catered to their needs in the rear of the resort at the spa, or by the pool and hot tub. Not to mention the multitude of services available at the brand-spanking new wedding and horse barns.

All those "rhinestone" cowboys were eager to fulfill a guest's every need. Why did this one, *real-life* cowboy have to make Tillie's goals more challenging?

People can be a trial.

Tillie set her fists on her hips and her chin in the air. "You need to leave, Keith." And when he didn't budge, she added, "Are you going to be difficult?" Tillie knew the answer to that. "Of course, you're going to be difficult."

Keith always eschewed maps and rode his own trail, a trait he claimed helped him come up with ideas for solutions to everyday problems, a skill he'd turned into a vocation as an inventor.

Tillie tried again to give him the boot. This time with a harder edge in her voice. "You can't be here."

Keith placed a hand over his heart, staggering back as if hurt. "Darlin', I'm the *best man* at this wedding. I brought my own horse and everything."

Because the Ambling Horse Prairie Resort had luxury accommodations for horses, too, and some of the activities this week were horse-related.

Tillie shook her head. "You *were* the best man." To her maid of honor, a reunion she'd been dreading. "Calling the groom *a money-grubbing minion of the all-powerful dollar* pretty much bans you from the wedding, Keith."

"Now, Tillie." Keith worked that smile of his with more charm, worked his boots a little closer to hers, worked to find a weakness in her determination—all things he was good at, darn him. "Just because Carter and Brad forced me out of *our* successful start-up doesn't mean I don't want to follow through on my family obligations or that Carter doesn't want me to stand up with him at the altar. We've been best buds since before puberty. Of course, we're going to have spats. It's happened before. Don't mean nothin' long-term."

That grin...

That charmer's grin plowed over Tillie's best intentions of staying cool, churning the soil in its wake to ready the ground to start romance anew.

Nope. Not again. No way.

"You can't win me over with that good ol' boy act, Keith." Tillie pointed toward the entrance to the resort lobby. "You need to leave. Last I heard, you were on the *Do Not Allow Entry* list."

"Turns out I have a non-refundable reservation both at the resort and by Carter's side." Keith tsked, moving closer once more, making Tillie's heart erratically *ka-thump, ka-thump*. "And you might need to update yourself on the wedding loop because I *will* be standing with Carter this coming Saturday." He ran his hand down her arm. "You'll see."

Ka-thump. Ka-thump. Ka-thump.

That fickle heartbeat had Tillie quietly standing still when she should have been loudly snapping back and pushing Keith away.

Ka-thump. Ka-thump.

That fickle heartbeat had blood buzzing in Tillie's ears so she couldn't hear Keith's arguments. Instead, she stared at that tempting mouth of his and remembered how tenderly his arms could hold her.

Warning! Warning!

If only self-talk worked where Keith was concerned.

"I've forgiven Carter for forcing me out of my own company," Keith was saying.

Tillie blinked as Keith's words sank in to her attraction-befuddled brain. And she blinked again as she processed their meaning along with what she knew about Keith.

Ah, yes.

Tillie scoffed, placing her palm on that firm chest of his and giving it a shove. "You've never forgiven anyone in your life. And before you go arguing with me, Mr. Grudgemaster, I present Exhibit A." Tillie used the same hand that had touched his chest to gesture toward herself. *"Me."*

A perplexed look flashed across Keith's face, as if he'd never held a grudge against her in his life. But it was quickly replaced by his stock-in-trade smile, the one he'd greeted her with.

I am immune.

For the first time that afternoon, Tillie almost believed it.

"There's your mama, Shay." Gran entered the lobby with Tillie's daughter, blowing in on a brisk winter wind.

"Mama!" Grinning, four-and-a-half-year-old Shay broke into a tottering run that had her thick glasses slipping down her thin nose. She wore her favorite blue princess dress, green dinosaur leggings, a brown jacket, pink cowboy boots and a matching pink cowboy hat.

Shay had been born nearly ten weeks early and still struggled with health issues, a fact that influenced every choice Tillie made. Despite her physical setbacks, Shay had latched on to life and a bushel full of interests as if she knew deep down how tenuous life really was. The last thing Tillie wanted to do was censor her precious baby girl and her clothing choices. The world would judge her darling soon enough.

"Mama, I'm here!" Shay carried a miniature

yellow dump truck in one hand, and a tote bag filled with Holly Explorers cookies in the other, more proof of her varied interests.

Next week, something else would catch Shay's attention. Perhaps fairy godmothers or fireflies. More likely airplanes and astronauts. Whatever it was, Tillie would support it.

"This must be that little filly of yours I've heard so much about," Keith said from behind Tillie—*too close behind Tillie*. "Looks like she's a pistol, *just like her mama*." This last bit was whispered near Tillie's ear.

His breath skimmed over Tillie's skin and she imagined Keith's strong arms coming around to draw her close for a breath-stealing kiss.

Hoo-boy. Being immune to him is going to be harder than I thought.

Not that she planned to let him know that.

"Stuff the fake flattery, Keith," Tillie said over her shoulder before bending and swinging her daughter into her arms. "Hey, pumpkin. Did you and Gran make sure Bixby, Barbara and Jam got unloaded?" Shay's pony, Gran's mare, and Tillie's gelding. Keith wasn't the only one to bring his ride to the wedding.

"Yes, Mama." Shay nodded solemnly, tucking her chin to her chest and giving Keith a guarded once-over out of the corner of her eye.

That's right, baby. Don't you trust him. He'll break your heart.

Keith faced Tillie's toddler with a welcoming smile. "Howdy, sunshine. Is Bixby your pony?"

Shay gave another nod, still playing the shy girl, which was completely out of character for her.

"I bet he's a great pal," Keith told Shay.

Shay nodded, the beginnings of a smile appearing on her sweet face.

Tillie's chin thrust out. It wasn't fair that Keith was winning Shay over so easily.

"I thought I spotted a familiar mug." Gran moseyed up to join them on long, stork-like legs. Tillie's maternal grandmother wore faded blue jeans, a pink button-down shirt and a shearling coat. Her thin, short white hair looked like bowl-cut fringe attached to her straw cowboy hat. She lived with Tillie, exchanging babysitting for room and board. "I didn't expect to see you here, Keith."

"He was just leaving," Tillie said, feeling ornery—more at herself than at Keith. She knew better than to be swayed by his cowboy charm and down-home magnetism. And yet…

Tillie was afraid Keith was swaying her with his cowboy charm and down-home magnetism.

"The best man doesn't shirk his wedding duties, Til." Keith gave Gran a mighty bear hug. "Besides, I wouldn't have gotten to see my best gal if I hadn't come. It's been an age since I've seen you, Velma." He kissed Gran's cheek before releasing her. "How are you?"

Tillie refused to feel slighted at Gran being Keith's best girl.

"It has been an age, Keith." Gran studied Keith from hat to boots, a twinkle in her faded brown eyes. "And in that age, it's been one heart attack and retirement—*mine*—one marriage and divorce—*Tillie's*—and one bouncing baby girl—*Shay*. A lot has changed."

Too much for me to restart a romance with you, Tillie wanted to say, recalling how devastated she'd been when he'd abandoned ship and left before they had any closure.

"Look at this." Shay held out her toy dump truck for Keith's inspection.

And darn it if the cowboy didn't take that toy, admire it with just the right amount of enthusiasm, and then carefully return it to Shay, as if he knew exactly how to make Tillie's daughter adore him. And darn it again if Keith's way with Shay didn't make Tillie's defenses weaken.

Tillie frowned. Two *darn it*s were never a good sign where Keith was concerned. It meant he was getting the better of her.

"Keith, we haven't seen much of you around Clementine since you, Brad and Carter moved to Dallas." Gran was intent upon catching up with Keith. "I bet your folks at the Done Roamin' Ranch miss you."

"Not as much as you might think. I saw Frank

and Mary a little over a week ago in Clementine," Keith admitted, surprising Tillie.

Hurting her, too. *I can't have it both ways.*

She glanced toward the slick-looking cowboy behind the check-in desk, wishing she could sweet talk the man into giving Keith a room refund. If Keith stayed, he was going to upset the apple cart this week. She was as certain of that as she was that a fox loved chicken as a midnight snack.

"Who knows. I might be spending more time in Clementine this year." Keith flashed his pearly whites at Tillie as if she meant something to him, making her want to slug him.

Because six years ago, he'd gotten up from bended knee, snapped a blue velvet ring box shut on a sparkling little diamond and driven out of Clementine, Oklahoma, without looking back.

Not once.

Not even to hear why Tillie had turned down his proposal of marriage.

IT FIGURED THAT the first time Keith would feel like smiling since his world was turned upside down last December would be with the woman who'd upended his plans for the future six years ago.

What is wrong with me?

He wasn't interested in getting back together with Tillie, even if she was as pretty as the picture he'd found in his home office desk drawer a few weeks back and as spunky as his memories of her from their time together reminded him. But that didn't erase the pain of her rejection of his ring.

And yet...

Just the sight of her makes me feel...lighter.

Which made no sense. As an orphaned foster kid, a boy both sets of grandparents and an array of other relatives had declined to raise, Keith had developed a code of sorts. If he let someone in and they hurt him, he shut them out, locked the door and threw away the key. Life was less painful that way.

Tillie was the only woman he'd ever considered a best friend. The only woman he ever confessed his dreams to. The only woman to win over his well-guarded heart.

And then, she'd returned it. Used and broken.

Keith had no reason to look at Tillie and smile, no cause to flirt a little and test the boundaries between them.

But he couldn't seem to stop doing just that.

Why? Wasn't this week stressful enough without him being unable to stop mooning at Tillie as if his heart still yearned for her affection?

Seeking a reason to stop smiling, Keith took a good hard look at Tillie.

She had long blond hair and golden bangs framing those too-serious blue eyes. She was taller than average and on the skinny side, taking after her svelte, maternal grandmother. She wore blue jeans and a stylish, baby blue wool coat that had seen better days.

That's what a camera would capture.

And beyond that...

Tillie still had that confident air of authority about her. She'd excelled and advanced at every job she ever had—coffee barista to shift manager, waitress to restaurant manager, grocery flower department manager to grocery store manager.

Her gaze still rattled the guardrails around his heart, seeking attention, demanding connection, calling for a door to be opened and her heart to be let through to the place where it belonged.

Next to mine.

He shook his head. Tillie had passed on that deal.

Keith forced himself to continue his critical assessment, looking for an answer to the question: *Why does Tillie Powell still make me smile?*

Analytically, in the detriment column, Tillie was...

He drew a blank.

This was harder than he'd thought it'd be.

Keith tried again.

Besides her rejection years ago, Tillie wasn't romance material because...

He had no answer.

Keith pressed his lips together and stared harder at the woman he'd once blindly assumed was his forever love.

Tillie held her little daughter in her arms and

stood next to her grandmother. That most likely meant she was a good mama and that Velma was still Tillie's sidekick, which said a lot about Tillie's love for, and loyalty to, others, as did bride Reese picking Tillie as her maid of honor.

Nothing for Keith to be worried about there.

But Tillie wasn't without her flaws. She was…

Wow. Pinpointing a flaw in Tillie is hard.

Her wit and attitude seemed as sharp as ever. She hadn't given up trying to put Keith in his place when she thought he needed it.

You can't be here, she'd said. Briskly, sharply, annoyingly.

That's it! Tillie is too bossy.

Keith grinned. He had news for Tillie. He'd already checked in. He'd made a promise to stand up with Carter. He wasn't going anywhere until his obligation was fulfilled.

"About you hanging around for the wedding…" Tillie was saying with a sly smile, bringing Keith back to the present and triggering his guard. "Why don't we play rock, paper, scissors to decide if you stay or not? If I win, you have to leave."

"And if I win, you'll quit telling me to go." Keith's smile broadened. "If that's what you want, darlin', let's play."

Keith had been throwing rock, paper, scissors with Tillie since they were study-buddies in high school. They'd played the game for a variety of reasons, whether they'd been friends or something more—for the last bar of chocolate in the school vending machine, for the last bronc ride of the day at rodeo camp, or for one last dance before leaving the Buckboard, Clementine's honky tonk.

And almost every time they threw, the outcome favored Tillie. Why? Because Tillie had a habit of closing her eyes when they played, while Keith kept his eyes open. That way, he had a split second to make a gesture guaranteed to please her.

And if he wanted to win… Well…

Dear Tillie didn't stand a chance.

"Game on." Tillie set her colorfully dressed daughter down, still smiling confidently.

"Play me, Gran. Play me," little Shay cried, rushing to Velma and eagerly grabbing her hands. Her big, round glasses slid precariously low on her pert little nose.

Velma straightened them, an action made harder because Shay tilted her head to one side and seemed to be trying to look at Keith without looking at Keith.

"Are you ready?" Tillie asked Keith, facing him with her right fist cradled in the palm of her left hand.

"Bring it." Keith mimicked Tillie's stance, her smile, her attitude that a win was all but assured.

But this time, I'm not going to let her have her way.

Tillie closed her eyes, jutted her stubborn chin, and started them off with, "Ready and…"

"Rock, paper, scissors, shoot!" they all cried at the same time.

Eyes still closed, Tillie kept her hand fisted.

Cheating, Keith made his hand flat, like paper.

Tillie opened her eyes.

"Paper covers rock. I win." Keith laid his hand over Tillie's fist, bursting with pleasure at having bested her. He hadn't had any wins lately. "Debate over. I'm staying."

"Me, too," Shay cried, dancing around Velma. She'd thrown a rock to her great-grandmother's scissors. "What do I win, Gran?"

"A hug." Velma bent and gave Shay an enthusiastic squeeze that had both laughing.

"You won," Tillie said softly to Keith, looking a bit awestruck. "You never used to win."

"I *seldom* used to win," Keith corrected her. "That must be a sign that I'm meant to be here."

Tillie nodded, brow furrowed.

Outside the grand entrance to the resort, a distinct clip-clop and soft jingle of bells heralded the arrival of another horse and wagon.

The cowboy concierge near the entrance glanced toward Tillie and her family. "Should I hold the wagon? Have you checked in, miss?"

"Not yet." Keith took gentle hold of Tillie's arm and led her to the front desk. "She needs to."

"Right." Tillie seemed to recover a bit of her characteristic bluster. "Just…promise me you won't start a fight or upset anyone by bringing up the past."

Keith promised her no such thing. How could he? He had no idea how he was going to be received by Carter and Brad when they arrived tomorrow.

"No promise?" Tillie muttered, tugging her arm free and marching up to the check-in clerk, dismissing Keith with her pretty nose in the air. "I thought so."

Keith bit back an apology.

If I'm going to salvage anything with Carter and Brad, I'll have to say something,

That thought brought back his headache. He rubbed one temple, turning his thoughts to more time-filling pursuits. Keith could grab a latte or a beer at the swanky bar, head over to the barn, saddle up Sable and go for a ride, or seek out the silence of his cabin and his blank idea notebook. Anything would be better than standing around pining for Tillie.

But Keith did so nonetheless, smiling as if he wasn't being torn up inside from long-buried contradictory feelings of betrayal (over Tillie's rejection) and longing (for Tillie's company).

"You were never this quiet when you dated Tillie." Velma came to stand beside Keith while Tillie checked them in. "You're either occupied with some new invention or…" she tsked "…you're thinking about the past."

Keith draped his arm over the elderly woman's thin shoulders. "You're right. I've got an idea for a new product banging around my head." That was a lie. His creativity had been stifled when Carter and Brad handed him his walking papers on Christmas Eve.

There'd been no ho-ho-ho that night.

At the check-in desk, Tillie's little ray of sunshine peeked around her mama's jeans clad leg to stare at Keith through those big, oval glasses, turning her head this way and that as if trying to find the right angle to study him.

Shay's vision must be poor. Keith had ring stains on his coffee table that were smaller than her large lenses.

Keith smiled and waved back at the cute tyke.

His overture emboldened Shay. "Wanna buy some cookies?" The little girl stepped forward, holding open a large, brown cloth tote bag that held several neatly stacked boxes of cookies. And then she smiled up at Keith with such pure innocence as she told him a price that Keith couldn't refuse.

"Give me a box of those chocolate striped ones." He whipped out his wallet. "Aren't you a little young to be a trooper?"

"She's getting an early start at being an entrepreneur." Velma glowed with pride.

Be careful who you trust in business, kid.

Shay took Keith's money and gave him a cookie

box. Then she danced around in a circle, arms raised, the train of her blue princess dress following her regally. "I sold some *coo-kies*. I sold some *coo-kies*."

Keith chuckled.

"Good job, pumpkin," Tillie told her daughter, still facing the check-in clerk. "Make sure you say thank-you."

"Thank you." Shay ran to Keith, flung her arms around his legs and squeezed tight. Then she lifted her face and stared up at him in that roving way of hers with adoring, bright blue eyes. And…

Keith was smitten.

His smile broadened. His headache receded.

The cookie-selling, cowgirl princess danced away, leaving an empty space inside Keith that had him thinking about mortgages and puppies and picket fences. With Tillie. With Shay. And with Velma as the cherry on top.

Ridiculous.

The headache pounded back, sharper than before.

Velma nudged Keith with her elbow. "Do you know what I miss about you?"

"My quick wit? My ready smile?" *My coming over for Sunday dinner with Tillie?* He missed that, too.

The old woman chuckled. "I miss the way you could rile Tillie."

"Best not let her hear that." Or she'd start in on

another round of him needing to leave, suggesting they throw rock, paper, scissors for the best two-out-of-three.

Velma gently elbowed him once more. "After you left town, I told Tillie not to marry that Wheeler boy. He was too agreeable about everything, from what Tillie wanted to what his ranch boss asked him to do. Never had an opinion on anything, from what to have for dinner to what he wanted to do with his life. In the end, his indifference nearly drove Tillie round the bend."

"And yet, she married him." Keith frowned. That hurt more to say out loud than he'd thought it would.

Unbidden, he recalled how hard the ground had been beneath his knee after he'd proposed to her and realized she wasn't going to say yes.

"Neil was her rebound. You don't marry your rebound." Velma sighed, stepping out from his embrace when Tillie was given her check-in receipt. "But would she listen to me? Nope. She had to do it. And Tillie must have known deep down it wasn't going to last because she never legally took his name." Velma tsked. "And just so you know… I. Blame. You." Velma poked his shoulder three times to emphasize those last three words.

"You blame me?" Keith scoffed. "Tillie turned *me* down."

"I wasn't witness to that proposal of yours. But it frightened her in a way I can't explain," Velma countered, frowning slightly. "You shouldn't have run off after just one try. Love doesn't always bloom on the first day of spring, even if it's a once-in-a-lifetime love." And with that, Velma followed Tillie and little Shay toward the lobby exit and the portico where a horse and buggy waited to take them and their luggage to their cabin.

Keith watched them go, memories of the past rising reluctantly to the forefront of his brain, like the first time he remembered noticing Tillie...

She'd put her head down on her desk in math class every time homework or test papers were handed back. She'd hunch her shoulders, trying to look invisible any time the math teacher asked for someone to work through a problem on the board. But in language arts...she'd smiled and held her head high when papers were returned, volunteering answers. Such an interesting contradiction. It had struck him then that they were opposites and could help each other. He was terrible at language arts. She was terrible at math.

And so, he'd made his first proposal to Tillie— study pals. And she'd accepted.

While they worked together, he'd discovered Tillie's sense of humor and her willingness to experience new things. She hadn't hesitated in agreeing to play Peter Pan for their homecoming float one year, even if it meant she'd be hoisted above a truck bed on a tether Keith rigged for the thirty minute parade. She'd gamely gotten on board the boat he'd constructed from two-by-fours and a large sheet of canvas for its maiden voyage in the Done Roamin' Ranch's pond. She'd even tried his "new and improved" hair straightener, the one he'd rigged from a rebuilt travel iron, one meant for ironing clothes.

Most things he built and she tried were a success.

But he could still recall the smell of burnt hair and see Tillie's horrified expression after she tried his hair straightener. To her credit, Tillie hadn't ended their friendship or teased him endlessly about that particular fail. Instead, she'd cut six inches off her hair and never spoken of it again.

He'd loved her then. As a friend.

Keith hadn't thought about Tillie romantically until he'd returned to Clementine after college and a six-year stretch where he, Brad and Carter had barely sold enough inventions to keep a roof over their heads. He'd bumped into Tillie at Clementine Coffee Roasters one morning when they were both intent upon getting a latte. The milk steamer had been broken and the lone, inexperienced employee hadn't known what to do. So, they'd walked over to the Buffalo Diner to grab a cup of coffee, taken the last two seats at the end of the counter and talked as if they hadn't been apart for nearly a decade.

It was then...while Tillie was sipping her coffee, occasionally brushing blond bangs from her frank blue eyes and smiling at Keith, that he'd been struck by the impulse to kiss her.

The same impulse had smacked into him again today, along with a bittersweet feeling of melancholy. Had he missed an opportunity?

Love doesn't always bloom on the first day of spring, even if it's a once-in-a-lifetime love.

True love took time, he thought Velma meant.

What he'd had with Tillie back then had felt real. Real enough to propose. But…

Keith shook his head, trying to shake off regret and what-ifs. Because no matter how he and Tillie had felt about each other, the past was in the past. He'd closed that door.

The same way he would with Carter and Brad when this wedding was through.

CHAPTER TWO

"WELCOME TO THE Ambling Horse Prairie Resort." The elderly buggy driver greeted Tillie and her family once they were seated in one of the resort's fancy, covered wagons. Then he set his draft horse into a walk, taking them from under the resort's big-timbered portico and toward the winding, single lane road that led to the guest cabins.

Bells jingled with every step the draft horse took.

"Did you bring a horse?" their driver asked.

"I brought Bixby." Shay bounced in her seat excitedly, sitting between Gran and Tillie. "He's a short horse but tall enough for me."

"Bixby is a pony, I'm guessing," their driver said, scratching the white whiskers on his chin as they passed beneath a spreading oak tree. Like other employees at the resort, he looked like a theme park cowboy in his un-scuffed boots and pressed brown-checked button-down. He tipped his tan cowboy hat back. "My name is Smidge. And this big fella pulling us today is Hercules.

You can always tell it's him coming because his harness has bigger bells than the other rig."

"Hercules sounds like he's pulling Santa's sleigh." Shay continued to bounce on the seat.

"And you're acting like a present in Santa's sack." Gran chuckled. "A jack-in-the-box, to be precise."

Shay stopped bouncing long enough to tip her head at an odd angle and give Gran an incredulous look. "A what?"

"We met last year, Smidge," Tillie said while Gran explained what toy she'd likened Shay to, and while Tillie tried to shed the residual, nostalgic funk over seeing Keith again, over being unable to shoo him away, of being torn that he was staying.

She shrugged deeper in her coat as a chill wind swept past, teasing the ends of her blond hair, the way proximity to Keith teased at her long-buried love for him.

That's all I'm feeling. Memories.

Tillie curled her toes in her cowboy boots. This was a test. A test she'd pass.

Everyone had a love they'd handle differently if given a second chance. Didn't mean Tillie had to give her feelings for Keith a second go-round. Her little family needed someone to stick around, through thick and thin, someone who wouldn't drain their financial resources, the ones they needed for Shay's medical issues.

Tillie expelled a breath, resolved to live in the

present, rather than to second-guess the past. "Do you remember me, Smidge? I came with my cousin Reese for a bridal tour last winter. You gave us a ride around the property."

Smidge glanced at Tillie over his shoulder before returning his attention to the narrow, paved road that twisted through the grounds. "I thought you had a familiar look to you. We've upgraded our wagons since then."

"This one is longer and grander than what I rode in before." Tillie studied the carriage with an eye toward things Reese would be pleased with.

The wagon had three rows of black leather, tufted seats for passengers. It was wide enough to fit four adults across, able to carry twelve of the wedding party. It was covered with a green and white striped awning. As a bonus, the wagon was well-sprung, riding smoothly on yellow-spoked wheels.

"As you know, there are no cars allowed past the lodge." Smidge settled into what sounded like a spiel as he drove the rig around a corner, startling chickens who were crossing the road. "You can either walk to your cabin or wait for a horse and wagon to swing by. There are two of us on the loop from six in the morning until ten o'clock at night. It takes us about fifteen to twenty minutes to complete a loop."

Fifteen to twenty minutes…

That was how long it had taken Tillie and Keith to realize they wanted to be more than friends.

Do not think about Keith, coffee, or those counter seats at the Buffalo Diner!

Tillie squared her shoulders. Going soft on Keith meant risking the job that would make living up to her family responsibilities easier.

"Smidge, do you eat cookies?" Shay wasn't paying a lick of attention to their driver's speech. She held up a box of mint cookies. "I'm a Holly Explorer and it's cookie sale season." She told him how much the boxes were. "How many would you like?"

Tillie smiled. Hours of cookie sale rehearsals on the drive from Oklahoma had paid off. Shay came across as a young professional.

Smidge held his cowboy hat on by the crown as the wind swept past. They all did. "Best cookie for dipping in coffee is shortbread."

Gran chuckled as the gust ruffled her fringe of short white hair. "They should use that slogan on the box."

"I'll buy one shortbread if you have them, young miss."

Smidge instantly won a place in Tillie's heart.

"I sold some *coo-kies*." Shay's voice twined with the jingling bells. She squirmed happily in her seat between Gran and Tillie, doing her sale dance from the waist up, arms waving and body moving so much that her glasses slid down her nose. "I sold some *coo-kies*."

Tillie righted her daughter's glasses, making a mental note to tighten them up again when they got home.

"This is the stop for the horse barn." Smidge gestured to the left where a sturdy bench sat at the base of a winding path, one that disappeared through the hedges and up the hill. A huge barn was set above them on a ridge, bordered by oak trees. "There's a bench in front of every stop—horse barn, wedding barn, pool—and every group of four cabins. Sit at a bench and we'll be by to give you a ride in no time."

Hercules jingled his way around a corner and up a slight rise.

"Where does that track go?" Gran pointed to a narrow trail leading down the hill between two cabins, where a small burro snacked on tufts of wild grass.

Smidge barely turned his head to look at the trail as they passed by. "You'll see those tracks all around the ranch. Our free range livestock make shortcuts, including our pair of burros. We recommend paying guests stick to the paved paths. Can't guarantee a track won't have a gopher hole."

"Nobody likes gopher holes but gophers," Gran observed.

"And snakes," Tillie added, to which Shay gasped.

But she recovered quickly. "What's the burro's name? Can I ride him?" Shay craned her neck to keep her eye on it, angling her head awkwardly to one side. "He's Bixby-size."

"That's Butler. But we'd prefer you ride Bixby," Smidge said with the patience of an experienced grandpa. "The free range stock haven't been saddle broke."

"That means no," Tillie explained to her daughter, to which Shay pouted.

As they trundled along, Gran pointed to another flock of chickens foraging beneath a bush. "Is there a lot of free range stock here?"

"Yep." Smidge nodded briskly. "The owners like the atmosphere of a homey ranch."

"Peacock!" Shay cried. She stood and pointed up the hill. "Mama, a peacock!"

"I'm proud of you for spotting that." Tillie gently brought Shay back down to the seat, noting the beautiful bird on the rise. "I didn't see him but you did."

Shay glowed at Tillie's praise.

The male peacock had his feathers spread and was strutting toward a female. Another peacock shrieked from the branches of an unusually large oak tree.

Shay seemed mesmerized by the exotic bird. "Do you have flamingos, too? I love flamingos. They're pink. And they can balance on one leg." She tried to get to her feet, presumably to stand on one leg, but Tillie quickly planted a hand on her daughter's shoulder and kept her seated.

"No flamingos yet," Smidge said, disappointing Shay. "But you never know what will happen on the next sunrise, do you?"

That's for sure.

"I don't remember as many free ranging animals on my last visit." And Tillie wasn't certain Reese would approve. Her cousin wanted a sophisticated wedding. "Do the peacocks return to a coop or the horse barn at night?"

"Or do they just screech from whatever tree they're in regardless of their location or time of day?" Gran picked up on Tillie's train of thought. "I'm hard of hearing but that squawk might startle me out of a good night's sleep."

Tillie nodded. "We'll want the peacocks to be as far away from the bride's cabin and the wedding barn as possible."

"They go where they go. We haven't had anyone complain yet." Smidge brushed aside their concerns as he guided Hercules around another corner. "Now, about where your cabin is located." Their driver took on the tone of a man on a mission to redirect guest attention in a more positive vein. "You ladies are lucky that you're close to the pool. In fact, there's a paved path between cabins eleven and twelve that you can take you right to the water's edge."

"It might be luckier if it was warm enough to swim." Gran was riding a sour horse now, probably put off by that shrieking peacock. She operated best on forty winks of undisturbed sleep.

Smidge made a poor attempt at a rich laugh. "The pool is heated, as is the hot tub, and there are heaters spread around the pool deck."

"That's a lot of heat," Gran murmured, shooting a speculative look at Tillie. "Maybe you could rekindle some heat with Keith."

SOON AFTER TILLIE left him, Keith followed a burro down the hill from the resort lodge.

The burro followed no path or trail, per se, simply plodding along a slight indentation of yellow grass to indicate someone—or something—had taken this way before. It was an almost trail.

Almost.

That was a fine metaphor for Keith's life. He'd almost been married. Almost been a success story. Almost been blessed with a loving, trustworthy pair of brothers after his parents died.

I feel a headache coming on.

The burro led Keith over a small rise and through a stand of oak trees before stopping at a tall, deep, A-frame structure with a wide, open garage door. The building was filled with workbenches and crowded with tools and machinery. From what Keith could see, there were several different types of table saws, a standing drill and a large lathe. There were odds and ends stacked against or hanging from the back wall—pieces of wood and metal, a shovel and pickax, lengths of rope and chain.

"Hello, Padre." An elderly man wearing faded overalls beneath a tan, grungy coat greeted the burro. And then he noticed Keith. "Howdy." He tipped his straw cowboy hat in greeting. "Can I help you find your way back where you belong?"

"Sure. At this point in my life, I'll accept advice and wisdom from anyone." Keith purposefully misunderstood the man's question. This was clearly the old cowboy's man cave and unlike Padre the burro, Keith wasn't welcome.

"You're looking for advice?" The old man produced a small carrot from his pocket and fed it to the burro. Given the remote location of the A-frame and his prickly attitude, he was probably someone who didn't like being disturbed. "Well, Padre here would advise you to keep going. If you followed this fine fellow here, you probably noticed how he kept on moving forward. And if you stay here any length of time, you'll notice he doesn't stay long anywhere. This little burro takes happiness—*and carrots*—wherever he can find them."

"And you?" Keith asked. "What life altering words of wisdom would you give me?"

"To help you get you back where you belong?" The elderly cowboy tsked. "First, I'd ask you if where you came from is really where you *want* to belong. No sense going back if it didn't bring you joy."

Keith was stunned into silence.

Was I happy working at Sunny Y'all?

Nope. Not that last year. Not after the buy-out offer from Durant Ranch Products came in, a contract that was estimated to take months to close, and still hadn't. Each detail from both sides was inspected by lawyers, management and the board. That inspection had led to more negotiation meetings, more contract revisions, more reviews. A seemingly endless cycle.

After that initial offer, everyone became so serious…so…so…self-conscious of every decision they made, from ordering paper clips for the office to requisitioning metal rings for production.

But it hadn't been happiness Keith had been searching for as an inventor. He'd wanted validation that the things he created had value… That *he* had value.

"Second," the elderly man continued, still with a touchy tone and get-a-move-on stare. "I'd advise you to find that one person who makes you feel like home is where they are, regardless of your location on a map."

Tillie…

Just the thought of her had Keith wanting to smile again, confound it all.

I'm not repeating that mistake.

"Now you're getting it," the old man told him,

rubbing a hand over his sharp chin. "Don't mean to be anti-social. But this is the resort's fix-it shop, not a playground. You've gotten your advice, now shake a leg." He waved Keith off.

"A fix-it shop?" Keith's interest was piqued. While the burro meandered around the side of the building, Keith moved closer to the A-frame's entrance. "What do you work on out here?"

"Anything that's broken. And any vision my wife dreams up." The old man made a broad gesture Keith assumed was meant to encapsulate the entire dude ranch. "She came up with the idea to turn our cattle ranch into this place when our kids showed no interest in keeping it running. She's the one who can't stop rescuing animals. And she's the one who is determined to make this more like a small community than a hotel. As for her latest idea…" He rested his hand atop a weather-worn, wooden water wheel that was a foot taller than he was. "She thinks this would be a great feature in the resort's wedding barn. And not just for atmosphere. She wants each set of spokes to hold a tray of cookies, chocolates, desserts or whatever."

Keith was definitely intrigued now, mind working toward what would need to be done to bring that vision to life. "You'll want each tray to stay parallel to the floor no matter where they are in the wheel rotation."

"I…" The old man bumped his hat brim up, as

if needing a bigger panorama to take Keith in. "That has been a challenge."

"Have you considered making a new one?" Keith poked at a wooden spoke that was more gray than brown on one end. A few dried out splinters fell to the ground. "If this was a working water wheel once, key parts of the structure might have disintegrated."

"The thought had crossed my mind but my missus is keen on upcycling. That is, making the old useful again. Like me." He smiled more genuinely at Keith. "I'm useful out here. My name's Woodburn. Do you putter?"

"I'm Keith." He smiled. "And yes, I've been known to tinker around. My parents had a little ranch before they died. Ranches always require creative fixes to equipment. And..." Keith decided not to tell the man he was an unemployed inventor. "That's how I got the bug. Are you going to make that wheel rotate with a motor?"

"You're thinking like my wife now." Woodburn chuckled, wrinkles working into a friendly spread. "I proposed hand rotation."

"It'd be a show-stopper if it continuously moved." Keith bet Tillie would appreciate it. But bride Reese? Not likely. Not anymore. It wasn't fancy enough. "What will the trays be made of? They could use some bling."

Woodburn chuckled. "My wife would like you. Not that I'm planning an introduction. You and she might build off each other's ideas and I've already got more projects than I can finish." He waved a hand again, this time to encompass the entire shop.

"You're complaining?" Keith liked the old man. He'd probably like Woodburn's wife, too. "We both know it's the tricky projects that make getting out of bed in the morning worthwhile."

"And going to sleep difficult." The old man tapped his temple. "A busy brain doesn't like to shut off."

"I couldn't agree more." Keith glanced around, taking in the workshop again, this time with an eye for the projects Woodburn had in the works—a rusty garden gate, a wheelbarrow with a broken handle, an old oil barrel, an antique cash register, and a dozen other parts and pieces of things Keith couldn't identify. "You've got a variety of items to repurpose."

"Yep." Woodburn hooked his thumbs in the straps of his faded overalls. "I fix. I fine tune. And I upcycle. Are you here with the Lonely Hearts? That Dallas singles club stays here every February. Nice bunch of folks looking for love. We get quite a few wedding bookings from their event each year." The old man gave Keith an expectant look.

"No. I'm not with the singles club. I'm the best man at a wedding." Reminded of his troubles, Keith removed his cowboy hat and ran a hand through his hair. "I'd much rather be down here puttering with you though." He set his hat back on his head.

Woodburn considered him a moment before smacking his lips. "I could use a hand getting this wheel presentable."

Keith poked at the disintegrating spoke once more, sending another sprinkle of wood splinters to the ground. "You could use a hand building a new one."

"Might be," Woodburn agreed, a friendly smile crossing his lined face. "I could use a little company, too. What's your greatest triumph, Keith? When my wife broke her leg inoculating cattle, I built an elevator in our first floor coat closet. It went straight up to our bedroom closet. Worked like a dream. And I didn't use a kit."

"I bet your wife appreciated that."

"Indeed, she did." The old man glowed with pride, resting his elbow on a workbench. "Now, tell me yours. You must have something to crow about."

"Well, I…" Keith lowered his voice because he hadn't even told Carter this idea. "I'm developing cooling boots for competitive horses." He warmed to his topic. "A horse's tendon heats up during a race or a rodeo, overheating to the point where cell damage occurs. Nowadays, folks put neoprene boots on their mounts to protect the front tendons from a rear hook strike. But that's like wrapping your ankle in plastic. It increases the heat in the leg."

Woodburn leaned forward, eagerness in his gaze. "And your fix is…"

"Simple. A sensor in the boot registers the temperature in the tendon and, if needed, activates a slim, chemical cooling pack. It's a simple fix using existing materials and technology."

The old man straightened, a look of surprise on his face. "You aren't just a putterer, Keith. You're a genius."

"Not hardly." Not if his closest pals could blindside him the way they had.

"No. You are." Woodburn took hold of Keith's hand and gave it a few good shakes. "I can replicate what others have made. But you… You're an inventor."

I was *an inventor.*

Past tense.

Keith didn't know where he was going from here.

CHAPTER THREE

"You ladies shouldn't joke about heat. True love happens at the Ambling Horse Prairie Resort. We're the chosen destination of the Dallas chapter of Lonely Hearts for a reason," Smidge said smoothly.

Tillie snorted. "We're not here to find love. We're here for a wedding."

Gran leaned forward, catching Tillie's eye. "But some of us wouldn't mind seeing others of us having a second chance at love."

"Do you mean you?" Shay asked Gran.

"She sure does," Tillie said quickly, giving Gran a reproachful look. "Wouldn't it be nice if Gran had a boyfriend?"

"Smidge, do you need a wife?" Shay hung her arms over the back of Smidge's seat and smiled sweetly at their driver. "Gran is a bad cook. But she knows all the words to Taylor Swift."

"Who?" Smidge asked at the same time that Gran cried, *"Shay!"*

"Look." Tillie shamelessly pointed at a flock of colorful hens running across the road. "Chickies!"

Shay was suitably distracted.

"And here we are." Smidge pulled the rig to a stop in front of a bench with the numbers 9-12 painted on the top rung in white. "Cabin twelve."

Tillie had seen a few of the attractive cabins last year, inside and out. But she still took a moment to appreciate their cozy facade. Each cabin was a tiny studio unit. Cabin Twelve was painted a light brown with teal trim and had a nice front porch edged with thick green hedges. Two white, wooden rockers invited guests to relax and watch time pass by. Other cabins were different colors—a deep redwood, a dark brown, a soft white or a cheerful yellow. The cabin next door had a narrow glider on the porch. The one across the road had a pair of Adirondack chairs.

There was a noise in the shrubbery in front of the cabin. And then a trio of baby goats—white, black and brown—leaped out, bouncing toward them as if their legs were springs.

"Goats!" Shay giggled, trying to climb over Tillie to reach them. "They're so cute. Can we take one home?"

"Sorry, cowgirl. This is where they live." Smidge looped the reins around a hook on the wagon front, and then hopped down from the buggy, spry for his age. "All the animals here are the resort's mascots. Permanent residents, like me. You can feed them if they stop by. You'll have a bowl on the counter of your kitchenette with a supply of carrots and bags of grain." Smidge lowered the buggy steps for his passengers.

"Goats don't eat cookies, do they?" Tillie climbed down, then turned to help Shay and Gran.

"Goats eat anything." Smidge grabbed two suitcases from the back and carried them up the walk toward the front porch. "And they're curious, too. I wouldn't leave your door open. They've been known to nibble on bedspreads, lipstick, purses, hair ties, remote controls…"

"What about bridal gowns?" Tillie murmured, not expecting the old man to hear.

But Smidge surprised her. "Just to be safe, I'd store your pretty things and cookies in the closet."

"Did you hear that, Shay? Better not let the goats get your cookie boxes," Gran advised, giving the bouncing goats a wide berth. She'd fallen last year and broken her hip. Since then, she was careful where she put her feet.

Shay didn't answer Gran. She was too busy bunny hopping with the baby goats, sending her blue dress swirling, her blond hair flying and Tillie's spirits soaring. Watching her sweet little girl, Tillie could imagine her growing up with the confidence and vision to take on the world.

And then, Shay hopped so joyfully and vigorously that her pink cowboy hat fell to the ground, along with her glasses.

Those glasses…

Coming back down to earth, Tillie snatched up

those glasses and checked for scratches. Shay's vision was severely compromised without them. Even with insurance, they'd cost Tillie a small fortune.

Thankfully, the lenses weren't damaged. Tillie breathed a sigh of relief.

Meanwhile, the white baby goat took Shay's pink hat brim in its mouth and then continued to bounce, now on a collision course with Shay.

"Hey!" Shay cried when struck, staggering and squinting.

Tillie grabbed her arm, steadying her.

The white goat landed on all four hooves, as agile as any competitive gymnast, but lost its grip on Shay's pink cowboy hat. It fell once more.

Tillie snatched up the hat and set if firmly on her daughter's head. "Baby goats may be cute, but they're still livestock. And what do we know about livestock, Shay?"

"I've got to be careful around livestock," Shay parroted, running toward the brown goat, who wasn't hopping. "Come here, baby. Let me pick you up."

"No, Shay," Tillie chastised, taking her daughter's hand and heading up the paved walk, towing Shay along. "That's *not* being careful."

"Mama," Shay protested, dragging her feet. "I want to hold them and cuddle them and love them, like they're my own."

"There's no harm in looking," Gran said from the porch, not much help.

"You can look at them all week. Let's get inside. Now." Tillie used her best parental obey-me tone. She hadn't counted on so many equilibrium-smashing surprises—Keith, baby goats and now an overly excited four-and-a-half-year-old.

"Dance with the goats at your own risk." Smidge had already opened the door to their cabin and returned to the fancy wagon to retrieve the rest of their luggage.

"That means no goat dances," Tillie explained to Shay, ascending the steps.

"But, Mama, they're so cute!" Shay dug in her heels on the porch steps, pulling her hand free and skipping joyfully back to the baby goats. "Look at them. Look!" Her laughter filled the air.

And Tillie did look. She stared long and hard, registering the sweet enthusiasm of her daughter's smile, the joy at her being able to see the goats spring about. And then Tillie snapped a few pictures with her phone for good measure.

Shay's glasses slipped down her nose.

Tillie extended an arm, as if she could catch them, as if she wasn't ten feet away.

But Shay shoved them back into place, for once.

Gran came out of the cabin and linked her arm with Tillie's. "That girl of ours is going to live a full life, whether we put guardrails on it or not."

"I know, but… Is it wrong to want those guard-rails?" Tillie wondered aloud.

"No matter what you try to do, she's going to see past them." Gran patted Tillie's hand before returning to the cabin.

With one last look at Shay and the goats, Tillie turned to follow her.

She knew the homey exterior of their cabin didn't give away the extravagance that waited inside. The door opened into a wide-planked wooden hallway. On one side was a closet and a large bathroom with both a white-tiled shower and a free-standing bathtub. The fixtures were gold. The countertops and flooring were black marble with white veining. On the other side of the hall-way was a small kitchenette with an intimidating-looking coffee machine and a yellow ceramic bowl filled with carrots and small bags of grain.

It wasn't anything like the budget motels Tillie chose to stay in on the rare occasions when she took time off.

But I could afford this type of lodging once a year if I make it successfully through this week.

"Look at the beautiful pool." Gran moved into the main part of the cabin, which had two queen beds with tan satin comforters and enough deco-rative pillows in a variety of colors to keep Shay busy building a pillow fort for an hour. Two small, gray barrel chairs sat in front of the windows over-looking the pool. "I can't believe so many people are out there poolside. Although I suppose it'd be harder to believe if they were wearing bikinis."

"The men or the women," Tillie teased.

"Both," Gran said, straight-faced.

"Those Lonely Hearts come every Valentine's week and they leave nothing on the table in their pursuit of love." Smidge deposited their remaining bags in a row along the kitchenette. "They've had two couples resign from the club already. I've never heard of an organization where the goal is to no longer be a member."

"I suppose you've got to kiss a lot of frogs nowadays until you find a prince," Gran allowed, still staring out the window.

"Mama, look at my goats." Shay ran into the cabin, pink boots clunking on hardwood. "They're following me."

Sure enough, those baby goats bounded inside, swarming around Shay's legs as if they were chicks and Shay was their much-adored mama hen.

"Shoo, babies." Smidge wasted no time herding the precocious goats out the door before turning back around and removing his tan cowboy hat, revealing a bald, sun-spotted head. "I'm sure the front desk told you the cabin doors only lock on the inside."

Gran chuckled, having turned away from the window to watch the goat drama. "I suppose this is the resort's nod to the Old West and today's small towns. We don't lock our doors in Clementine either."

Tillie always locked her doors but didn't think now was the time to point that out.

"Do you have any questions for me, ladies?" Smidge asked, hat still in hand.

"No, sir." Tillie tipped him in cash, some of which he made a show of giving to Shay for his box of cookies, sending her into another performance of her cookie dance.

"It'll take you about fifteen minutes to walk to the lodge from here." Smidge put his hat back on. "Dinner service begins at five. Bar closes at midnight."

They all bid him farewell.

Tillie glanced out the front door—not for a chance to glimpse Keith. And she wasn't disappointed when only Smidge and Hercules were visible. Further, she wasn't going to be looking for him the entire wedding week.

Right. She rolled her shoulders back. *I just need to keep telling myself that.*

"Mama, who is Keith?" Shay pressed her nose to the window facing the pool. "He's so big, he could eat lots of cookies. Boxes and boxes."

Gran chuckled. "Keith was your mama's one true—"

"Friend," Tillie cut her grandmother off, coming to look out the window, too—not to look for Keith at the pool. But she did notice he wasn't

there. "Keith and I used to be good friends in school. We hung out with the same crowd."

And when he'd returned to Clementine, they'd hung out together. Every day. For over a year. He'd gone back to work at the Done Roamin' Ranch, moving stock for their rodeo business while dreaming up ideas he, Carter and Brad tried to build and sell. For a time, he'd been her one and only.

Shay struggled to climb onto one of the slippery, satin-covered beds. Once on top, she removed her pink cowboy boots, letting them drop to the floor. "Tell me Keith's story," she demanded.

Recently, Shay had become fascinated with people they knew, wanting to hear everything about them—where they came from, how Tillie met them, stories about their presence in Tillie's life. And for the most part, Tillie had indulged her daughter's curiosity because she believed empathy for others was to be encouraged.

But that didn't mean Tillie wanted to share her history of Keith with her daughter.

Gran hung the garment bag with her and Shay's dresses for the wedding in the closet. Her straw cowboy hat went onto a hook by the door. "I'd like to hear Keith's story, too."

Keith's story?

Tillie didn't know what to say.

She could say she'd been surprised by the strength of her feelings for him. She could say he'd broken her heart when he left town. But she definitely wouldn't say he could still make her heart *ka-thump* with just a smile.

Tillie tossed her brown cowboy hat on a pillow, stalling. "Keith's story…"

"Mama…" Shay flung her pink cowboy hat onto one of the barrel chairs, then flopped back on the bed. "Tell me Keith's story."

"I want to hear it, too." Gran laid her suitcase on the empty bed across from Shay and unzipped it. "I'll let you in on a secret, Shay. Keith is one of my favorite cowboys in the whole wide world."

Shay gasped, sitting up. "Really and truly?"

"Really and truly." Gran nodded. She began transferring items from her suitcase to a small dresser. "He's a keeper."

Tillie gaped at her grandmother in disbelief. A man who wasn't willing to talk things out wasn't a keeper, no matter how feverishly he made her heart *ka-thump*.

"I have to hear Keith's story, Mama." Shay flopped back onto the bed and began making imaginary snow angels with her arms and legs. "'Cause he's a keeper."

There's no getting out of this.

"Okay. Um… Keith and I went to school together when we were kids." Tillie was determined to keep this story in the friend zone. They'd spent most of their lives there, after all. Being friends. Being friendly. Until the first press of his lips to hers. Until they both sighed afterward and said, *"Wow."*

In that moment, Tillie's heart had proclaimed him *The One*. The man who could make her feel safe— emotionally, physically, financially—and could make her heart *ka-thump* and would forevermore.

"We liked a lot of the same things." Riding. Rodeo. Hiking. Clementine. "We liked trying new things." His inventions. Fantastical food combinations and scary rides at the county fair. "And we both believed in working hard to secure our future."

"I witnessed this *friendship*." Gran carried her toiletry kit to the bathroom. "I was their language arts teacher in high school. They tended to like the same people."

And be annoyed by the same people as well— haters, fakers, backstabbers.

Had Carter and Brad stabbed Keith in the back? Tillie hadn't thought about Keith's departure from Sunny Y'all in those terms before.

"We helped each other academically." Tillie hefted her suitcase onto the bed Shay lay on. "We studied together." How comfortable they'd been around each other back then.

Would it be possible to return to that friendship? Would it be wise to try?

No.

Shay sat up, blond hair mussed in the back. "Was Keith your boyfriend in school? Did he kiss you?"

"No." Tillie's cheeks felt hot. "Keith was too

busy in school being...*busy*...to have a girlfriend. He was on every sports team and in every club, plus he worked part-time. He was always coming and going." Determined to earn a college scholarship somehow. He'd had more drive to succeed than Tillie had. And that was saying something.

Because Tillie was also driven to succeed. She didn't like having to count pennies and coming up short. She'd been determined to have a more stable life than her parents had provided. She didn't want to move to a smaller place or a sketchy part of town or a new town in the middle of the night when bills totaled more than rent. She didn't want to face the decision of whether to pay the rent or to keep the heat on or to put food on the table.

Her parents and brother had decided to leave Clementine the summer before Tillie started high school. She'd begged them to let her stay with Gran. Her brother, Dan, had told Tillie not to abandon them, while Gran had told her that sometimes you had to think of yourself.

Tillie had made her choice. Dan hadn't talked to her for a long time after that.

And since then, Tillie's family had continued to move west every year or so, whenever they dug themselves into a hole of debt. Currently, they were living in Beaver on the western side of Oklahoma, still barely getting by, and only exchanged calls on holidays and birthdays.

But Keith...

He could outwork a hamster on a wheel.

Had he worked his way out of his business with Brad and Carter? Was that even possible?

"I'm always coming and going, like Keith." Shay got to her stocking feet and bounced on the bed, slipping on the slick, tan satin and nearly falling off.

"None of that, pumpkin." Tillie hurried over to encourage Shay to sit back down. She smoothed Shay's hair and repositioned her wayward glasses. "Beds aren't for bouncing. You know the rules."

"I know what's fun." Shay curled into a ball, rolling side to side on the bed, wound up with baby goat excitement, no doubt. "Was Keith fun?"

Tillie nodded, smiling a little. "He was. And he was nice to everyone. He was voted most likely to succeed." Tillie frowned. How odd that it was Keith, the boy with the pie-in-the-sky imagination, who had been voted most likely to succeed rather than Carter, the boy who could sell bottled water to mermaids.

"I'm nice to everyone." Shay pulled the skirt of her blue princess dress up over her face, kicking her green dinosaur legging-clad legs like she was swimming. "And I'm good at everything."

"You're good at trying everything," Tillie allowed indulgently.

"Do you know what, Mama?" Shay finally came to rest, skirt still covering her face. "I'm going to sell the most cookies *ever.*"

"You give it your best shot, pumpkin." Tillie set about unpacking, glad that Shay was on to other things besides Keith, because the next part of his story was where they'd ventured past the friend zone.

Gran emerged from the bathroom, whispering to Tillie as she passed, "I saw what you did there—avoiding the real story about Keith."

Tillie ignored her comment.

Why wouldn't she? Tillie had been ignoring her history with Keith for six years.

There was no need to revisit it now.

"EVERYTHING'S GOING TO be just fine."

A muttered phrase caught Keith's attention, the woman sounded like she was sending up a quick prayer after discovering herself in a tight spot.

After helping Woodburn for an hour, he'd found a quiet corner in the resort's lobby with a latte and had been trying to enjoy the expansive vistas out the back window. But even the peaceful view of rolling hills couldn't ease the feeling in his gut that said he wasn't welcome here—not by his foster brothers or his ex—and that the idea for a wrap cooling equine tendons, the one Woodburn had praised, had little chance of seeing the light of day without the proper sales and manufacturing experience Carter and Brad possessed.

"Just fine," the mutterer continued.

Recognizing Tillie's voice, Keith turned, taking

in her ruffled blond hair beneath her brown cowboy hat and her furrowed brow beneath the brim.

"Are you worried, Til? Is there anything I can do?" The words were out before he could admonish himself into silence. Tillie's well-being was no longer his concern.

Tillie eased her cowboy hat back as if a decision had been made. "I've just finished a meeting with the person filling in for the resort wedding planner."

"Bad news?" Keith guessed.

Her frown deepened, almost to a scowl. "Probably not for you."

That scowl and sharp tone pierced Keith's composure, releasing a burst of frustration. "What's that supposed to mean?"

Tillie crossed her arms and planted her boots hip distance apart on the hardwood, unwittingly emphasizing those long legs of hers. And then she snapped, "Like you care that Reese won't get the flowers she had her heart set on."

Air exited Keith's lungs, seemingly without intention of returning because he wheezed, "You think I don't care? She's been my friend as long as you have."

"I… That was mean." Tillie rolled her eyes upward, rolled her head around, rolled her shoulders back. And all that rolling seemed to roll that frown completely away. "I'm sorry. It's just… I'm stressed. I told Reese I'd double-check on a few things before she arrived. Good thing I did, too. There was an ice storm in south Texas last week. The resort's flower supplier suffered damage to its hothouse and the calla lilies Reese chose for her bridal bouquet were destroyed. Unfortunately, that vibrant orange and yellow color is hard to find in a different flower."

"There's got to be another grower of calla lilies somewhere." Keith dug his phone from his pocket, intending to search for a florist.

"I appreciate your concern, Keith, but I have nursery contacts from Oklahoma that I'll reach out to later." Tillie made a weak gesture toward the bar. "I'm pressed for time. The bartender is expecting me for the final specialty drink taste testing. I was supposed to be there five minutes ago."

"Booze." Keith stood. "I'm in."

"I didn't… I wasn't… You aren't…" Tillie sighed, gathering her long blond hair, twisted it and rested it over one shoulder.

Keith wanted to run his hands through those thick, golden locks, tangling his fingers in the silky softness as he drew her closer for a—

"Come on, then, Keith." Tillie interrupted his wayward thoughts. "You'll tag along whether I want you to or not."

"Yep." Keith followed Tillie across the lobby, smiling because…

He didn't want to dwell on the whys.

He cleared his throat instead. "Did you arrive

early to ensure everything runs smoothly for the wedding?"

"Yes." Tillie waved to the bartender and took a seat at the bar. "Uncle Boone wants everything to go as planned. And if Reese is happy, he's going to hire me to be his ranch manager." She spoke briskly, like she was in charge and he, her underling, was only on a need-to-know basis when it came to the finer details. "I've held Reese's hand through the wedding planning for nearly a year, but only received Uncle Boone's job offer in January. And for a few weeks, I thought it was in the bag." She gave Keith a long-suffering look. "And then came you. You're going to ruffle feathers just by being here."

"Ah. You've got money on the line." Taking the bar stool next to Tillie, Keith gave her what he hoped was a reassuring look. "Is that why you're casting me as a villain?"

"Partly. Plus Uncle Boone mentioned you specifically when last we talked." Tillie smirked at Keith, not dimming her appeal to him in the slightest. "You can't blame my uncle. You and Carter had a falling out. The last thing Uncle Boone wants is your disagreement with the groom tumbling like a landslide over Reese's dream wedding."

Her uncle Boone had been an early investor in Sunny Y'all and now served on their board of directors. Keith had planned to talk to him face-to-face about the events of December, but Tillie's comment didn't bode well for that.

"Are you ready for a Gin Flower and a Whiskey Punch?" The bartender served them each two drinks over ice in crystal tumblers. One was a soft yellow color. The other was deep red.

"I'm ready for something." Keith took a whiff of the red liquid and then a sip. "Oh, that's good. The taste definitely delivers on whiskey."

"That's too strong," Tillie said in a coarse voice, accented with a cough. "We don't want the guests to be incapacitated after the reception."

The bartender checked his notes. "That's what the bride and groom requested."

"They approved the drinks without tasting based on the bar menu sent over." Tillie coughed again, blinking watery eyes. "The groom is more of a lightweight than I am."

The bartender looked doubtful.

"It's true," Keith confirmed. "Carter can't hold his liquor. Are there two shots of whiskey per punch glass? If so, one shot of whiskey will do it."

"Agreed." Tillie leaned over the counter to tap the sheet of paper with the wedding's bar order. "Can you make note of the change, please?"

The bartender nodded. "Will do." He scribbled something illegible on the paper. "What about the Gin Flower?"

Tillie and Keith sipped from their second tumblers.

The gin-based drink had less bite and met with Tillie's approval, even if it wasn't something Keith would ever order. Gin was his least favorite spirit. The bartender moved away, putting the sheet with his notes into a binder.

Some of the Lonely Hearts were in attendance, gathered at a large table near a small stage at the back of the bar. A sign indicated karaoke was available every night after ten.

All adult fun happens after ten o'clock, Tillie had once told him, arguing that they should stay at the Buckboard, Clementine's local honky tonk, and dance until the band stopped playing.

Keith had loved holding her in his arms. She'd been his person. The woman who understood his humor, his quiet moments, his drive to invent and thrive.

My arms are empty now.

They had been for far too long.

Keith raised his empty whiskey punch glass, catching the bartender's eye and silently requesting another.

Not that I need another drink...

Not that I need an excuse to linger with Tillie...

He lingered anyway, angling toward her, leaning his forearm on the bar, taking in the graceful lines of Tillie's neck and that mass of touchable blond hair resting over one shoulder while he swallowed his pride enough to ask, "Did Reese say anything about me?"

Tillie turned in her seat to face him, giving him a tiny smirk. "Are we in high school?"

Smooth, Keith. Real smooth.

"Let me rephrase." Keith backpedaled. "Did Reese say anything about what happened at Sunny Y'all before Christmas?"

"Besides what you called Carter? No." Tillie sipped the gin drink, expression giving nothing away. "I was told you left the company."

"That's it?" Keith swiveled his stool around to face Tillie head on. "Brad and Carter forced me out and all Reese had to say was that I *left*?"

The bartender set another whiskey punch on the bar and removed Keith's empty glass.

Keith took a generous sip. *Nice.* The bartender had made this one just as strong as his first.

Tillie peered at Keith in a way that implied the wheels in her head were turning double-time. "What did you do to Brad and Carter?"

"To them? *Nothing.*" The need for answers pressed upon the back of his throat. Did she have them? "Nothing I know of anyway," he muttered.

"You don't know why..." Tillie combed her fingers through all that blond hair, making him want to do the same. "Why did you show up here?"

"I gave my word to Carter."

More singles wandered in, filling the bar with more high-spirited chatter. They had bright eyes and wide, eager smiles. Those Lonely Hearts were searching for that elusive magic, like the magic he'd had once with Tillie.

"You gave your word to Carter," Tillie repeated softly, her gaze fixed on him, her smile nowhere to be found. "And yet, you don't sound happy to be here. You don't look happy at all."

"I'm not." He shook his head. "I'm feeling cautious. This will be the first time I've seen Carter since he handed me my walking papers." Keith swallowed thickly.

"You're still upset," Tillie surmised. "If I were you, I wouldn't have shown up."

Keith set his jaw, unwilling to admit he'd felt the same way.

"That's interesting," Tillie set her elbow on the bar and rested her chin in her palm. "It wasn't until you left me that I realized you don't usually stick around for a fight."

"That was different," he said through gritted teeth.

"Was it?" Tillie finished her gin drink and set the tumbler on the bar. She hadn't touched her whiskey punch after that first sip. "We hadn't even talked about marriage when you proposed."

"We didn't need to talk," he protested, getting hot. He shrugged out of his lined jeans jacket. "We were on the same page."

How could Tillie not know I was going to propose?

"We weren't. And maybe you weren't on the

same page with Brad and Carter either." She shook her head, frustrating him further with her insights. "Did you blindside them with something the way you did me? Did you assume they'd agree to produce a product you had an idea for? Did you act without running your ideas by the team first?"

"No." But there was a heavy feeling in his chest that said otherwise. "I did my job. When the sale goes through they'll get plum jobs continuing to run Sunny Y'all as a division of Durant Ranch Products, while I'll just have…"

"Your share of the sale." Tillie rolled her eyes. "They'll go their way and you'll go yours. But you won't be empty handed."

"They took something from me, Til," Keith ground out. Something he was trying hard to get back—his self-worth. "I'm going to get to the bottom of what happened here where they can't run away from me. And when I have those answers, you'll see I wasn't to blame and that they were in the wrong for squeezing me out." For making him feel unwanted.

"Wow." Tillie slid off the bar stool, looking hurt. "It sounds like you're ready to dig in and take a stand for what you want with Sunny Y'all when you weren't at all interested in doing that for me. See you later, Keith."

And from the sounds of it, she hoped it was much, much later when they met again.

If ever.

CHAPTER FOUR

Tuesday, four days until the wedding

"EVERYTHING'S GOING TO be just fine," Tillie murmured, smoothing her black sweater dress in the resort's lobby while she waited for the bride and her entourage to arrive Tuesday afternoon.

Gran and Shay were taking naps in the cabin.

"Of course, it's going to be fine." Keith appeared at her shoulder, unsettling Tillie's equilibrium and causing her to sway toward him. "You're great at multitasking."

"Please, go away." Tillie righted herself. She hadn't seen Keith since yesterday afternoon in the bar. She'd spent too many hours last night staring at the ceiling and pondering his naivete when it came to his botched marriage proposal. Maybe she should have driven down to Dallas all those years ago, the way Gran had recommended, and told Keith she loved him but—

"I won at rock, paper, scissors." Keith interrupted her thoughts. "I'm not going anywhere."

How could he be so stubborn?

She drew a calming breath. For the next five days, Reese was the priority. Tillie's feelings had to be put on the back burner. She had to be unflappable but honest with him. "Keith, if the bridal party walks in here and you're standing next to me…"

"Yes?" He arched a brow, looking more attractive than a man had a right to be with his black cowboy hat tilted at a jaunty angle.

She grit her teeth.

I don't need attractive. I need the manager job at the Rocking P.

"Are you worried about Reese's reaction to seeing me?" Keith asked, gaze drifting toward a desk clerk cowpoke putting a log on the already roaring fire in the giant fireplace. "Or are you worried about your uncle Boone's reaction and that job he's dangling in front of you? I'd wager it's the latter."

Tillie bit her lip. Keith was right. It wasn't Reese she was worried about. At least, not completely. "Even if there wasn't a job on the line, I'd still be concerned about Reese. She's been stuck on edge lately and questioning all her wedding decisions. Your presence here will probably throw her for a loop."

"I'm not here to make waves," Keith insisted, losing a bit of that smile. "I don't want to miss Carter's wedding and have regrets months from now if it takes us that long to work through our differences."

He wants to make things right with Brad and Carter after they ousted him? Is he sincere?

He seemed to be.

Tillie couldn't afford to let her guard down if he wasn't. "Are you going to apologize for the harsh words you exchanged with Carter? Do you think Carter is going to apologize for forcing you to leave?"

"Tillie… Look… I know this reunion isn't going to be easy," Keith said stiffly. "But nothing worth saving is easy."

Tillie felt the impact of those words like a blow to her heart, a one-two knockout punch. But she kept her head high as she called him out. "I guess you didn't think *we* were worth saving."

I need to let that go.

And not because Keith's frown was fierce. "Til-lie, I…"

A sound from the portico drew Tillie's attention. Uncle Boone's new, silver Suburban pulled up at the door.

"The bride and her family are here," Tillie announced to Keith, trying to encourage him to leave. "Please go."

He didn't budge, of course.

Moments later, Reese entered the lobby wearing a short blue skirt, a long, silver sweater and high-heeled, white cowboy boots. Her thin, white-blond hair was in an intricate French braid. And her cowboy hat was white, wide-brimmed and floppy.

She'd become a citified cowgirl since she moved to Dallas, dressing more for fashion than function, a change that made Tillie feel left behind.

Reese hailed Tillie, rushing over to give her a hug. "That drive was exhausting. Daddy was…" And then her gaze fell on Keith and all her happy vibes dropped to the floor. "Keith. What are you doing here?"

"I'm the best man." Keith resorted to his standard line of defense. "You don't want to tell me to go away, do you? It's bad luck to have regrets about a wedding."

Bad luck?

"Of course, you'd play that card," Tillie muttered, taking note of Reese's frown. She'd caught Reese muttering about luck several times recently.

The three bridesmaids entered next—Crystal, Jane and Sophie Jean, the last of which was also doing everyone's hair and makeup. The bridesmaids were as different as different could be.

Crystal was a Dallas socialite with big blond hair. She'd begun dragging Reese to galas and inviting her on yacht trips in the Gulf of Mexico, excursions Reese gave lip service to, as if she didn't really enjoy them. Crystal always wore high-heeled, impractical boots *not* made for riding or walking and had an annoying habit of rubbing Tillie the wrong way.

Crystal was the type of person who posted every bit of their life online with the best lighting and the most unrealistic poses. She'd encouraged Reese to do the same.

Fluff and nonsense. Tillie had no idea what Reese saw in her.

Keith and Crystal exchanged brief nods. Crystal's regard of Keith was more speculative than Tillie liked.

Not that it's any of my business.

Tillie turned toward the other bridesmaids.

Crystal's opposite in the bridesmaid department was Jane. As a nurse, Jane was as practical as they came, as evidenced by her no-nonsense sneakers and short brown hair. Sophie Jean fell somewhere between the two—sweet as honey, a clotheshorse, and a woman who loved styling hair. Today she wore her long, dark hair in a soft, romantic bun. Both Jane and Sophie Jean were from Clementine, and both looked around the swanky Ambling Horse Prairie Resort lodge with wide eyes, not having been there before.

Tillie hugged Jane and Sophie Jean with heartfelt welcome. They were her best allies when it came to calming Reese's bridal mood swings. Crystal only seemed to make things worse.

Uncle Boone and Aunt Eleanor entered the lobby.

Tillie's paternal uncle had made his fortune in cattle ranching and stock market investments. He was a barrel-chested man with a cowboy hat some said was too small for his big ego. He wore nothing special or expensive—no fancy boots, no new jeans, not even a new shirt. He may not have been brash in appearance but he was brash in manner and when it came to watching out for those he cared for.

Tillie's aunt Eleanor was yin to Uncle Boone's yang, soft to his stormy bluster. She wore a long denim dress beneath a multi-colored Southwestern coat. Her short blond hair was windblown and her smile was scattered.

Tillie suspected Aunt Eleanor was the real reason Uncle Boone had enlisted her help this week.

Greetings, hugs and dark looks were exchanged, the last between Keith and Uncle Boone. And then between Uncle Boone and Tillie, although his dark look wasn't reciprocated by Tillie.

"It's not my fault," Tillie wanted to say. But why defend herself when the reason Keith was still here was because Tillie had lost at rock, paper, scissors? That was no excuse for letting the bull into the china shop.

"I'm disappointed, Matilda. I thought I told you to handle any and all emergencies," Uncle Boone whispered to Tillie before heading to the check-in desk.

"There's Carter and the groomsmen." Reese checked her smartwatch before nodding toward the trucks pulling beneath the portico. "Right on time."

Keith went out to greet the men, walking slowly, as if he was headed toward his doom.

Although Tillie didn't want Keith here, her heart still went out to him. This had to be hard.

Laughter drifted from the bar where a group of Lonely Hearts were day-drinking.

"There's a big singles event this week," Tillie explained when the ladies stared curiously.

"They're having a *crafting* mixer on Friday." Laughing, Jane pointed to a sign on the check-in desk. "That's what it says, right? *Crafting?* Who still needs a date for the reception? Sophie Jean, haven't you always wanted to date a knitter?"

Sophie Jean shook her head, laughing a little.

"There's no time for romance, girls," Reese said briskly. "I know each of you has the online link to our itinerary this week. But I got so anxious before I left that I printed it out." She produced a sheaf of papers from her tote and handed one copy to each member of the bridal party, last of all Tillie, whose page was filled with scribbles next to each of the scheduled activities, sometimes including phone numbers and emails. "Tillie, I hope you had a good breakfast. I received your message about the resort's wedding planner having her baby a month early. I was beside myself with worry. But Daddy said you'd pick up her slack. So I wrote down everything I could remember that she was supposed to do for me. You'll help, won't you?"

"Of course, I will." Tillie smiled as if this was no big deal. That was how much Tillie loved her cousin.

And how badly I want the Rocking P's ranch manager job.

Feeling like a hypocrite, Tillie kept on smiling as she read the plethora of listed duties Reese had jotted down for her, including dates and times, if applicable.

Final review of wedding decorations. Tuesday, 3 p.m.

Receive delivery of bride and bridesmaid gowns. Wednesday, 8 a.m.

Confirm picnic lunch is delivered for first trail ride, Wednesday. 9 a.m.

Make sure everyone attends all events, including dance rehearsals every afternoon at 4 p.m.

Receive delivery of wedding favors and add chocolates. Wednesday, 10 a.m.

Receive and distribute wedding flowers on Saturday morning.

Make sure everything is in the bride's cabin on Saturday morning.

"I'm sure I've left off something," Reese was saying, fussing with Tillie's hair where it fell over her shoulder. "But I know you. You'll manage perfectly. It's what you do."

"Everything will be just fine," Tillie murmured. It had become her mantra.

She appreciated the fact that Crystal, Jane and Sophie Jean promised to help.

"Sophie Jean." Aunt Eleanor pulled the bridesmaid beautician closer to Reese. "I can't believe my daughter hasn't decided on a hairstyle for her big day but I'm still voting for Reese to go with a less fussy look, like that bun in your hair. Isn't it pretty, Reese?"

"Yes, but I need to make my own decisions about my hair and dress." Reese cocked her head and her hip as if ready to diss her own sweet mother. "Mom, just because I said I wanted to wear your wedding dress when I was a six, doesn't mean I want to wear it now that I'm thirty-six." It felt like there was more to come. But unexpectedly, Reese paused.

Tillie held her breath.

And then, instead of going into full-on bridezilla mode, Reese smiled and hugged her mother. "I love you, Mom, but I'm not your little girl from Oklahoma anymore. I'm marrying a good man from Dallas, a fine man who's going places. I have to look chic and modern."

"Hear, hear," Crystal said, earning a smirk from Tillie.

"You keep saying that, Reese." Aunt Eleanor held her daughter at arm's length, worry furrowing her brow. "But no matter who you're marrying, you should still be the same person, inside and out."

"Hear, hear," Tillie murmured, earning a thumbs up from Jane.

"People grow and change, Mom." Reese's smile seemed strained. "Let's not fight about this."

"You can't fault me for holding out hope for nostalgia, Reese. You'd look beautiful in my gown." Aunt Eleanor had tears in her eyes.

Reese drew her mama in for another hug.

"Parents of the bride, the bride, and all her bridesmaids are checked in." Uncle Boone announced. He'd generously paid for all their rooms, including Tillie's. He headed toward the portico without so much as a glance Tillie's way.

There goes my job.

Reese settled her purse strap on her shoulder and walked after him, leading the rest of the women.

Tillie stayed where she was, studying the agenda for the week, giving herself a pep talk.

I can do this.

Tillie reviewed the list again, realizing she wasn't sure what "everything" meant in terms of items Reese needed on Saturday morning. She hadn't given Tillie those details and Tillie was afraid they'd matter.

She walked across the lobby toward the grand entrance and the portico. The glass doors slid open silently at her approach.

"Tillie is my maid of honor," Reese was saying to Crystal, her back to Tillie. "I would have chosen you but my parents expected me to choose her. It's a family obligation I can't shirk. I'm sure you understand."

"Believe me. I understand family duty all too well," Crystal said in that uppity voice of hers. "And besides, after losing your wedding planner, Tillie is more like staff anyway."

Tillie backpedaled, moving out of sight as her cheeks flamed with sudden heat and her eyes filled with tears. She felt like Aunt Eleanor must have a few moments before—like she didn't know who Reese was anymore.

An obligation? Staff?

Hurt raked its way down Tillie's throat, making it hard to swallow back those hot tears. She turned and strode toward the lobby restrooms.

An obligation? I bought Reese tampons when we were fourteen and she was too mortified to pay the male sales clerk. I was her alibi when Reese ditched Uncle Boone's big business dinner and went on a date with Carter instead. I used up all my vacation time to help Reese plan this wedding and I never complained. Not once!

Tillie stumbled into the ladies' room and locked herself in a stall, unrolling a good three feet of toilet paper before burying her face in all that tissue and releasing a tortured sob. She let herself wallow briefly before wiping her tears and blowing her nose.

Because no matter how much Reese's comment stung, it made no difference to what Tillie had to do. She had to make sure Reese was the happiest of brides.

It was her obligation. If not to Reese, to Shay and Gran.

CARTER GOT OUT of his truck, put his straw cowboy hat on, spotted Keith and strode forward, smiling as if nothing bad had ever happened between them. "You came."

"I did." Keith hesitated, wondering how to greet his foster brother. He extended his hand. "You asked me to be your best man and I said yes. I need to honor my commitment."

"Meaning Mom and Dad talked you into keeping it." Carter ignored Keith's outstretched hand and hugged him instead. "I didn't think you'd show. It says a lot about you as a man that you did."

"I'm here to make this the best week of your life." Keith nodded toward the approaching groomsmen—Brad, Luther and Van. The men all worked for Sunny Y'all and were former fosters at the Done Roamin' Ranch. "Just like the rest of the guys."

Brad made a non-committal noise but nodded. No apology. No empathetic looks.

Was Tillie right? Did I do something wrong?

Regardless, Keith bared his teeth in the best attempt at a smile he could make at the moment, because *this*—seeing his foster brothers again after what they'd done to him—was the really hard part of being here. Regardless, he had to pretend—pretend that all had been forgiven and that he'd moved on, pretend that he wanted to be here to love and support Carter, the money-grubbing minion.

Keith pulled his lips up even farther, revealing more teeth. "I hope we can put the past behind us."

"We'll catch up later," Carter promised, which was the same as saying nothing.

Keith nodded.

Carter and the other groomsmen entered the lobby without looking back. Theirs wasn't the kind of body language that encouraged Keith to follow them inside. Or to stay outside waiting for their return.

Before Keith could decide whether to stay or go, Boone Powell appeared before him.

"I need to talk to you. Come on." Tillie's uncle led Keith away from the resort entry. He was an imposing man physically, wearing a compact cowboy hat and a shiny belt buckle that marked a win as a bronc rider. When he reached the edge of the portico, Boone crossed his arms and frowned at Keith. "*You* will not make a scene at my daughter's wedding."

"I won't, sir," Keith assured him, feeling tension knot in his shoulders.

"I invested in your vision long before you three left Clementine for Texas," Boone continued, puffing out his chest with what Keith assumed was pride. "I've waited a long time for a payout. And when Carter's guidance finally brought us to where we are now—on the brink of closing the sale of the company—you nearly ruined everything for all of us."

What?

"I don't know what you mean." Keith's headache was back, the one he'd had since Christmas. And it was more pronounced than ever.

Boone scuffed the soul of his boot on the pavement, much like a bull considering trampling an intruder in his pasture. "As a board member, I keep a close eye on Sunny Y'all's operations. And when I heard about what you were doing, *I* proposed a change. A change that Carter and Brad fully supported."

"You..." The blood roared in Keith's ears, increasing the hammering of his headache. "You heard what *I* was doing? It was you? *You* wanted me out."

"Yes. And you can't complain about the consequences. The partnership contract you made with Carter and Brad allows you to be voted out if two *partners* agree." Boone settled his cowboy hat more firmly on his head. "Yes, I said *partners*.

Not brothers or friends. There are no family or friendships stronger than your signature on that contract's dotted line. In December, you received a generous buy-out, including shares in the company, plus you'll get a healthy check when we finally sell Sunny Y'all. If you've made peace with what happened, you're welcome here. If not, it's time for you to leave."

Without waiting for an answer, Boone strutted off.

Keith watched Boone go, noting he ignored Tillie at the entry doors as the older man passed. Keith didn't like that hurt look on Tillie's face any more than he liked the way his head was pounding, protesting Boone's revelations.

I did nothing wrong.

Keith had come to the Ambling Horse Prairie Resort to keep his promise and hopefully obtain closure regarding what went down at Sunny Y'all last December. But suddenly, he realized those answers might not make him feel any better.

Was I to blame?

In addition to his headache, his stomach was making knots. And they weren't slip knots either. They were the kind of bonds that didn't want to loosen and become undone.

Now would be a good time for a head-clearing ride. And afterward, he'd ask for a few minutes alone with Carter. Ask him some pointed questions. Calmly listen to his answers. And then he'd hightail it out of here tomorrow morning.

Because being a bigger man was overrated.

But just then, his foster parents pulled up, smiling and waving, seemingly happy to see him. They'd expect Keith to soldier on. To make them proud. To do what was necessary to make things right on a family level.

Even if he did feel like a pebble stuck beneath someone's bootheel.

CHAPTER FIVE

"WHAT ARE YOU doing here?" After a long ride to clear his head, Keith found Tillie sitting on a bench in the resort's shiny, new horse barn. In the stall nearest to her, a strawberry roan poked his head out and looked at Keith. "I didn't mean you, Jam." Tillie's gelding.

He gave the horse a pat on the neck anyway.

Jam turned heads. He looked like a once dull white horse that had been splattered with a case of strawberry preserves by an overly-energetic toddler. The red streaks, dots and splotches had no pattern to them. But the gelding's character was as steady and predictable as they came.

Tillie sat on a bench near Jam's stall nursing a beer and looking like she didn't want to be disturbed. She'd changed since he'd seen her this afternoon. No longer in a black dress, Tillie wore jeans, a black turtleneck and that baby blue coat. Her brown cowboy hat brim was pulled low and her long, blond hair looked as limp as Keith's spirits.

Keith could relate to her defeated mood, even if he didn't know what had befallen her.

"Shouldn't you be at dinner with Reese and the rest?" Keith asked, not rejecting the notion that he felt better just seeing Tillie. Sometimes a man needed to take comfort wherever it could be found. "Did something happen?"

"Something happened all right. And then I needed some space." Tillie scrunched her face into an unhappy expression, reaching up with her right hand to stroke Jam's neck. "Or at least, I told Gran I needed space. She didn't interrogate me as to why, but she didn't argue. She just took Shay to dinner." Tillie patted the bench next to her, then reached into a cooler at her feet and removed a bottle of beer—one of several buried in the ice. She offered it to him. "What's your excuse for skipping out on supper?"

"I went on a long ride searching for elusive answers and lost track of time. Rode back after sunset." Not the wisest of moves, especially in unfamiliar territory. Keith took the beer, wiping off ice chips before cracking it open. Then he had a sip of the satisfying cold brew and sat to her left on the bench. "Not very proud of skipping a group dinner and I'll probably hear about it later from my folks. Why didn't you want to go?"

"I didn't feel comfortable attending. Me being the unpaid wedding planner and all. In other words—*staff*." Tillie accented the word with air quotes. Then she gestured toward Keith with the hand that held her beer bottle, blue eyes glinting with stubbornness. "And before you say anything sarcastic, I know that as maid of honor I am supposed to pitch in on principle. And, also, by accepting Uncle Boone's deal with a job hanging in the balance, I agreed to help. And I suppose that's not really what's bothering me." Her unhappy expression reappeared. "It's just easier to moan about being *staff*."

"I'm a good listener to gripes." Hers, anyway.

"Really?" Tillie's bright blue eyes seemed to say she had more gripes than he'd ever want to hear. "Reese gave me extra wedding duties when she arrived. After that, she and Crystal reviewed the wedding flowers, linens and decorations." Tillie tsked. "They couldn't find fault with the flowers since I was able to contact another florist with access to calla lilies. But Crystal rejected the ribbon the resort provides to mark the wedding aisle. She said it was more ivory than white. She said it'll clash with Reese's white wedding dress. She said, she said, she said."

Keith sipped his cold beer, letting Tillie sort through her list of grievances.

"Anyway." Tillie sighed. "One of the desk clerks helped me dig through the storage room for alternatives." Tillie sipped her beer once more, tension radiating from her like a heat lamp on high. "The *so-called* storage room is just a shipping container, which I don't think is airtight given the number of spiderwebs in my hair." She shivered, running her fingers through her blond ends as if checking for gossamer threads.

"Bugs are your kryptonite." Keith tried to lighten her mood while simultaneously trying not to think about how much he'd loved Tillie once. He failed at both, if her frown and his aching heart were any indication. He tried again. "Who said this was a luxury resort? Luxury resorts don't have cobwebs."

"Oh, yes, they do. They have all sorts of creepy crawlies." Tillie reached up to scratch her gelding's red-and-white speckled cheek. "I stepped on what I *hope* was an already dead scorpion. That bugger was huge. I'm not lying, Keith. He was tarantula-size." She sucked in a breath, taking hold of her beer bottle with both hands. "I'm actually quite proud of myself. I didn't bolt. The desk clerk took one look at it, screamed and made a run for it. I swear she ran so fast, I felt a breeze when she passed me."

Keith was trying hard not to smile. Growing up on a ranch meant bugs were an everyday thing. But not for Tillie. Never for Tillie. "Why would she run if the scorpion was dead?"

"Keith..." Tillie muttered his name as if he was a disillusioned bug-lover. She gathered all her blond hair with one hand and twisted it over

one shoulder. "It's a well-known fact that bugs don't travel alone."

"Tell that to the one dead fly on my window-sill at home." Okay, now he had to smile, if only a little.

"You know what I mean." Tillie nudged him with her shoulder, the way she used to when they were friends in high school as well as later when they'd been romantically involved. And then Tillie became animated, waving her hands in that energetic way of hers as she explained, "Bugs are either *looking for* a mate, or a place to lay eggs *after they've eaten* their mate, or all of their eggs are hatching *at the same time* and they're *eating their mama*." She sipped her beer before repeating, "Bugs don't travel alone. Ever."

Keith discreetly brushed a small spider from the bench between them, hoping she wouldn't notice. "You know that's not true of all bugs."

"It's true of the bugs that have venom," she argued, nose in the air.

Keith's smile broadened, deepened, refused to dim.

I missed this.

Their easy banter. Their teasing back-and-forth. The way being with Tillie lifted a weight inside of him. Not to mention the tug of attraction and deep rooted feeling that he was supposed to be by her side.

It was confounding. She'd rejected him. He

shouldn't be open to any of these nostalgic emotions because they'd only loop back on a dead end track toward hurt. And yet…he was.

Does Tillie feel it, too?

Further down the breezeway, a horse nickered, bringing Keith back to the present.

What had they been talking about? *Oh, yeah. Bugs.* Venomous bugs traveling in packs.

That was Tillie's phobia talking.

Keith tried to find a suitable retort. Failed. Conceded to her. "I'm not going to win this argument, am I?"

"Nope."

"I can live with that."

They drank in silence, listening to the soft sounds of horses in their stalls—moving across straw, slurping water, bumping into stall doors as they poked their heads over them to snoop on the two humans who'd stopped talking. It felt like déjà vu. Once upon a time, they'd been good with silences between them, content with their own thoughts and being near each other.

And now, Keith was happy to sit quietly while he concerned himself with Tillie's problems rather than his, content to be near her while he waited until she was ready to talk again. Because it wasn't just spiders and scorpions that had her making an escape. She'd said *staff* earlier, as if the word and its connotations undercut her sense of self-worth and she resented it.

I feel you, babe.

Keith wanted to feel her—her soft lips, her soft breath on his skin, the softness of her filling his arms.

But that didn't mean he was going to act on that impulse.

Because whatever Tillie had felt for him once, it wasn't strong enough for a happily-ever-after.

I DIDN'T EXPECT THIS.

For Keith to treat me kindly after I tried to take him down a peg or two and shoo him off.

That Keith was willing to listen to her vent said something positive about the man. The Keith she used to know didn't do well with rejection. She knew that firsthand.

And she knew it secondhand, as well.

In high school, Tillie had asked Keith why he didn't spend Christmas with family. His blood relations, she'd meant.

Imagine your grandmother had a chance to take you in but decided she wasn't up to it, he'd said. *Imagine your uncle told you he couldn't afford another mouth to feed,* he'd said. *Imagine your aunt begged off raising you because you were a boy,* he'd said.

And then hurt had filled his orphaned blue eyes.

Now imagine how it would feel to spend the holidays—or any day—with people who'd felt you were inconvenient, too much trouble and a bur-

den, all the while knowing they don't love you, he'd said.

And Tillie had imagined that very thing. His hurt. His pain. And it had gripped her insides and wrung her out.

That would sting, she'd managed to say.

Back then, she'd mislabeled him as holding grudges. Now those long-ago comments combined with the vulnerability he'd shown her the past few days helped Tillie understand why Keith had walked away when she'd said no to his marriage proposal. His pride… His guard… His survival instincts… Whatever it was that Tillie's unfinished rejection had triggered, Keith had wanted to avoid it completely.

It served no purpose to go back now and wonder what would have happened if Keith hadn't been leaving town the afternoon he'd proposed, embarking upon a new life and career in Dallas. All Tillie could do was acknowledge their souls would always call to each other. But for now…for this week, she needed to respond to him with friendship of some kind, not googly-eyed romance.

And that meant wrapping up her gripes so they could spend time on his. He'd taken a long, solo ride. That was what he did when he needed to clear his head. Friends griped to friends. Griping shouldn't be one-sided.

Tillie set her beer on the ground. "Scorpion or

no…things turned out all right in the end with the ribbon. I found a color that pleased the bride, or at least, Crystal. But after that, I needed some time alone to collect myself for the week ahead." Tillie set her cowboy hat on her knee and leaned back against the barn wall. "But now, of course, I feel guilty. You know how Reese gets when she's stressed. She eats chocolate. And then zits pop up faster than mushrooms in spring grass."

Keith nodded, blue gaze direct, giving nothing away.

"There's a triple chocolate cake on the resort's dessert menu, by the way," Tillie told him. "And Reese has no willpower."

"Now is not the week for a bride to be blemished." Keith nodded once more. "Not with pictures of her being taken every hour of every day. As I recall, the photographer arrives tomorrow."

"Yes." Tillie turned to study Keith, trying to see if he was making fun of her cousin. She'd have to take him to task if he was.

But his blue eyes didn't shine with a tease. His wide mouth didn't grin with mischief. All in all, Keith seemed sympathetic to Reese's plight.

Or at least, he looked like he was sympathetic. But then, he added, "Reese is a grown woman. She doesn't need you to be a member of the chocolate police."

"She's my beloved cousin," Tillie ground out, although the word *obligation* came unbidden to mind, contradicting *beloved*. "We've spent many a night talking about boys, imagining our careers and planning our dream weddings."

"You forgot to include naming your children." Keith was teasing now, smiling in a way that made Tillie's heart *ka-thump*. "In high school, you and Reese were always considering what to name your children. Although… I don't recall you ever mentioning *Shay*."

"Like you remember any of my ramblings from my childhood." Tillie scoffed, trying to ignore her rapidly beating heart.

If he does recall…what does that mean?

"You wanted to have three kids," Keith said without missing a beat. "You were going to name them Thomas, Justine and Beatrice. You'd all live on your own ranch where you'd raise chickens and cattle while you renovated an old farmhouse." He snapped his fingers. "Oh, and you wanted to work as a school librarian."

Tillie's jaw dropped while her heart kept *ka-thumping*.

"How did you remember all that?" she asked in a breathless voice before composing herself. "No. Strike that. *Why* do you remember all that?"

Keith shrugged, resettling his black cowboy hat on his head and a private smile on that too handsome face. "It's one of those useless pieces of information I retain. You know, like how to solve the algebraic equation for the third length of a tri-angle or how many cups make up a quart."

She angled toward him, knees nearly touching his. "Cups to quarts isn't useless information." And remembering all that about her meant something. Exactly what, she didn't know and shouldn't dwell on.

Keith scoffed. "Cups to quarts is useless if you don't make any meal from scratch."

"You don't make…" Tillie's hands rose in the air, forming small circles. "Cookies? Surely, you make cookies." Everyone did now and then.

Keith stared at Tillie as if he was about to explain the greatest of his inventions and he was certain she wouldn't understand. "I buy pre-formed dough to bake cookies. Great idea, by the way. You get it in the refrigerated aisle and it's super convenient. Now, what's so hard to believe about me remembering things you told me in school?"

Tillie's cheeks were starting to feel uncomfortably warm. This wasn't friend-zone conversation. "It's not about you retaining what I said that's hard to believe. You're brilliant. But… Why would you waste any brain cells storing details about me?"

"Tillie…" He spoke her name in a hoarse voice, as if she was questioning his feelings toward her and he didn't believe she'd dare.

Oh, I'd dare. But only because you make me forget myself.

A change of subject was required. Because if

Tillie didn't change the subject, she might do something more foolish than probing into the past. She might act on an impulse in the present and kiss him. And if she discovered he still kissed like a dream?

Trouble.

Tillie cleared her throat. "Moving on… What's your excuse for taking an overly long ride? Did you and Carter have a dust-up?"

"Nope." Keith lowered his head, along with his shoulders, clearly demoralized. "Your uncle Boone warned me not to make waves this week." He tilted his head, sorrowful blue gaze catching hers, holding hers.

"Uncle Boone is as stressed out by this wedding as Reese is. But you don't usually let something like that bother you." Tillie looked deeper into Keith's eyes, trying to see what was really bothering him. But she couldn't read him this time. "That can't be all that's upset you. I basically told you the same thing about the wedding, plus I told you to get lost. More than once. What else did he say?"

Keith shifted on the bench, moved his booted feet slowly back-and-forth across the barn floor, probably arguing with himself about how much to share with her. If anything.

"I swear, Keith, you haven't changed." Tillie gave a wry laugh. "You'd overthink which radio station to play while showering on a Sunday morning."

Keith's smile returned. "No. You've got that wrong. I'd hesitate to choose one station because I'd be trying to figure out how to solve the problem of how to change the radio station during commercials while I'm in the shower," he amended, capping off his comment with a laugh.

"I hate to break it to you," Tillie told him in mock seriousness. "But there are electronic devices now that change stations using voice commands."

"Right." Keith's smile turned into a tempting grin. "I'm behind the times."

"What you're behind on is telling me why you let my uncle get to you." And why he'd recalled so much about her. Tillie plopped her cowboy hat back on her head. "Get talking, cowboy."

"It was Boone's delivery," Keith admitted without overly hesitating, although he did frown slightly. "The way Boone said it… It was like I was an already dead scorpion being ground to dust beneath his boot."

"Ouch. My uncle does have a knack for the put-down, doesn't he?" Tillie resisted the impulse to take Keith's hand and give it a reassuring squeeze. "There's more, though, isn't there? More that's bothering you about your conversation with Uncle Boone." Because he hadn't been walking around with a thundercloud over his head before the wedding party arrived.

"You noticed?" Keith's eyes widened, as big and blue as an Oklahoma summer sky. "We shouldn't get into it."

"Oh, but we will. And do you know why?" At his shrug, Tillie continued, even if a small voice in the back of her head cautioned that this overshare was unwise. "Because misery loves company. I haven't told you all that's bothering me either."

Keith stared at her the way Tillie imagined he stared at a problem he'd identified that he had no inkling—*yet*—as to how to solve. His smile may have disappeared but his lips were no less tempting. "You go ahead, Til. Because I'm not in the mood to share and we…" Keith looked apologetic at his incomplete sentence.

"We are no longer a couple," Tillie finished firmly for him, dragging her fingers through the length of blond hair over her shoulder. "I know that. But it's going to be a long week. You and I might make a habit of hiding out in the barn and—"

"You and me? Like we were before?" There was an odd note in Keith's voice, as if he was asking if she still had feelings for him.

Ka-thump. Ka-thump.

Don't get carried away.

"Which before?" Tillie asked in a painstakingly neutral voice, afraid of his answer but eager for it as well. "The friend zone before or the—"

"The friend zone before," Keith blurted. *Although... Is he staring at my lips?*

Ka-thump-ka-thump-ka-thump-ka-thump!

"Do you remember how to be friends?" Tillie asked. Again, carefully. Again, with mixed feelings about the answer to her question. One did not rush toward a platonic relationship with an ex-boyfriend, just as one did not run blindfolded into a rodeo arena during a cowboy's bull ride.

"I remember how to be friends," Keith said earnestly. Defensively. His chin jutted out. "I do."

Good heavens. I do?

Those two words were a foreshadowing of Carter and Reese's vows a few days from now when they'd promise to love each other 'til death did them part.

I can ignore two words.

Tillie cleared her throat, as if that would clear away her compulsion to reacquaint herself with the rough feel of Keith's five o'clock shadow. "Okay. We'll overshare in the name of a partnership to help each other through the week." Tillie gave a jerky nod, took a deep breath and then said briskly, "I don't think Reese knows who she is anymore. She waffles between being my cousin from Oklahoma and trying to be like Crystal from Dallas. She's put off several decisions about the wedding—her hair, her makeup, possibly even her wedding dress. And if I try to help her make a decision, she becomes touchier than a bronc that can't throw its rider." She closed her eyes briefly.

"I get that. If it makes you feel better, it's been going on for some time." Keith nodded. "Her morphing into a Crystal clone, I mean. She was dragging Carter to black-tie events a few times a month last fall."

Oh, that was bad news.

"Forget I said anything." Tillie pinched the bridge of her nose. "Truly. Forget the last five minutes entirely. I've just committed maid of honor blasphemy. If Reese heard me, she'd be hurt and I'd never forgive myself." Even if her cousin didn't reciprocate and feel the same way. "Of course, Reese knows who she is. It's just pre-wedding jitters."

"It's not jitters. But you can try to tell yourself that until we get through this thing." Keith rubbed his hand back-and-forth across her shoulders.

His touch was brief but Tillie could have sworn his fingers tangled in her hair.

Her entire body felt charged with electricity. She reached for Jam instead of Keith, giving the gelding a pat on the neck. "Your turn."

Silence.

"I said…" Tillie turned to stare at him, trying to convey annoyance while hiding longing. "It's your turn, Keith. Spill your guts."

"Boone told me…" He pressed his lips together, as if reconsidering his confession. But then, he blurted, "It wasn't Carter and Brad's idea to boot me out, but they agreed to let me go without a fight when Boone and the board pressed them. They could have fought for me but they didn't. They dumped me. Me. Their foster brother. And for what? Power? Prestige?"

Tillie shifted away, trying to glimpse all of Keith as if that would help her see the big picture in his situation. "That's so..."

"Slimy?" Keith supplied.

Tillie shook her head, gaze tangled with his.

"Dirty?" Keith tried again, so intense, so angry, so...darn good looking.

"No." Tillie shook her head, vehemently this time.

Focus, Tillie. Focus.

"Underhanded?"

"No." She held up a finger, hoping he'd understand she needed quiet to find the words through the fog of attraction he caused whenever he was near. "No. That's so...out of character for Brad and Carter."

Keith scoffed. "People change. And not always for the better. Black-tie affairs, remember?"

"People don't change. Not really. They get boxed in until there are no other choices available but the wrong ones." Tillie touched Keith's forearm for a quick second. "You know this. You saw it when your foster brothers were younger, when they felt threatened."

His brow furrowed.

She kept talking. "Brad and Carter aren't spending gobs of money on fancy trucks or limited edition cowboy boots. They may not have explained their actions to you and maybe they couldn't at the time. But—"

"You're giving them too much credit," Keith groused, crossing his arms over his chest. "I was betrayed."

"Oh, yeah. I get betrayal. Reese felt *obligated* to choose me as the maid of honor because of her parents. I'm the sole relative." Despite Tillie's best efforts, her voice sharpened as she repeated, "She felt *obligated* to the family. Just hearing her say it… That's a betrayal."

"Speaking of betrayal…" Keith said slowly. "Boone said I did something that put the company at risk. *Me.* One of Sunny Y'all's founders. If so, I did it naively."

Jam stretched his nose toward Tillie and blew a raspberry.

"Exactly, Jam. Keith isn't often naive." Tillie gave the gelding a scratch beneath his ruddy forelock. "There's only one thing that frustrates me more than technology and that's—"

"People," she and Keith said at the same time, with the same ironic sentiment, and the same emphasis.

They exchanged the kind of smile that spoke

of a cherished, private connection, of inside jokes and laughter, of days growing old together.

Him, Tillie's heart ka-thumped, heedless of the wound he'd made when he left her.

This, Tillie's soul whispered, forgetting her goals and responsibilities.

Now, Tillie's inner joy expanded, bubbling as if she was a little girl diving into her Santa-stuffed stocking on Christmas morning.

Tillie opened her mouth to say something— *what, she had no idea*—but Keith beat her to the punch.

"I think we can do the friend thing," he said.

Oh...

His statement contradicted every feeling Tillie had just experienced, shattering them the same way he'd broken her to pieces when he left Clementine six years ago. A jagged pain tore through Tillie's heart.

"It's the wedding thing we need to worry about," Keith was saying. "Me getting through it without biting someone's head off and you keeping it running smoothly despite Reese second-guessing herself."

Tillie drew a slow, steadying breath, trying to regain a feeling of neutrality where Keith was concerned. It was a tough task.

"Don't you agree, Tillie?" Keith smiled, but it was an inquisitive type of smile.

"Yes. Yes, of course, I agree that it's going to

be a long week." Needing something to do with her hands other than reach for him, Tillie removed her brown cowboy hat and brushed imaginary lint from the brim. "I can't work miracles as a wedding planner. There might be an ice storm coming on Friday. Nothing I can do about that." But there was something she could do about her attraction to Keith—shore up her defenses.

"An ice storm… Carter and Reese shouldn't have chosen Valentine's Day to get married." Keith extended his long legs out in front of him and sipped his beer. "They planned a lot of outdoor activities this week that will be chilly due to prairie wind gusts or canceled due to bad weather—a picnic tomorrow, outdoor games the next day, a horseback scavenger hunt on Friday."

"We're doing all this outdoor stuff because Reese and Carter always wanted a summer wedding," Tillie explained, trying to lose herself in the wedding details and the reminder of her *obligation*. "Crystal talked Reese into Valentine's Day because she said it'd get more traction on social media." Tillie rolled her eyes. "Who bases decisions about the most important day of their lives on social media?"

"Crystal does." Keith finished his beer. "I think she's trying to mold Reese in her image. She's always encouraging Reese to come up with ways to work Sunny Y'all into her posts."

Tillie frowned. "Somehow…ranch livestock

products don't fit the city girl image that Crystal portrays."

"Agree. But what are you going to do? After all, Crystal is *people*." He smiled at his little reference to their shared complaint earlier that people could be annoying, but Tillie wasn't amused.

She set her hat back on her head. "Yes, people are annoying." Especially men who sent mixed messages.

Especially me when I misinterpret his meaning.

Tillie's cell phone pinged. She checked her screen, neck stiffening with tension. "Gran says Crystal ordered triple chocolate cake for everyone for dessert. I need to text Reese and find out the guests' dietary requirements. Oh, and I have to tell her to use an acne facial mask tonight to prevent blemishes." Tillie quickly sent a note to the bride.

"I haven't heard a lot about the wedding recently." Keith put his empty beer bottle in the cooler, perhaps considering taking a second one since he paused. But then he closed the lid instead. "Crystal isn't the only one meddling with wedding plans. When I was home two weeks ago, my parents had given Reese and Carter a pair of matched paints. They seemed to have forgotten that Carter told them last summer he and Reese don't want to keep horses in Dallas. And yet, Mom said she'd heard Reese mention that she wanted to ride off into the sunset from the wedding reception with Carter. Mom said dreams are important."

"Crystal would say images are important." Tillie tucked her cell phone back into her coat pocket. "She encouraged Reese to add a choreographed wedding party dance to the reception festivities. You know Carter isn't much of a dancer."

"I was hoping that dance wasn't happening." Keith wasn't twinkle toes either.

"You're not alone in wishing for a different wedding experience this week. Aunt Eleanor is still holding out hope that Reese will wear her wedding dress." Tillie opened the cooler and set her empty beer bottle inside. "It's no wonder Reese is getting stressed out and can't make a decision. Everyone has a different idea of how her wedding should be."

"It sounds like it's going to be a rollercoaster ride. I predict at least one disaster."

"I hope we have none." Tillie mirrored Keith's position, resting her elbows on her knees, thinking about how much she needed the job Uncle Boone was offering rather than dwelling on her cousin's hurtful words. "What would you do if you had a say in the wedding proceedings? If you could advise Reese on what to do in a way that would ease her mind."

Keith shrugged. "I have no opinion."

"Oh, *please*." Tillie scoffed. "You've already said you didn't want to dance. Even I wondered why we had to have a horseback scavenger hunt outside on Friday in the middle of February. They have a spa here. Can't we have a spa day?"

"That does make more sense." A smile took shape on Keith's face, a dear, familiar smile. "But a poker match would be fun."

"That would be appropriate since it's what you Done Roamin' Ranch boys did on Saturday nights." Tillie could definitely see that.

"And no fancy duds. No shimmering gowns or formal tuxedos." Keith was feeling it now. "Let's all wear blue jeans and ride off after the ceremony into the sunset." He was endearing when he got into the spirit of things.

Tillie smiled. "Maybe I should suggest these changes to Reese."

Keith laughed. "Make any more suggestions for change and you'll lose your chance at that job your uncle's offering you."

A wave of apprehension rolled through Tillie. She ran her fingers through her hair, looking away.

"You do want that job, don't you?" Keith asked softly. "Or… Could it be…deep down…you don't really want it."

Bingo.

Tillie didn't answer at first. And then she looked at him hard, with truth and a defense at the ready. "You're not a parent. You wouldn't understand. I need that job. Rent free living for a single mom… That will make such a huge difference in what I'm able to provide for Shay." More special glasses.

More appointments with specialists. And all the eye surgeries that the doctors predicted she'd need

"Yeah, but do you want to work for Boone?" From Keith's tone of voice, Tillie gathered he wouldn't.

"I want to give my daughter a better, more secure life than I was provided. No coming home to find my mother packing up for an unexpected move. No eating lunch alone at a new school while other kids stare and try to figure out if they should be friends with me or not. I moved four times before we landed in Clementine." Tillie didn't sugarcoat anything as she continued, voice rising, "If I have to take a job that isn't ideal *for me* in order to give Shay stability, so be it."

"Wow. I get it now. Security. Safety." Keith studied her face, his scrutiny bringing heat to her cheeks. "You've always been touchy about money, saving more than you would ever spend, and not loaning what you have to others."

"Yes," she told him, refusing to feel guilty about that. "I wouldn't even give you money to invest in Sunny Y'all. Do you remember?"

Keith's brow clouded. "I asked you for an investment in our future."

His statement needed correcting. "You didn't ask, Keith. You assumed my money was your money when you proposed."

He shook his head ever so slightly. "I'd never do that."

"You did. And you shocked me speechless." Making her wonder if she'd be forever counting their pennies and worrying about a roof over her head.

Keith moved closer on the bench, staring into Tillie's eyes, giving her the more-than-friends vibe once again, darn him. "Tillie, when I asked you to marry me, I talked about us pooling resources to help launch Sunny Y'all. I was looking toward the future with you. With us. As a team."

How had she thought they had a connection where they knew what each other was thinking? Keith didn't seem to know her at all. It was time to have that conversation they'd postponed for six years.

"First of all, that wasn't much of a marriage proposal. You made me a business proposition, Keith." Tillie glanced away from him, embarrassed that it hurt to bring everything back to the surface—the memories of that day, his big smile, that sweet little diamond ring, her disappointment as he stumbled over his words. The wrong words. "You talked about all the ideas you had for the business, the things you could do if you had an angel investor, how we'd be living hand-to-mouth at first." She wrapped her arms tighter around her torso. "You never even told me during your pitch that you loved me."

"I didn't…" He made a sound that seemed like a denial. "Okay. Maybe that's true. We were leaving for Dallas—me, Carter and Brad. And yes, we needed money to tide us over. But I was just so excited to have another shot at the future I wanted that I... I completely blew it with you, I'm sorry." Keith took her hand, undoing the knot her arms made over her chest. "I didn't realize how I'd made it all sound, that I'd forgotten the really important words. And, of course, your savings would have meant a lot to you."

"No need to apologize, Keith. That was then. We're back in the non-relationship zone now." But her cheeks felt as if they'd been sunburned and her heart was racing faster than it had a right to because he still held her hand.

Yet, they seemed to sit worlds apart.

"Are we firmly in the friend zone?" Keith had somehow managed to move close enough that she could breathe in his scent—musky cologne, horse leather and hay. He hooked a lock of hair around her ear. "I keep getting mixed signals."

Me, too.

But maybe all these mixed signals were a sign, a sign that they needed to set aside a long-abandoned attraction in favor of more adult decisions and friendship.

"Let's look at this practically." Tillie willed her heartbeat to slow. "Things are different now, Keith. I have a little girl and a life in Clementine. Your life is in Dallas. You don't want to start up with me again."

"I've made mistakes, Tillie," Keith whispered, tilting his hat back before placing a soft kiss on her cheek that tested her resolve. "But you know what they say about mistakes. That's how we learn. Those mistakes are why we can be friends again."

"Friends?" Tillie opened her eyes and turned her face toward his, prepared to reinforce the boundary she needed to be a responsible single mom. Instead, she said, "Who said I want to be friends?"

And then, she kissed him.

CHAPTER SIX

Wednesday, three days until the wedding

"MAMA, IT'S TIME to wake up." Shay climbed onto Tillie's back, straddling Tillie like she was a horse. "I want to go riding today."

"We ride at lunchtime." Tillie's head and left arm were hanging over the edge of the bed. She squinted and croaked, *"Gran? Coffee?"*

"Almost ready." Gran made the fancy coffee machine whir and hiss. Yesterday, she'd claimed to know what to do, having read the instructions. And based on the smell of fresh coffee, Gran was succeeding.

"Thanks." Tillie's mouth was dry and her head felt heavy.

But she wasn't hungover. She was sleep-deprived, having tossed and turned all night long because...

I kissed Keith.

Tillie tugged her pillow over her head and groaned.

Not only had Keith kissed her back but then

she'd scampered off like a skittish colt afterward. Not exactly projecting the I-don't-want-to-start-up-with-you-again image she wanted to.

What am I going to say to him later?

Tillie tugged the pillow more firmly over her head, feeling more like a teenager than a woman of thirty-five. Kissing an ex-boyfriend was a young person's mistake. And yet...

That was one heck of a kiss.

"Be gentle with your mama." From the sounds of it, Gran set a coffee mug on the bedside table. "She looks like she might need more...*space*." Chuckling, Gran lifted the pillow and kissed Tillie's cheek. "Sometimes mamas need to be handled gently, Shay. Or left alone, like your mama was last night, while we ate triple chocolate cake." There was innuendo in Gran's voice.

She suspects something happened between me and Keith.

Tillie groaned a second time because Gran was Team Keith and had been for years. "Time to dismount, Shay. Mama needs coffee."

Yes. Perhaps two cups. Because avoiding Keith was going to take all her wiles.

"What time is it?" Tillie rolled over, sending Shay tumbling onto the bed where she giggled happily. "I'm supposed to meet the dress delivery man at eight in the lobby." Per Reese's notes. "And then there's breakfast at eight-thirty." And picnic confirmation with the staff at nine.

"It's five past eight." Gran tsked. "I'll call the concierge and ask them to hold all deliveries for us."

"Great idea." Tillie sat up so fast she gave herself a head rush. "Thank you."

Shay slid off the tan satin bedspread and ran around the bed to grasp Tillie's hand. "Can we sell cookies later?"

"We might have time after breakfast." Tillie got to her feet, staring at what her daughter had chosen to wear today—blue jeans, an orange sweater with a kangaroo stitched on the front, and a black tutu at her waist. "Hey, pumpkin. Maybe we should leave the tutu in the room."

"No." Shay's bottom lip stuck out, as prominent as her owlish lenses. "I'm gonna ride with it. Bixby loves my tutu."

"Pick your battles," Gran murmured. "The dress code today is blue, remember?"

Tillie wished she could forget. Crystal had talked Reese into assigning colors for each day of the week. Today was blue. Thursday was green. Friday was tan. And the dress code sent out to all wedding guests was red, white or black for Saturday.

"Right." Tillie had ten minutes to get ready. She hurried into the bathroom, calling over her shoulder, "You can wear the tutu, pumpkin. But you need to put on your blue sweater today."

"My dinosaur sweater! Goodie!" Thankfully, Shay moved to make the change.

Twenty-five minutes later, Tillie leaped out of the buggy almost before it stopped beneath the portico at the resort's lodge. She rushed inside to the concierge desk, fidgeting and huffing while waiting for the cowboy concierge to finish talking to a burly man about a flower order for a special woman who'd agreed to resign from the Lonely Hearts club with him last night.

"Good morning," Tillie said when the concierge turned toward her. "I was expecting a delivery of dresses this morning at eight. My grandmother called about it."

"Ah, yes. They never arrived." The concierge smiled expectantly, as if awaiting further instructions.

"Whew. I didn't miss it." Tillie sagged against the desk in relief. "I'll be in the restaurant. Can you come get me when the delivery man arrives?" She gave him her name and cabin number, just in case.

"Did they come?" Gran entered on a gust of winter wind, holding onto Shay's hand.

Tillie shook her head, falling into step with Gran and shoving her hands into her coat pockets.

"Enjoy your breakfast," the concierge called after them. "Try the blueberry pancakes."

"Pancakes!" Shay excitedly thrust one fist in the air. "Pancakes are almost as good as ice cream but better than cookies."

"Says who?" Tillie teased.

Another gust of wind blew in, the way it did when the resort's main doors opened. Tillie glanced over her shoulder.

Keith strode into the lobby, looking chipper and chill, like he'd had a good night's sleep after a woman he used to know kissed him before bedtime. "Morning, ladies."

"Morning," Tillie mumbled, hurrying toward the restaurant and away from Keith.

"Do you wanna buy another box of cookies, Keith?" Shay asked, dragging her feet while contorting herself to look back at Tillie's ex.

"Shay, I haven't finished the first box yet. Ask me later." Keith caught up to Tillie, giving her a nearly tangible, curious inspection. "Everything all right? You look—"

"Careful there, cowboy." Gran held him back with a hand on his shoulder. "Tillie looks lovely this morning. Doesn't she?"

"She looks lovely all day, every day," Keith recovered quickly, smiling brighter. "But my question stands. Is everything all right? You look worried, Til."

"I'm fine." Why stress? The fact that the bride and bridesmaids' dress delivery was late was nothing to worry about. The resort was miles and miles away from Dallas on a two lane state highway. It made sense that the delivery wouldn't arrive first thing this morning. Why worry?

But Tillie was worrying.

I'd rather worry about the wedding dresses than me kissing Keith.

"Wanna ride together to today's picnic?" Keith asked, all sunshine and innocence, the calm blue of his shirt matching the tempting blue of his eyes.

The toe of Tillie's boot caught on an imaginary obstacle on the floor.

"No, thanks," Tillie choked out as she recovered her balance.

"I was asking Shay." Keith took Shay's free hand. "What do you say, cowgirl? May I have the privilege of escorting you on our trail ride later?"

Tillie wanted to tap her bootheels together three times and magically whisk herself to a quiet corner, one without handsome, full-of-themselves cowboys who knew how to get under her skin.

"Are you gonna ride in front?" Shay asked Keith with a four-and-a-half-year-old's swagger. "I like riding in front. There's no dust. If I ride behind, I can't see past the butt in front of me."

"The butt in front of you?" Keith glanced toward Tillie for clarification.

"The *horse's* behind," Tillie ground out.

"Now I get what you're saying, Shay." Keith smiled. He smiled as if he found Tillie's daughter adorable. And then he smiled at Tillie, as if he found her adorable, too. As if she'd kissed him last night and she hadn't run away.

He's supposed to be the runner, not me.

"I need more coffee." Frowning, Tillie led the

way into the resort restaurant, where they were seated in a section reserved for the wedding party all week.

They were the first ones there. The rest of the restaurant was filled with chattering Lonely Hearts. Tillie floundered, searching for a distraction.

The restaurant had white tablecloths, black napkins and fresh flower centerpieces. The chairs were black wood with tan, leather cushions. The hardwood floors continued in here. Large windows overlooked the rolling Texas hills.

It was nothing at all like the Buffalo Diner back home. There were no booths with sagging springs. No scuffed linoleum floors. No sneakered waitresses carrying creased order pads. Just fit cowboys and cowgirls wearing matching Western wear and memorizing orders rather than writing anything down.

The restaurant was beautiful, high class, and felt well-run, just like the rest of the resort. This was a place for folks to set their cares aside and feel at ease.

So it made no sense that Tillie had a feeling that everything was unraveling and had been since she'd first set foot in the Ambling Horse Prairie Resort.

And seen Keith.

"REESE, WHAT DO you think of the horses my parents got you?" Doctoring his coffee with cream,

Keith made nice with the bride-to-be at the breakfast table when she came in, giving Tillie the space she so obviously needed.

He'd responded to her kiss last night enthusiastically. And when that kiss had ended, they'd both been breathless. And when he'd brought that fairy tale moment to an end, he'd waited for Tillie to open her eyes, to smile and admit she still had feelings for him.

Wasn't that why he'd read those mixed signals? Wasn't that why she'd kissed him?

Instead, Tillie had opened her eyes, gasped, launched herself off the bench and sprinted for the exit, leaving Keith with only Jam for company.

Jam had blown another raspberry.

"That's putting it mildly," Keith had told the roan, wondering if this was how Tillie had felt when he'd dashed away after she'd rejected what he now knew was the worst marriage proposal in the history of bad marriage proposals.

For years, he'd believed Tillie hadn't loved him as much as he'd loved her. He hadn't taken his poor delivery and her financial fears into account. And then with one kiss, she'd reignited the spark he'd felt upon first seeing her yesterday. For a short time, he'd forgotten about being done wrong in business. Instead, he'd been thinking about the things he wanted to tell Tillie, things that had happened over the past few years. He'd been imagining taking her to his favorite restaurants, riding with her on the open range, driving her down to Austin for a music festival.

And then, Jam had head-butted Keith's shoulder, knocking him back to his senses.

Nothing has changed.

Tillie was still striving for financial security while Keith's future was up in the air. If he started a new business, he'd need a backer. Money would be tight. And there were more investors to be found in Dallas than there were in Clementine.

Still, that hadn't prevented him from having the best night's sleep in months, falling asleep thinking about Tillie rather than what happened last December. And it didn't prevent him from whistling a happy tune on his walk to the resort lodge this morning. Or being drawn back into Tillie's sphere when he'd seen her in the lobby.

"But I want double whipped cream," Shay said in a tense, raised voice that brought Keith back to the present.

"You can't have blueberry pancakes *and* hot chocolate with double whipped cream for breakfast, pumpkin," Tillie told her daughter gently. She sat across from Keith and wore that baby blue coat over a touchable, fuzzy blue sweater. "That's too much sugar, even for you, Shay."

The little cowgirl pouted, sinking in her seat and staring at the ceiling through those thick glasses of hers. "Gran would let me have both if you weren't here."

"True," Velma murmured, shedding her shearling coat to reveal a white yoked blue button-down. She was sitting to the right of Keith, her endearingly wrinkled face a reassuring boon to his senses. "Spoiling kiddos is what grannies were put on this earth for."

"I'm sorry, Keith," Reese said from the seat to the left of him. The bride-to-be wore a thin blue sweater set and a frown. She seemed unusually scattered, glancing from her phone to Keith to the door, and back to her phone. "I was checking social media. What did you ask me?"

"About those horses my parents bought for you and Carter. I saw them in the barn." Keith gave Reese an encouraging smile. "Real lookers, those paints. Black on white."

"We saw them in the barn yesterday." Velma's gaze turned dreamy. "They look just like Joe Cartwright's horse on *Bonanza.* I used to have the biggest crush on Little Joe."

"Have you ridden them, Reese?" Keith asked, not wanting to get sidetracked by Velma's imaginary romance.

"We're going to ride them for the first time today." Reese had her blond hair pulled into a ponytail, making her look more like the girl he'd grown up with than the spruced up woman she'd become over the past few years. "Carter is super excited."

"For the first time…" Tillie had been lifting

her coffee cup to take a drink but she set it back down. "Maybe Keith and I should give them a go first, Reese."

"Bless your heart, Tillie." Reese chuckled, turning her phone over and then reaching for her water glass. "That's very sweet. But Carter and I are good riders."

Keith and Tillie exchanged glances at this fib.

Tillie looked like she wanted to roll her eyes but all she did was mouth the word, *"People."*

This was the first time they'd been on the same wavelength since her sweet kiss last night. Keith couldn't help but smile back and extend his hands out as if to say, *"What are you gonna do?"*

"Just because I couldn't ride a bareback bronc for eight seconds doesn't mean I'm not a good rider in the saddle," Reese was saying.

"I'm sure they're well trained." Keith couldn't imagine his parents buying horses above Reese and Carter's skill level. But he'd try to get to the barn early just to make sure.

The Powells and the Harrisons entered, parents of the bride and groom, respectively.

"We missed you last night at dinner." Mom leaned over to kiss Keith's cheek, smelling of lavender. She was dressed to ride in a blue denim shirt, blue jeans faded nearly to gray, and serviceable, black cowboy boots. No cowboy hat sat as yet on her short white hair.

"Keith's the one who missed out." Dad patted

Keith's shoulder, his wide white cowboy hat brim practically blocking out the light above them. "The triple chocolate cake was the star of the show."

"It was heaven," Reese said half under her breath, rubbing her hands over her face as if she were tired.

Tillie made an indistinguishable noise and drank more coffee. That woman ran on caffeine.

Back when they were dating, Keith used to meet Tillie at the Buffalo Diner for coffee or lunch breaks during her shifts on his days off. They'd sit at the counter, fingers twined together, leaning in close to talk about Keith's ideas or Tillie's challenges running a little ranchette while working full time at the grocery store and trying to squeeze out every penny of profit.

"Did we interrupt something?" Mom asked after placing her breakfast order. "What were you talking about?"

"Those beautiful paint horses you bought us," Reese gushed. "I can't thank you enough."

"A cowpoke without a horse ain't much of a cowpoke." Dad tipped his wide-brimmed white cowboy hat back and gave Reese a kindly smile. "We don't want you to forget your roots."

"You told me once about your dream to ride off after marrying Carter." Mom leaned her head on Dad's shoulder. "There's nothing like a good ride with your honey to work out your differences. Isn't that right, Frank?"

"I wouldn't know." Dad stroked Mom's hair, a tender expression on his face. "We've never had any differences to work out."

Everyone laughed at this obvious fib. But Tillie's laughter seemed strained.

Velma inched closer to Keith to whisper, "My granddaughter isn't much good at hiding her feelings. Tillie's been worried about something all morning."

"I noticed."

"Something happened last night between you two," Velma continued to whisper. "I'd be counting down the days to that wedding if I were you. That's how long you have to make things right."

To kiss Tillie and not have her run away? That was his idea of heaven.

"Message received, Velma." Keith nodded, trying to get Tillie to meet his gaze. Or at least acknowledge his existence. "But it's a long shot."

Velma tsked. "That's what folks said about you and your friends leaving for Dallas with dreams of starting a successful company."

Carter shuffled in, looking hungover. He kissed Reese's cheek, then collapsed into the seat next to her and gulped water from the glass in front of him.

"Crystal and I bought these gorgeous saddles and bridles for the paints." Reese picked up where she'd left off. "They're trimmed in silver. When our children and grandchildren look at our wedding pictures, they're going to think Saturday was a fairy tale."

"That's the way you used to look at our wedding pictures," Reese's mother said quietly. "My wedding dress went on a ride off into the sunset, too."

Reese bit her lip.

"Both wedding dresses are lovely." Tillie played peacemaker, smiling at both the bride and her mother.

The groomsmen funneled in, all but Brad anyway, looking as done in as Carter.

The waiter delivered food, although all Reese ordered was a hard-boiled egg. More coffee was poured. More food orders taken. Carter drank a second glass of water, eyes practically closed.

Tillie stared at Reese with concern, then shifted her gaze to Keith, making a subtle gesture that he took to mean he should talk to the bride.

Keith cleared his throat. "How does that work exactly, Reese? You riding in your wedding dress, I mean." He hadn't really thought about the logistics before but now his riddle-solving brain latched onto the idea. "Do you ride side-saddle? Or hitch up your skirts?"

"I'll wear white leggings to ride. My skirt is wide enough to drape on either side of my horse so that only my boots show."

"Does your dress cover your horse's butt?"

Shay piped up, noticed her mother's look of disapproval, and then course corrected. "His *behind*?"

"No." Reese frowned. "That would be…"

"Wedding dress demise," Keith guessed, earning a smile from Tillie.

I could use a lifetime more of those.

Keith reined in his enthusiasm. "No one would wear that wedding dress again if it went over a horse's tail."

Everyone around the table agreed.

Tillie set her coffee cup down. "Reese, did you change your mind then? Are you riding off after the reception? Last I heard, you weren't."

"I'm still debating." Reese didn't look happy to admit this, or perhaps wasn't happy to still have things up in the air when the wedding was a handful of days away. "I read my horoscope today but it was no help."

"It never is," Velma murmured.

"Which is why I'm still pulling for her to wear my wedding dress," Eleanor said in a chipper voice.

Crystal entered in time to hear this last bit, breezing past them all to take a seat at the far end of the table, the only empty seat left. "Your dress is cowgirl chic, Eleanor. But times have changed. Reese is wearing a dress I'd wear if it was me getting married."

Tillie rolled her eyes.

Carter seemed to see Keith for the first time,

glancing from him to Tillie. "Where were you two last night? I bet Brad a new laptop that you were getting back together."

"Ha!" Tillie released a shout of laughter that horse collared Keith's pride. She took note of Keith's frown, and sobered. "I needed some time alone. As for Keith… You know how he gets when an idea strikes. I bet he stayed up for hours trying to solve the world's problems with a new invention."

Before Keith could decide what to say to that, Reese's knife clattered on her plate.

"Tillie?" Reese thrust out her chin and brushed over it with her fingers. "Tillie? Look at my face. What is this? Is it a zit? A rash? A…a…whisker?"

Tillie came around the table to inspect her cousin's chin. "It looks like a zit." She took hold of Reese's hands and lowered her voice. "But there are still days before the wedding. No reason to panic. No more chocolate, though."

"I only had one slice of chocolate cake last night," Reese said, eyes wild.

"And that chocolate milkshake in the car on the drive over here," her father pointed out. "Can't start a road trip in Clementine without picking up an ice cream."

"And that candy bar when we stopped for gas," Jane added.

"Oh, and don't forget the mocha Frappuccino when we stopped for coffees," Sophie Jean put in.

With a wounded cry, Reese ran out of the restaurant.

Carter drained his glass. No one watching would have chosen him as the happy groom.

"She'll be fine," Tillie promised the table, leaning on the back of Reese's chair.

Only the women agreed with her, which only made Tillie look more worried.

So, Keith leaped in with the least controversial thing he could think of. "Isn't this coffee great? The waiter said they grind every cup when you order."

"I'd expect as much with the prices they charge," Boone grumbled in that buzz-kill way of his.

Tillie excused herself and hurried off.

"It hasn't arrived, miss."

"But... It's after nine." The delivery truck was an hour late. Tillie had a bad feeling in her stomach. Like when she put too many hot peppers in a batch of chili. If she was Reese, she'd say it was a sign of bad things to come.

Tillie whipped out the folded sheet of paper with Reese's agenda and footnotes from her back pocket. Thankfully, Reese had scribbled a contact number for the delivery company.

Tillie walked outside, heading toward the parking lot as she made a call from her cell phone to the delivery company and quickly explained who she was and what she was looking for.

"Yes." The woman at the delivery company tapped what sounded like a keyboard. "I see in our system that delivery was completed at eight a.m."

"Eight? But...it's after nine." Tillie glanced around the parking lot as if expecting to find the dresses draped over a truck bed. "Did someone sign for them?"

More pounding of the keyboard. "Yes. It was signed for by... Keith Morgan."

Tillie gasped. "Are you sure?"

The woman assured her she was.

Tillie thanked her and stormed back inside, clutching her cell phone, intent upon finding Keith and having a word, not caring that she had to make that request in front of their friends and family, who'd think—like Carter and Brad had—that they were getting the band back together.

Never. Ever.

She marched into the restaurant and went directly to Keith's chair.

"Can I talk to you for a minute, Keith?" Tillie didn't wait for him to answer. She just tugged him up and out of his chair, and then towed him out to the lobby, where she whispered angrily, "That was really low."

Keith tipped his black cowboy hat back and looked at Tillie with faux innocence. "What?"

"Don't pretend." She was so angry, so hurt,

so…so disappointed that it took great effort not to grab hold of his arms and try to shake some sense into him. "This isn't funny. My job with Uncle Boone is on the line here. What have you done with them?"

"Them?" Keith frowned. "Who?"

"Not who. *Them!*" Tillie stomped her foot, giving into impulse and taking hold of his arms—those strong, sturdy arms—and holding on tight enough to convey she meant business. "The dresses, Keith. Reese's wedding gown and the bridesmaid dresses."

Keith shook his head. "I have no idea what you're talking about." And the worst of it was that he still looked angelically innocent.

Tillie released his arms, took a step back and regrouped. Facts. She needed to stick to the facts. "I just called the delivery company. They say the dresses for the wedding were delivered at eight o'clock this morning to the resort. They say one Keith Morgan signed for them." Tillie poked Keith's chest—his firm, sculpted chest. "Keith Morgan. That's you."

"That's my name but…" Keith shook his head again, frowning this time. "It wasn't me."

Tillie scowled. "Just last night, we joked about the wedding changes we wanted to see. You wanted to get rid of the dresses and tuxedos. And now… You know how Reese is lately. Fragile. You saw her run off this morning because of a blemish. The loss of a wedding dress could be the straw that breaks Reese and stops the wedding. No wedding for Reese. No job for me." Tillie poked Keith's chest again. "What have you done with them?"

"Tillie…" Keith placed his hands gently on her shoulders. "I swear to you. I barely rolled out of bed by eight this morning. I walked here because I missed the buggy." He dragged her over to the cowboy concierge. "Did I come in early this morning? Any time before Tillie talked to you?"

"No, sir."

The concierge had barely spoken those two words, before Keith dragged Tillie away from the desk. "I did *not* steal those dresses. I'm being framed." He glanced toward the restaurant, an uncharacteristic frown on his face, a combination of displeasure, disappointment and disbelief.

The frown of a man who'd been struck by surprise.

And yet…framed?

"Let's not go jumping to conclusions." But what he said about being framed made sense. No one had expected Keith to show up. And everyone knew he was upset about what had happened with Sunny Y'all in December. He was the perfect fall guy. "I have an idea. Let me call the delivery company again."

A few minutes and one phone call later, an email pinged Tillie's cell phone. She opened it and the attachment—an image of the delivery invoice, including a signature at the bottom. She made the image larger, showing the screen to Keith. "Look at this."

Keith brought his head close to hers, gently bumping her cowboy hat brim with his. "I bet you believe me now. I've never dotted my *i*'s with hearts in my life."

Tillie nodded. "I don't want to stereotype, but that's something a woman would do."

"Are you thinking what I'm thinking?" Keith asked.

Tillie tilted her head to one side. "If you're thinking there are a lot of women in the bridal party, then yes. I'm thinking what you're thinking."

They walked toward the restaurant, stopping at a place in the lobby where they could see inside.

Conversation had lightened at the breakfast table since Keith and Tillie left. People were laughing, smiling and looking as if they were having a good time. Not one female glanced their way with a guilty look on their face.

"These are our friends," Tillie said, feeling hollow. "Reese's friends. Our families. They couldn't have done it."

Keith stared at Tillie with an inscrutable expression. "Do you watch any detective shows or true crime?"

Tillie put a hand on her hip, energized despite herself. "Keith Morgan, I'm a single working mom. I don't have time to watch TV much less listen to a true crime podcast." Or pursue long-distance relationships with too-handsome cowboys.

"That's too bad. Crime-solving experience would come in handy right about now." Keith escorted Tillie back into the restaurant. "We need to locate the dresses and identify the culprit before Reese finds out anything is wrong."

"I agree but...we aren't Holmes and Watson," Tillie grumbled. "We're more like Laurel and Hardy."

CHAPTER SEVEN

"BUT I'M NOT supposed to sell cookies door-to-door." Shay stomped along between Keith and Tillie after breakfast, making as much noise as a pair of pink boots could on the paved lane. "Mama, you said so. Over and over before cookie season started."

"And now I'm saying different." Tillie's mouth formed a grim line.

As far as Keith was concerned, Tillie had good reason to be in a snappy mood.

After breakfast, they'd begun visiting cabins assigned to the wedding party, ostensibly to sell cookies. But in truth, they were looking for the missing wedding dresses. And they were looking among their friends and family.

Grim business, that.

They'd sold boxes of cookies at every stop and wormed their way inside cabins under the pre-text of fawning over the view from each person's back window. But they hadn't found any wedding dresses. And because they didn't want to cross anyone off their suspect list, they were stopping at every cabin, not just those occupied by women.

"Someday..." Shay began with all the gusto of a child who felt she'd been wronged "...when I'm a mama... I'm gonna say and do whatever I want." The little girl kept stomping ahead, the sides of her brown coat flapping like short wings in the wind. And with every heavy footfall of her pink cowboy boots, her black tutu bounced over her blue jeans.

"Someday...when you're a mama...you're going to find out that so-called freedom no longer exists for you." Tillie tramped right next to her daughter, hands jammed in her blue coat pockets, brown cowboy hat firmly on her head. Only her blond hair tossed and tumbled in the wind. "You've got to keep a roof over your head, food on the table and the doctor bills paid. And to do that, you have to go to work on your boss's schedule."

"Unless, of course, you're your own boss," Keith pointed out, earning a frown from Tillie.

That frown. She'd greeted him with it first thing this morning.

It wasn't an expression that encouraged a man who was searching for friendship or, possibly, something more.

Am I looking for something more? The smart answer was no.

But if Keith could smooth things over with Tillie in any way, shape or form, there was hope for him smoothing things over with Brad and Carter. And yet, that frown...

He raised his gaze skyward, hoping for heavenly intervention.

But all he heard was his own voice in his own head: *fat chance*.

Tillie's frown said she had no time or inclination for anything with him. And frankly, they hadn't been able to overcome their differences before. Who said they could now?

A trio of baby goats came bouncing around the side of the cabin they approached. The white goat bleated and leaped enthusiastically toward Shay.

"My babies!" Shay dropped her cookie tote and skipped toward the cabin, sending her large, round glasses sliding down her little nose. Soon, Shay was jumping about the grounds in front of the cabin as if she, too, was a baby goat and thrilled to be alive.

Tillie stopped frowning. Stopped walking. And stopped emitting waves of snappy concern. "Look," she whispered.

And he did.

The sun was out. The sky was blue. And the air was crisp and fresh. Shay's laughter was blissful. Tillie's blond hair fluttered in the breeze, tempting Keith to touch it. It was an idyllic moment, the kind of moment that made a man want to try and overcome obstacles so these moments happened more than once in a blue moon.

"You're so pretty," Shay cooed to the goats. "Look at them, Mama."

"I'm looking at you, pumpkin," Tillie said softly as if bouncy, energetic moments with Shay were few and needed to be appreciated.

Without thinking about it, Keith draped his arm over Tillie's shoulders, resting his hand on her arm.

Tillie glanced up at him, tears gathering in her big blue eyes. Without speaking, she moved closer, taking hold of his hand on her arm, as if she needed and appreciated his support.

What's this all about?

Keith's chest cinched, pressing in on his heart. There was something going on here. More than he could fathom. Outwardly, there was love and bittersweet joy emanating from Tillie. And inside of Keith…there was a longing to be a partner in those feelings. To be on the inside of this picture instead of on the outside looking in.

This could be my life.

And what a sweet life it would be. If only he and Tillie could find their way back to each other.

If only…

A couple they didn't know walked by on the lane, interrupting his train of thought.

Tillie stepped away from Keith, moving purposefully toward the cabin they'd targeted for their next cookie sale—Brad's. It left Keith with nothing to do but follow.

They walked past bouncing Shay and leaping kids.

"I'm going up the steps, Shay," Tillie said in a

tone that implied Shay should stop playing and get down to business. Tillie rested her boot on the first step, glancing back at her daughter, who didn't pay Tillie a lick of attention.

"I'm headed up the steps, too." Keith trotted up the stairs to the porch. "Grab your cookie tote, girlie."

Shay kept hopping about with the three baby goats on the grass in front of the cabin. Her pink cowboy hat was balanced precariously on her head, and her thick round glasses balanced precariously on the tip of her nose.

"We're knocking on the door, Shay." Tillie stomped up the steps.

"Yep." Keith rapped his knuckles on the door. "Hear that, Shay?"

The little dynamo kept right on bouncing, moving one hand to her hat, and one on her glasses.

Brad opened the door enough to lean on the doorjamb and smiled at Tillie. Then his gaze landed on Keith and his smile dropped.

Brad was tall and lanky. If he hadn't been raised on the Done Roamin' Ranch in foster care, he probably would have been a full-on nerd. As it was, he wore a blue polo with a curled collar, and wrinkled jeans that were tucked into his worn brown cowboy boots. His dull brown hair was thinning, and he wore Clark Kent glasses that disguised his greedy, evil alter ego, the one that double-crossed unsuspecting foster brothers.

Keith sighed.

That's me and my overactive imagination.

Brad wasn't 100 percent evil. He was just wicked good at engineering the production of Keith's inventions and greedy enough to force Keith out the door at Boone's request. *Talk about biting the hand that feeds you.*

"What's up?" Brad asked, blocking the entrance to his cabin with a hand on the interior doorknob, which made it hard to get much of a look inside, although Keith certainly tried.

Tillie gave Keith a brief, commiserative look before turning her attention to Brad. "My daughter, Shay, is selling Holly Explorers cookies." She gestured toward the little ray of sunshine and her happy goats.

A stiff breeze blew past, rustling the leaves on the hedges.

Frowning, Brad tapped the bridge of his black nerd glasses, an indication that he was impatient. "I'm not interested in cookies."

Keith didn't believe him. "You know you'll get the munchies late at night while you're working, Brad. You always do."

"We have plenty of chocolate options," Tillie increased the sales pressure with a rehearsed pitch before Brad could send them away. "Chocolate chip, chocolate stripes, chocolate raspberry cream, and the classic chocolate mint."

"Mint are the best," Shay called from below them, proof she was paying attention.

"I shouldn't." Brad doled out the smallest of smiles.

Oh, he was tempted, all right.

"You absolutely should, Brad," Tillie told him. "You know how quickly these cookies sell out. You snooze, you lose."

"Okay. I'll buy a box of chocolate chip." Brad released his hold on the interior door handle, letting the door open just a bit more.

"Oh, look at your view." Tillie nudged Brad's door open wider and entered his cabin, walking all the way to the back and stopping in front of the picture window. "It's so different than mine. I get to watch the Lonely Hearts try to find love at the swimming pool."

"View? What view?" Brad scoffed, digging into his wallet for bills. "It's all shrubbery and trees."

"There's a peacock out there," Tillie insisted. "Come see, Brad."

Yes. Go see, Brad, so I can search for stolen wedding dresses.

When Keith's former business partner moved to look, Keith entered the cabin. It was the same setup as his—a long entry with a luxurious bathroom, a closet on the left and an upscale kitchenette on the right.

"Where's the peacock?" Brad asked Tillie.

She took him gently by the shoulders and moved

him out of Keith's line of sight. "Up in the tree. See there?"

Keith tiptoed toward the closet and opened the door a crack. There was nothing inside. No wedding dresses. No suitcase. No hanging polo shirts. Not even Brad's tuxedo for Saturday's wedding.

That's suspicious.

"I don't see anything," Brad complained. He could get testy when he felt out of step with something.

"Your glasses are smudged," Tillie told him. "Here, let me clean them."

Keith smiled. Tillie was good at this investigation business, distracting folks so he could snoop around. Brad couldn't see ten feet away without his specs.

Keith crept to the end of the entryway, peeking into Brad's room. He spotted a carry-on sized suitcase on the bed. But there was no tuxedo or garment bag in sight.

Does he know something about this wedding that we don't?

"What are you doing?" Shay asked, startling Keith since he hadn't heard her ascend the porch stairs. She stood in the doorway with three curious baby goats behind her. The tote full of cookies sat at her feet.

"I'm looking for peacocks." Keith tried not to appear guilty.

Not that Shay had time to pay him close attention. The white baby goat bounded inside, ping-ponging from wall to wall, followed by the brown and black goats. Shay scampered after them, her laughter filling the air.

"Shay, can you give Brad a box of chocolate chip cookies?" Tillie asked, returning Brad's glasses to him. "And take your goats outside?"

"Goats! Don't let them near my computer power cords!" Brad sprang into action, enlisting Keith and Tillie's help in trying to herd the kids toward the door.

Shay climbed on Brad's bed where she started bouncing and directing the action all while looking out the window. "Coffee's in the corner, Mama. Bear's behind the curtain, Keith. Butter's in your suitcase, Brad." She must have named them. Shay's feet slid out from under her and she fell on her bottom. But she giggled her way through it, managing to call out more instructions.

For wearing such thick glasses, the kid had really good peripheral vision.

They finally succeeded in driving the black and brown pair toward the door. The kids were followed closely by Shay. The two goats crashed into Shay's tote, spilling cookie boxes across the porch. The brown goat grabbed a box of chocolate chip cookies by one corner and trotted down the steps after the black goat, happy as could be.

"Noooo!" Shay wailed, tearing after the mischief maker. "Cookie thief! Mama, help!"

Tillie ran to her daughter's rescue, nearly tripping over the white goat as she sprinted by Keith.

The white goat must have realized it was being left out of the fun because it also charged toward the door, leaped over the threshold and landed on some cookie boxes, before bounding down the steps after Tillie, Shay and the other baby goats.

From the way the goats and goat chasers were circling each other, it was hard to tell who was chasing whom.

Brad came to stand beside Keith, watching the spectacle unfold. "I don't suppose I can pay less for damaged goods."

"Nope." Keith shook his head. "I seem to recall crushed chocolate chip cookies are your favorite ice cream topping."

"If only I had some ice cream," Brad lamented.

"I can take care of that." Keith made a mental note to log an order with the concierge. He placed a hand on Brad's shoulder, the way he had a gazillion times before. "Hey, can I ask you something?"

Brad stiffened and moved away. "We said all we had to say last December."

"No. Not that." Keith hoped he hid his hurt and disappointment behind a hard-won smile. "I was going to ask you why you missed breakfast this morning."

"Oh." Brad's expression became less guarded. "I slept in. You know me. I'm a night owl."

"That you are," Keith agreed, noting Tillie winning the cookie box war. The goats scattered like autumn leaves on a blustery day.

"Did something happen at breakfast?" Brad asked, looking interested.

"There was a delivery, one that Tillie was supposed to pick up." Keith shrugged, trying to downplay the theft. "It's gone missing. I was just wondering if you'd seen something."

"Not even a peacock in the trees behind my cabin," Brad said wryly. "What was in this package?"

"Brad, you don't mind a nibbled cookie box, do you?" Tillie interrupted with a significant glance Keith's way. They'd decided earlier not to let anyone know the dresses had gone missing in case someone blabbed to Reese.

Tillie and Shay hurried up the porch steps.

"As long as Keith comes through with ice cream, I don't mind." Brad handed Shay some bills.

"Consider it done." Keith nodded.

Meanwhile, Shay did her cookie dance, shimmying in a circle with her arms raised to the sky. "I sold some *coo-kies*."

"Well, we better be going." Keith headed down the porch stairs. "Lots more cookies to sell before our lunchtime ride. Nice to chat, Brad."

"Yeah…uh… It was for the best." Brad sounded apologetic, not that Keith wanted to look back.

But Tillie did. "Was what happened at Sunny

Y'all for the best? You don't look like you mean it, Brad. And I bet you'll be regretting what you did for a very long time."

"What *I* did?" Brad sounded defensive. "The board did what needed to be done to ensure the continued progress of the sale. By voting with them, I was continuing to present Sunny Y'all as an attractive buy-out prospect."

Is that what Boone meant about me putting Sunny Y'all at risk?

Keith couldn't fathom what he'd done to risk their sale. "Come on, Tillie." He needed time to think. His boots rang on the walkway leading back to the narrow road.

In the distance, the jingling of bells announced a buggy's approach. A small hand took hold of his. A precious face glanced up at him, smiling reassuringly, blue eyes large behind round lenses.

This is my future. Shay and Tillie.

With the pair by his side, he could weather any storm, even this accusation that he'd almost put the company he'd built on the road to financial ruin.

But Tillie wasn't by Keith's side. She was still on the porch, whispering furtively at Brad, fighting Keith's fight.

Unacceptable.

Keith stopped and bent to Shay's height. "Why don't you wait here to see which horse and buggy are coming our way. I'll go back and get your mama."

"Okay." Shay went to stand at the end of the walk and stared toward the sound of the approaching horse and wagon.

With the little girl suitably distracted, Keith returned to the porch.

The conversation between Brad and Tillie stopped when he joined them.

"I did nothing to risk the sale of the company." Keith planted his boots, taking a stand. "If anything, I was thinking about the future value, putting the next generation of products for Sunny Y'all in the pipeline."

"You were a wild card," Brad admitted slowly. "Moving too fast on a road no one planned to travel until the sale went through."

"What's that supposed to mean?" Keith wondered aloud, tipping his cowboy hat back. "Companies innovate to stay alive."

Brad's cheeks were ruddy and his lips pressed together, as if he was trying hard to hold back a dam of emotions or information. Or both. He pressed the bridge of his Clark Kent glasses. And then, the dam broke open. "We were supposed to pull back on the reins. The new products weren't supposed to be produced or launched until after the sale happened."

"And if the sale fell through?" Keith was flabbergasted. He removed his cowboy hat and ran a hand through his hair. "We would have been vulnerable to the competition."

"Everyone but you understood that in order to close the sale, expenses had to be kept to a minimum and the buyer had to be kept happy." Brad's tone resembled Mr. Castor's from their high school science class. He'd been a condescending know-it-all. "You stopped one production line to retrofit it for one of our new products." A sensor to track mare fertility.

"The parts were delivered early and you and Carter were on vacation," Keith argued. "I picked up the slack. Your slack. We planned to launch the new product after Christmas. I was keeping to the timeline, ahead of it even."

"You're always thinking ahead," Brad countered in that same smarmy tone. "And that's the problem. You don't think enough about now. The company interested in buying Sunny Y'all wants complete control over new product production and marketing."

"Cheapen the materials and cut the price, you mean," Keith griped. "Our names are still attached to Sunny Y'all. If shoddy product goes out the door, what's that going to say about us?"

How was that for forward thinking?

Sometime during the conversation, Tillie had taken Keith's hand. She gave it a reassuring squeeze.

He appreciated the support, feeling calmer just from her touch.

"Thinking ahead is one of your strengths," Brad continued, this time in a more compassionate voice. "But one of your weaknesses is accepting things you can't change. It's not like I'm happy about the direction they're planning to take Sunny Y'all. In fact, they may drop the Sunny Y'all name in favor of something else after the sale."

"Keith," Tillie said quietly. "We should go."

"I just…" Keith faltered as the world seemed to tilt on its axis. His gaze sought Tillie's. "I just want anything associated with me to be top-notch." Not something sold cheaply and soon tossed away. "I thought… I guess I thought they'd approve our quality standards if the production line was in place." He hadn't realized until this moment that he had other motivations besides the efficiency.

"Mama, here comes Hercules!" Shay cried over the increasing sound of bells. "I see him!"

"This isn't the entire story, Brad." Keith wasn't sure how he knew that, but he felt it deep in his gut.

Instead of arguing, Brad took his box of cookies and closed the cabin door.

"SHAY WANTS TO sell cookies to Reese. I need you to keep things civil when we get to her cabin," Tillie told Keith as they approached the bride's unit.

He'd been dealt a terrible blow by Brad. And Tillie knew it because Brad had spoken the truth. Most days, Keith didn't see the trees for the forest.

"I'm not going to take out my frustrations on the bride." Keith walked a few feet away from Tillie, hands in his jeans jacket pockets, a dejected look on his face. "I'm beating myself up now."

Shay skipped ahead.

Tillie's heart ached for Keith. His was a perfect example of the truth hurting. And it would sting until he accepted it. Frankly, it would most likely sting afterward, too.

"Brad is right, isn't he?" Keith's gaze sought Tillie's, blue eyes ringed with the sorrow that comes with a negative self-assessment. "About me. That's why I proposed to you the way I did."

Tillie nodded. "I think so."

"It's why you rejected me." His gaze shifted toward Shay. "She could have been mine."

Oh, Keith.

"No one ever found happiness by dwelling in the past." Tillie rested her hand in the crook of his arm. When he didn't speak, she added, "Look, it's not like forward-thinking is a bad thing. Even Brad acknowledged it as one of your strengths."

"But not being fully present…" Keith shook his head. "That's a relationship deal-breaker every time, whether it's romance, family or business."

"Do I hear tiny violins playing?" Tillie teased, receiving an unappreciative look from Keith. "What I mean is that your family loves you. You have scores of friends who love you. Even me. I…" *Love you.* Tillie caught herself, backing off. Their time had passed. "Admittedly, sometimes you put the cart before the horse. That's why you needed Brad, wasn't it? Because he was able to translate your visionary ideas into reality without you having to think about the nuts and bolts? And Carter? To make the sales deals so you wouldn't have to leave your workshop?"

"And by doing so, I had blinders on." He sounded miserable.

"Well, there's got to be a reason you put blinders on in the first place."

That seemed to get him thinking.

They proceeded in silence.

"After my parents died," he said in a gruff voice, "I had to endure meetings about their funeral and where I was going to live. I was passed from one relative to another, never having a space of my own. I didn't like the here and now. I kept looking ahead to when I could be my own person, have my own home, make my own rules."

"I…" Tillie rested her head on his shoulder for a few steps. "I'm so sorry you grew up like that."

"And I'm sorry I didn't see the impact it had on me before," Keith said, still in a tone as rough as pine bark.

Tillie left him with his thoughts.

A bird swooped past, disappearing into a shrub.

"Is Brad a bad man?" Shay spun in a circle, swinging her cookie tote. "You were arguing with him, Mama. What's his story?"

"Stop spinning, Shay." It exasperated her eye condition. "And no, Brad isn't a bad guy." The last thing Tillie needed with a job on the line was Shay getting an idea in her head about members of the wedding party being bad. "Brad just… He made Keith upset last Christmas. And I wanted to let him know how to do better this Christmas."

Oh, the things moms have to say to keep the peace.

Keith made a low noise in his throat, like a hound dog's unhappy growl. "It's me who should do better."

Tillie had the strongest urge to comfort him with a word, a touch, a supportive hug. But there was curious Shay. And she wasn't listening to Tillie's commands. "Shay, stop before you fall, please."

Too late. Shay plopped down on her bottom on the narrow road, swaying around like a slowly spinning top. "Keith, were you mad because Brad didn't get you good Christmas presents?"

"Yep," Keith said in a grumbly voice, a frown set deep on his handsome face as he and Tillie came to a stop on either side of Shay. "Brad isn't a bad man. He's just a man who stinks at…buying presents."

The only person on this earth who'd believe that speech was a dizzy little girl wearing pink boots and a black tutu.

"Good. I like Brad. He bought a box of cookies from me." Shay tugged her pink cowboy hat brim down over her face. "Santa always brings me good presents. Maybe Brad should take lessons from Mr. Claus."

"What a great idea, pumpkin." Tillie tilted Shay's hat back. "Look at me. Is the world still spinning?"

Shay squinted up at Tillie, eyes unfocused. "Your face is smudged."

Tillie fake laughed, kneeling next to her daughter. "Remember what Dr. Gibbs said. Close your eyes and take a deep breath."

"Who's Dr. Gibbs?" Keith asked.

Tillie ignored him, focusing on her precious gem. She removed Shay's glasses. "Keep your eyes closed, pumpkin." Using a cloth in her pocket, Tillie cleaned Shay's lenses, all the while aware of Keith's inquisitive stare. And when she was satisfied that she'd removed all the smudges, she put the glasses carefully back on Shay. "One more breath, pumpkin. Then open your eyes."

Shay took a deep breath and then looked up at Tillie. "Mama! You're so pretty!"

"Not half as pretty as you." Tillie helped Shay up and dusted her off. "Now we're going to ask Reese if she wants cookies."

"Okay." Shay marched forward, dragging the Holly Explorers tote bag behind her. And then she stopped, gasped and pointed. "Chickies!"

Three chickens of various colors scurried in front of them, crossing the narrow resort road and heading up the walk toward Reese's cabin.

Shay strutted after them toward Reese's cabin, flapping her elbows and doing her best funky chicken walk.

"What just happened?" Keith's intent gaze on Tillie was nearly palpable.

"Shay was dizzy." Tillie forced herself to smile. The last thing she wanted was for folks to treat Shay differently because of her eye disease. It was why she kept it under wraps.

"Hang on. You were as white as a freshly painted picket fence a minute ago." Keith lowered his voice as they entered the cabin yard proper. "Is there something wrong with her?"

The protective mama bear inside of Tillie reared up with fearsome intensity. She turned to face him. *"There is nothing wrong with Shay."*

Keith drew back, blue eyes wide. "I didn't mean—"

"It's just a vision thing, Keith. You've seen her glasses." And then Tillie stopped herself from blathering on.

It's early onset Stargardt disease, she wanted to say.

She may or may not end up being partially or totally blind, she wanted to say.

Depending upon whether I have enough money and insurance for her surgeries, she wanted to say.

And she's too young to be told, she wanted to say. *Which is why Gran and I let her be just a normal, independent, precocious girl.*

Thankfully, the cabin door opened, preventing Tillie from having second thoughts and spilling her guts right there at Keith's feet.

"I heard voices." Reese leaned against the doorframe, half closing the door behind her, the same way Brad had, like she didn't want them to come in.

Tillie hadn't thought to inspect Reese's cabin until now.

"Hello, Shay." Reese looked like what Tillie was coming to think of as Clementine Reese in her ranch riding clothes with two pigtails. Even the bandage on her chin covering her unexpected blemish was endearing to Tillie. "To what do I owe this pleasure?"

"I'm selling cookies." Shay stumbled up the porch steps, black tutu bouncing, and nearly fell.

Tillie caught her breath, taking a step forward in case Shay needed a rescue.

But Shay righted herself, banging her cookie tote against each step on her way to the porch proper. "Every bride needs cookies, Miss Reese."

"Careful with the merchandise, pumpkin," Tillie cautioned, grateful that the cookies were well packaged. But even Holly Explorers couldn't package cookies well enough to withstand goat nibbles and stair bouncing.

"Every bride needs cookies." Reese repeated Shay's words, adjusting Shay's hat to sit further back on her crown. "That's a great sales pitch. Two boxes, please."

"Cookie crumbs are great over ice cream," Keith whispered to Tillie, warm breath wafting over her cheek.

"Shush." Tillie gave him a dirty look and whispered, "Are you trying to jinx my daughter's cookie sales?"

"No. I'm giving you a backup sales pitch so you don't get any customer returns." Keith held her gaze in a way that said he'd set aside his questions about Shay's vision. For now. "That's what friends do. They help each other. They offer a shoulder to their friends when they need to lean on someone."

I don't have enough friends like that.

Tillie blinked back a sudden rush of tears. "Thank you. But…we're fine." All Tillie needed was that job from Uncle Boone.

"Fine." Keith scoffed. "The word most commonly used to lie about one's emotional condition."

"Stop." Tillie crossed her arms over her chest and rested one foot on the bottom porch step.

"Two boxes!" Shay was saying to Reese at her door. "No one's ever bought two boxes from me. Not even Keith."

"I'll buy anything that isn't chocolate." Reese knelt in front of Shay, fluffing her black tutu. "What do you have left?"

"Snickerdoodles… Sugar cookies…" Shay drew

boxes out of the tote, unceremoniously dropping them on the porch without regard to the impact. "If you buy three boxes, Aunt Reese, I'll love you forever and ever."

"Wow." Reese beamed down at Shay, picking up a snickerdoodle box. "That's practically a proposal of marriage, sweet girl. Do you love me?"

"I love you forever and always." Shay nodded solemnly.

"Now, that's a marriage proposal," Tillie whispered to Keith.

He made that low, grumbly noise once more, sending a shiver down her spine. And then he smiled at Tillie as if his conversation with Brad had never happened and her snapping at him for implying there was something wrong with Shay had also never happened.

He's smiling at me the way he might have if I hadn't run off after kissing him last night.

And Tillie must have been smiling back the same way, because Reese caught Tillie's eye and said, "Now last night's absence makes sense."

Biting her lip, Tillie shook her head, earning a chuckle from both Reese and Keith and setting Tillie's teeth on edge. She reassured Reese she'd confirmed the logistics of the picnic lunch later and was about to ask if there was anything else her cousin needed when Shay interrupted her.

"Are you sure you only want two boxes, Aunt Reese?" Shay asked, organizing her wares on the porch floor, oblivious to the adult tensions around her. "Three is a lucky number."

"Three boxes it is, Shay. I need all the luck you can give me. I'll get my wallet." Reese retreated into her cabin, closing the door firmly behind her.

As if she has something to hide?

Tillie turned toward Keith, frowning. "I don't think Reese wants us to see inside her room."

Keith nodded, also frowning. "I think you're right."

"She wouldn't have taken those dresses." Tillie chewed her bottom lip once more. "Maybe she's hiding Carter in there. He wasn't in his cabin."

"Maybe." But Keith didn't sound so sure.

By unspoken agreement, they walked up the steps of Reese's cabin together, coming to stand on either side of Shay, who was humming to herself and swaying from side-to-side.

Keith reached over and rubbed the small of Tillie's back briefly before dropping his hand to his side. "I'm sorry about… Well, you can apply my apology anywhere you see fit, past or present."

"Thank you for apologizing," Tillie said softly, taking a moment to appreciate the warmth of his touch. "We can be firmly in the friend zone because we have a better understanding of each other now."

"You mean, I'm now more self-aware of my flaws." Keith ran a hand around the back of his neck where his hair curled enticingly.

"It's not like I'm perfect." Tillie reached over and gently touched those curls, trying to lighten his mood. "No one else is either. You don't have to be a drama queen."

He didn't so much as smile. "My situation—*based on my flaws*—seems pretty dramatic from where I'm sitting. I lost you *and* my company. I think I'm allowed to be a royal mess."

"Your situation from where you're sitting… Cowboy, I think you need to find a new chair to sit in." Tillie resisted rolling her eyes. "Wasn't it you who was talking about mistakes as a way to learn?"

"Yes," Keith grudgingly agreed.

"Ant!" Shay stomped the porch over and over, before squatting to assess the poor ant's condition. "He tried to eat my cookies." She squirmed. "I hate bugs."

"You come by that bug-o-phobia honestly, kid," Keith murmured, earning a shoulder nudge from Tillie.

Shay glanced up at them. "Is Aunt Reese coming out soon?"

"Yep," Tillie reassured her daughter. But it was taking her cousin a long time to find her wallet.

"She better come out," a woman's voice said authoritatively.

They all turned to find Crystal strutting up the walk. She was dressed in a ruffled blue skirt and an oatmeal-colored fisherman's sweater. Her hat was a coral fedora with a silver and turquoise hatband. Her boots were coral suede. She was dressed for a photo session, not a country ride.

"Reese needs to be ready to go soon, zit or no zit." Crystal held up a small vial. "I brought concealer."

"Okay, Shay. Here you go." Reese stepped out onto the porch with bills in her hand, pulling her door nearly closed behind her. "Oh, hey, Crystal."

Shay completed the exchange, taking the money and handing Reese her cookies.

"Girl, what are you wearing? You need to get changed." Crystal charged up the steps. "Plus we have to do your hair and makeup. You look like the day I first met you in Dallas. Did something happen to make you regress? Or was it *someone*?" She raised her neat brows while staring at Tillie.

Before Tillie knew what was happening, Crystal had whisked Reese back inside the cabin and shut the door in their faces.

CHAPTER EIGHT

"I'M ALMOST OUT of cookies, Mama." Stopping in the middle of the lane, Shay held her nearly empty tote out for inspection with a bespectacled smile that charmed Keith enough to smile in return.

Yes, Keith was enchanted, even as he wondered what had caused Shay's vision loss and why Tillie had such a guarded response to him asking about it. Granted, he'd asked about it as flat-footedly as he'd delivered his marriage proposal. Being thirty-five didn't necessarily mean a man had developed the proper conversational tools. But still...

"We should sell door-to-door every day." Shay lifted her face to the sky and began to spin. "I'm gonna sell a million-trillion cookies."

"No more spinning," Tillie warned.

And this time, Shay came to an immediate stop.

"Shay is determined to be right about her cookie sales strategy," Keith murmured to Tillie, who had stopped beside him, blond hair fluttering in the breeze beneath her brown cowboy hat.

They'd stopped at three other cabins since they'd visited Reese. No one had the dresses.

At the top of the rise stood Keith's cabin. It was white and the first in the next cluster of four cabins.

"Kids always want to grow up too soon," Tillie murmured back, adding in a louder, yet gentler, voice, "We sold to family and friends, Shay. When I say no door-to-door sales, I mean to strangers." And then, Tillie released a soft sigh.

Everything about her had been subdued since Reese had shut them out of her cabin, much like everything about Keith had been subdued since his conversation with Brad.

Well, almost everything. He and Tillie still managed an occasional tease, a soft, if brief, supportive touch. How quickly he'd taken to relying on that lighthearted aspect of their relationship.

"I think you're reneging on a promise," Keith told Tillie. He took her hand, lacing his fingers with hers. When she glanced at him with brows raised, he chuckled. "We agreed to lean on each other to get through the week, remember?"

He had a feeling she didn't lean on many people. Tillie had always been one to go it alone and power through.

"Are you gonna marry my mama?" Shay asked, letting the cookie tote fall to the ground, letting her jaw drop open as well. It only took the little spitfire a moment to collect herself. Well, her jaw, at least. Shay put her hands on her hips above that black tutu. "I'll let you marry Mama if you buy the rest of my cookies."

"Shay." Tillie tried to covertly tug her hand free, but Keith was having none of it. After a short attempt, Tillie gave up and asked her daughter, "You're partnering me with Keith till death do us part for all your cookies?"

"Uh-huh." Shay nodded, narrowing her eyes and angling her head to look at Keith through thick, critical lenses. "He's good at buying cookies *and* he's good at selling them."

Keith disguised a chuckle behind a cough and eased closer to Tillie, who also seemed locked in a struggle to keep from grinning. Her lips twitched.

"Seems like there should be more criteria for marriage than cookie buying and cookie selling skills," Tillie tried to grouse, but she gazed up at Keith with a speculative look in her eye. "Don't you think?"

Honey, you have no idea what I'm thinking.

Frankly, that was because his thoughts where she was concerned were a jumble.

Shay shrugged. "At least, Keith is good at something. I don't know what Aunt Reese sees in Carter."

Shay sounded so grown up that Keith could no longer disguise his laughter. And neither could Tillie.

"What's so funny?" Shay stomped her pink boot, making her black tutu bounce.

Tillie and Keith quickly contained themselves. Or tried to.

A stiff, chill breeze had them all reaching for their cowboy hats. The gust tangled and tossed the long ends of Tillie's and Shay's blond hair.

"You're full of opinions," Keith said to Shay when the wind died down. He fought to keep a straight face. "What about when you grow up? What qualities would you want a prospective fella to have?"

"Well..." Shay tapped a finger to her pursed lips, looking like the question required serious consideration. "He should have a good horse or two. And have won some rodeo competitions."

Keith raised his hand. "So far, I qualify."

"Not you." Shay scoffed. "You're *old*."

Tillie snorted.

"Ouch." Keith clutched his jean jacket over his chest. "That's hurtful."

Shay performed a mega eye roll she must have learned from watching her mother. "It's not hurtful if it's true."

"From the mouths of babes," Keith murmured, struck by the profound nature of Shay's comment. Because now, Keith could take Brad's comment about his strength being his ability to look ahead as a compliment. It was his strength. And it was something he liked about himself. That part wasn't as hurtful as it had been at first. Not anymore.

It was his own fault for not listening generously

and wholeheartedly to the subtext of the conversations they'd had at Sunny Y'all during contract negotiations. He hadn't wanted to sell. And he'd quickly learned that his voice was a minority in his partnership and with the board. The company they'd chosen to sell to had plans to distribute their current product catalog worldwide but not without changes that meant a decrease in price and, inevitably, in quality.

"It's my fault," he said. And this time, the words didn't carry the burdensome weight they had before.

Tillie reached up and tapped Keith's temple beneath the brim of his cowboy hat. "Have you just had an epiphany, Einstein?"

Keith nodded, then shook his head. "It's more like...self-forgiveness. I am who I am."

"I don't know what that means." Shay picked up her cookie tote and began to swing it around once more. "But I do know *I'm* not marrying you *or* Carter."

"It means..." Movement by Keith's cabin caught his eye. "Look! Did you see that?" Keith ran up the rise. "Someone came out of my cabin and disappeared into the brush."

"It was probably a staff member," Tillie called after him.

The feeling in Keith's gut doubted that. It was stupid of the resort to have an open door policy.

Keith's laptop was inside. It had every idea he'd ever had saved in various documents and files.

Keith charged up the porch steps, opened the cabin door and ran in.

Everything looked the same way he'd left it. Bed unmade, wet towel from his shower hanging on a hook, empty water glass in the sink, laptop still in his laptop bag.

Nothing was missing but no one had been inside cleaning either.

"Is this your room?" Shay wandered in, dragging her cookie tote as she moved toward the picture window in the back. "Do you share with anybody? Do you snore? Gran snores. But I sleep through it." She pressed her nose to the rear window. "Mostly."

Keith followed Shay to the window, brain still racing through possibilities—*maybe someone saw us approach and lost their nerve to rob me, maybe they'd only just opened the door when they realized I was nearby, maybe it was staff and they got called away.*

"You don't have anything fun outside your window," Shay said sadly, although it seemed like she was still searching for critters. "Just bushes."

"I had a burro outside my window this morning." He'd gotten out of the shower and been surprised to find the curious creature staring at him. "I think his name is Padre."

"It's Butler," the little girl said with certainty.

"Where is he now?" Shay placed her palms on his window on either side of her face, knocking her pink hat brim back. "I don't see him. I don't even see a peacock. Mama saw a peacock at a lot of cabins this morning."

No. She didn't.

That had been Tillie's ruse to get inside the cabins where they'd sold cookies so that she could search for dresses.

"I bet the peacocks are up by the barn," Keith told her. "That's where I saw them yesterday afternoon."

"I want a peacock feather." Shay pressed one cheek against the window and then the other, knocking off her pink cowboy hat and bumping her glasses on the window as she rotated her face from side-to-side. "Can you get me one?"

"I like you, Shay, but I'm not going to pluck a peacock for you."

Shay picked up her cowboy hat, plopped it on her little head and then turned toward him, head tilted and glasses askew. "Will you buy another box of cookies from me? *Please.*"

"All right." He couldn't resist this kid.

Shay nodded. "Okay. You can marry my mama."

Keith chuckled. "I didn't ask." Not recently anyway. And despite all the hand holding this afternoon, there were still obstacles that made a permanent relationship with Tillie…near impossible.

"Stop matchmaking, Shay. You're worse than Gran." Behind them in the entry, Tillie opened Keith's closet door, perhaps out of habit after their search of everyone else's room, perhaps because she was curious about him.

And then she said ominously, *"Keith."*

"What?" He left Shay at the window and joined Tillie at the closet.

"Look at this." Tillie drew out a garment bag.

But instead of revealing his black tuxedo, the clear garment bag held a ruby red gown. In fact, there were three others just like it hanging in his closet next to his tux. But no wedding dress.

"I told you someone ran out of my room," Keith said, feeling set up and boxed in. "You believe me, don't you?"

Tille stared at him, speculation in her blue eyes.

"Those dresses weren't there before, Til," he said firmly. "I told you. I saw someone run off. Whoever took the delivery must have placed the dresses in here." Struck by an unpleasant thought, Keith unzipped one of the garment bags holding a red dress.

"What are you doing?" Tillie demanded.

"Making sure the dresses aren't ripped or ruined in some way." He didn't really know what he was looking for but he drew the delicate skirt of the dress out of the garment bag anyway. "Why else would they swipe them?"

"That's a horrible thought." And yet, Tillie

opened another garment bag and conducted the same inspection he was. "You're not very trusting."

"I've learned a hard lesson about trust recently." Regardless of whether his own actions had led to his downfall or not.

Thankfully, the dresses all seemed fine.

Keith took Tillie's hand. "You do believe me, don't you, Til?"

Tillie stared at their joined hands, and then she nodded, raising her pretty blue gaze to his. "I believe you. I did see someone. Just not enough to identify anyone."

"Thank you." He breathed a sigh of relief, then impulsively lifted her cowboy hat and pressed a kiss to her forehead. "Thank you," he said again, returning her brown hat to its place on all that golden hair.

"What do we do now?" Tillie eased her hand from his, blushing.

"Mama! Keith!" Shay cried. "Come look at the peacock. It's so pretty and it's making a big fan."

"What do we do now?" Keith considered reclaiming Tillie's hand but decided she wouldn't want him to, if only not to encourage Shay. "First, we go look at a peacock to see if he drops a feather. And then we go for a trail ride and picnic." He led the way to the back of the cabin. "And then we find Reese's wedding dress by circling back around to the odd things we noticed today."

Brad's lack of a tuxedo and Reese's determination to keep them from seeing inside her cabin.

"Hey, I can finish that." Keith arrived at the barn after pausing the dress search with Tillie to find that the staff were saddling his horse. He walked over to the young cowboy tending to his black gelding. "I'm not used to anyone doing the work for me."

"That's for sure." Carter appeared nearby, leading a flashy white and black paint out of a stall.

Keith wasn't sure how to take that remark. So, he didn't answer. Instead, he checked Sable's bridle, and then his girth strap. The stable hand seemed to know what he was doing.

And Tillie...

She was a kind, smart, attractive woman capable of knocking him off his game, even if his game felt as if it was on pause, both personally and professionally.

Carter tied up his horse next to Sable using the next hook in the barn wall. "I meant that we always saddled our own horses growing up."

"You meant..." Keith let those two words hang in the air between them before continuing. "That implies there could be two meanings to your statement. Such as, I also did a lot of work for myself elsewhere... Say at Sunny Y'all?"

Carter grunted, taking a brush from a shelf and running it over the paint's sleek back.

"I talked to Brad about what led to my…leaving." That felt like it needed to be said.

Carter's grunt deepened.

"You could have told me outright to stop moving new product production forward, Carter. You didn't have to give me the ax."

His foster brother shook his head. "We did it to protect you."

Two months of resentment tried to push its way up Keith's throat. With effort, he swallowed it back down, wanting answers more than the chance to vent. "Of all the reasons I imagined you giving me for forcing me out…protecting me wasn't one of them."

Sable bumped Keith's arm with his nose, as if to say, *"Lighten up."* As if to remind Keith that he'd imagined much darker, self-serving confessions coming out of Carter and Brad. He should be happy with this more altruistic version. And he might have been if it wasn't so hard to believe.

Carter brushed his flashy horse. "I saw the signs. You were getting twitchy about the sale. So, yes. When I voted with the board to oust you, I was making sure you receive the payout you deserve for over a decade of hard work."

"I'd rather have the choice than have you make it for me without explanation."

Keith's mind drifted back to the days when he, Carter and Brad were in high school. As teens, they'd had each other's backs. They'd battled the enemy on the football field. Keith and Brad blocking for Carter in a primitive version of the tush-push. Quarterback Carter celebrating touchdowns with backflips. They'd helped each other improve their technique in riding bulls and broncs. And although they had dreams of winning weekend rodeos to finance college and then a company, they'd laughed when they'd spent more on entry fees than they'd won.

When had the laughter stopped? Keith couldn't remember.

He focused on less enigmatic issues. "We should take the paints out before the trail ride."

"Good idea," Carter agreed.

The stable hand returned with Carter's saddle and bridle. It was the special tack Reese had talked about at breakfast—dark leather with lots of shiny silver accents.

"Fancy," Keith noted. And not at all like the Carter he'd grown up with. Or Reese, for that matter.

Carter looked at the elaborately decorated tack with a resigned expression. "The things we do for those we love."

The sound of women's laughter drifted to them from the other end of the barn, Reese's distinctive chuckle among them.

"We'll talk more later," Carter promised Keith, putting a smile on his face for the approaching wedding party. And then his smile fell. His brow clouded. And he glanced at Keith.

Keith turned and experienced the same shock.

Reese and Crystal led the bridesmaids through the barn. Unlike the other women, Reese and Crystal wore long flowing dresses, and had styled their hair in a fussy fashion. Reese looked nothing like the woman Shay had sold cookies to an hour ago, nothing like the woman Carter had proposed to.

And as Keith studied Carter's closed-off reaction, he realized that his foster brother noticed it, too.

And didn't like it.

CHAPTER NINE

"I'M DANIEL. I'll be your tour guide today." A cowboy who looked barely old enough to drive sat on a sturdy-looking bay at the front of the mounted riders in the wedding party. "We always ask that you take a guided tour of the property before you set out riding on your own."

Daniel's gaze landed on Keith, who'd gone out riding yesterday on his own.

Keith, who'd chastely kissed Tillie's forehead after she'd found the bridesmaid dresses in his closet and told him she didn't suspect him of stealing them.

Keith, who'd taken her hand after Reese had shut her out and reminded her of their agreement to lean on each other to get through the wedding week.

Keith, who her heart pined for and her head adamantly rejected.

'Nuff said.

Tillie looked away from temptation.

"Gran, can we ride in front? Daniel looks like he could eat a lot of cookies." Without waiting for her grandmother's permission, Shay guided her pony Bixby onward.

"I guess I'm riding with the bride and groom." Tugging down the wide brim of her straw cowboy hat, Gran guided her gray mare after Shay.

Tillie eased up on the reins, allowing Jam to take a couple steps forward, closing the gap left when Gran and Shay moved ahead.

Keith brought his horse abreast of Tillie's.

His horse Sable was a tall, black gelding with a competitive nature. He liked to run and he didn't like to lose. He also had a playful streak, which was how he fit as Keith's mount. When they were leading their horses out to the ranch yard, Sable had plucked Shay's pink cowboy hat off her head.

Not only had Keith won Shay over, his horse had as well.

Keith gestured toward Shay. "Shouldn't we keep Shay with us? Reese and Carter are supposed to be at the front of the line."

"Gran won't let Shay steal anybody's limelight." Tillie stared at Keith's boot in Sable's stirrup. It was a worn brown boot and an equally worn stirrup. Both signs of a true cowboy. "And technically, Mike the photographer is at the front of the line."

The aging cowboy shutterbug rode a grizzled gray. He held the reins in his teeth, his camera with both hands, and had already choreographed

Reese and Carter into several staged poses as he guided his horse in a slow circle around them.

And Reese…

Keith nodded toward her. "I can tell by that look on your face that you're as shocked as everyone by Reese's costume change."

"She looks beautiful." And for that, Tillie was happy for her cousin. "Like she could be on a magazine cover."

Reese's white-blond hair was gorgeous, barely lifting as the wind swirled about. She wore a feminine-cut denim jacket. The skirt of her blue, ruffled dress was spread out over the saddle and hindquarters of her flashy white and black horse. Not even Crystal could compare to Reese.

Tillie took small pleasure in that.

Ahead of them, Shay reached Reese's side and said something that Tillie couldn't hear.

Reese glowed as she said something back.

"If I was a lip-reader," Keith said, deep voice low, as if he had something romantic only Tillie should hear. "I'd tell you Reese just told Shay she was pretty, too."

He says all the right things.

But Tillie knew he wasn't the right man for her. Not anymore. He was no longer a fine citizen of Clementine. And his future was up in the air, while Tillie's was at stake here on the ground.

"We're not in Clementine anymore, are we?" Keith asked, bringing Tillie back to the present.

"No cowgirl in Clementine would wear a dress like that on a trail ride. And news flash. The skirt covers nearly all the silver on her saddle."

"Sourpuss. Reese may look different, but she's still my Clementine Reese inside," Tillie said softly.

"I hope Carter sees that, too," Keith said cryptically.

The group set off at a walk. Keith and Tillie lingered at the back.

Daniel led them to what seemed like an ATV path. There were ruts on both sides of the dirt road. Chickens escorted them down the trail to a gate, where they clucked excitedly, going no further.

Keith tipped his hat to a noisy hen. "I think these chickens expect us to toss them some chicken feed."

"We'll have to bring some on our next ride." Tillie passed through the gate, noticing that the chickens didn't venture out of the ranch proper. "There must be coyotes in the area. Chickens aren't the brightest animals on the planet, but they can learn where it's safest."

The wind kicked up, swirling dust around their horse's hooves.

Keith settled his black cowboy hat more firmly on his head. "This missing wedding dress is like a puzzle."

"You've always enjoyed puzzles." Tillie would rather watch him solve them. He was something to behold when his creative juices started flowing. His eyes flashed and his mouth puckered, as if he was in need of a kiss.

Best not think about kisses.

Keith let Sable pick his way around a large dip in the path. "Whoever signed for the dresses had to think about what name to put on the delivery form, then carry them somewhere, then come to breakfast acting as if nothing was amiss, and then put them in my cabin."

They'd since moved the bridesmaid dresses to Tillie's cabin.

"The thief used your name and planted dresses in your closet." Tillie clucked her tongue, causing Jam's ears to swivel around toward her. "That does seem like a heavy handed set-up, perhaps by someone who doesn't want you at the wedding."

"Boone? Carter? Brad?" he guessed.

Tillie nodded. "Although it's hard to imagine my uncle signing your name with a heart over the *i*. Or him risking upsetting Reese this way. I'd cross him off your list."

"Point taken. The only one of those three still upset with me is Brad." Keith squinted skyward, as if the heavens held the answer that eluded him. "All that carrying around of the dresses…" Enthusiasm built in his voice. "There are resort employees everywhere. Someone had to see something."

Tillie snuck a glance at Keith's handsome face, then admired the way he sat tall in the saddle. She had a weak spot for handsome, skilled cowboys. "We can ask the employees when we get back."

"Good idea." Keith nodded. "I want to question Brad on this ride. He didn't have a tuxedo in his closet. Did he forget it or does he think there won't be a wedding?"

"Oh, there will be a wedding," Tillie said firmly.

Ahead of them, the wedding photographer asked for a pause as he set up a shot with a sprawling pasture as a backdrop. The rest of the wedding party halted their horses.

"And then there's Reese." Keith brought Sable to a stop, turning his attention to Tillie. "She didn't want us to see inside her cabin this morning. Do you think she'll let you in later?"

"I can try." Tillie thought on that task for a moment before adding, "Gran is loaning her a blue handkerchief to pin beneath her skirt for the wedding. We could deliver it after our ride."

"Hi, Mama!" Shay drew her feet from her stirrups, rose to a kneeling position on her saddle, then brandished her pink cowboy hat in the air, waving like mad. "I see you! Look at me!"

"Sit down in your saddle, young lady," Tillie called back, causing all sorts of laughter and comments from the rest of the bridal party.

"You've got a trick rider on your hands, Matilda." Uncle Boone rode about four horses ahead of them next to Aunt Eleanor.

"She's outgrown that pony," Keith's father told Tillie. He rode behind Boone and next to his wife, Mary.

"You're as adorable as your mother at that age," Gran told Shay, earning a grin of approval from Tillie's pride and joy.

After a few minutes, the photographer was satisfied and they continued with their trail ride. The air was brisk and the sky a soft shade of blue. It felt good to be on horseback. Tillie could pretend the wedding dress wasn't missing, the wedding week was proceeding smoothly toward its conclusion, and that she wouldn't fall back in love with Keith.

That was a lot of pretending. Otherwise known as denial.

Tillie sighed.

The lead riders broke into a slow gallop. Not one to have good technique, Reese bounced in the saddle. Shay's pony had a dislike of galloping. Bixby trotted at a quick clip, giving Shay a bouncy ride, too. Tillie didn't need much cuing to put Jam into his smooth lope.

Nor did Keith, although his problem was reining Sable in. He gave Tillie a curious look. "Why did you marry Neil Wheeler?"

Tillie frowned, guard coming up.

Her ex-husband was ancient history. He'd moved out of state, provided a small amount of child support and only saw Shay a few times a year. And yet, Keith's question was as uncomfortable as a cheap wool sweater.

"Why did I marry Neil? For one thing, he didn't ask me for the money in my savings account when he proposed."

Keith shook his head, not looking perturbed. "You're avoiding the question."

She was. It was painful to admit that she'd made a mistake with her marriage. She hadn't loved Neil to the moon and back the way a bride was supposed to love her groom.

The way I loved Keith.

"This isn't a conversation I want to have, Keith." But he'd owned up to his contribution in his ouster at Sunny Y'all. How could she not own up to her own mistake?

Tillie eased back on the reins, shortening Jam's stride, slowing them down for a little more privacy.

Keith did the same with Sable. "As if any of our conversations in the last twenty-four hours weren't difficult."

Tillie spared him a glance. "Neil was nice to me and he stuck around."

Keith stiffened in the saddle, scowling at a point between Sable's ears. "That's it? That's all it took to forget me?"

I didn't forget you.

"Of course, that's not all." Tillie gave Keith what she hoped was a withering look, not that he saw it given he was still staring ahead. "After you left… After you wouldn't return any of my messages… Something clicked in my head. Call it my biological alarm clock ringing. Call it the need to nest. Whatever. Neil was there and you weren't. It was a brief courtship, a brief marriage, and I'd regret it more if I hadn't had Shay."

"I should have stuck around after I proposed," Keith admitted, surprising Tillie. Was this him taking Brad's words to heart? "And I should have listened to or read your messages. I had my blinders on."

"I appreciate you saying that." And Tillie knew how much it cost him to admit he'd been wrong. But that wasn't enough to start anew.

They approached the end of the pasture. The trail ahead disappeared beneath some trees. Riders were reining their horses in, bringing them to a walk. Puffs of dust rose from the horses' hooves as the riders closed ranks.

Keith and Tillie didn't say anything to each other as they rode through the trees and into the next pasture. One by one, pairs of riders took off at a gallop again, giving them privacy once more.

Keith held Sable to a slow pace, despite the gelding tossing his head and trying to run with—or past—the herd. "Did you hear what I said?"

"Yep." Tillie eased Jam into a controlled gallop, his smoothest gait. "When I turned you down, I didn't mean you to take it as a forever no. I would have waited for you the way Reese has waited for

Carter. But it's too late now. And… I can't be certain you won't disappear without hearing me out if things get tough." And with Shay's health issues, things were always tough.

Keith held Sable even with Tillie and Jam, looking as if he disagreed with her.

And then Keith loosened his reins and let Sable run. Full tilt.

As if he couldn't get away from Tillie fast enough.

FUNNY THING ABOUT HURT. It made a man act like an utter fool.

Keith wanted to rein Sable in and apologize to Tillie. Again.

He wanted to tell her he was a changed man.

But hurt had lit a fire beneath the feet of his vulnerable self-worth and that had him galloping away from Tillie with blinders on, overtaking his parents on their horses, Reese's parents on their mounts, and a few of the bridesmaids riding resort horses. It took him across the pasture to the gentle rise of a hill where riders were pulling their horses back into a walk. It took him right next to Brad.

"Pretty place, isn't it?" Keith began when he drew even with Brad, who was looking at his phone and letting his horse pick his way as they rode beneath another tree line. "Reminds me of the Done Roamin' Ranch back home in Clementine."

"Huh?" Brad looked up from his phone, glanced around. Shrugged. "There are more trees here. And if you're wanting to talk more about what happened, the answer is no."

Keith scoffed. "I'm just shooting the breeze. How'd you sleep last night?" Might just as well make idle conversation. It was preferable to thoughts of Tillie running roughshod through his head.

"If you must know, I didn't sleep well. I was up late going over production schematics. Something isn't right. We've had too many quality standards fail since we downgraded our materials." Brad tucked his phone in his jeans pocket, then pushed his prescription sunglasses up his nose. "And no. I'm not going to go into the details of that either."

"I'm out of Sunny Y'all. I get that." Keith's pride was a bitter lump moving at a snail's pace up the back of his throat. He tamped it down, along with the impulse to ride ahead to a more welcoming Velma and Shay. "So, you weren't drinking with Carter last night?"

Brad shook his head, looking more at ease. "No. I had work to do. Carter is as anxious as a pup waiting at the vet's for this wedding to be over. He started drinking at dinner and didn't seem interested in stopping."

"I don't blame him. There's hardly a moment to relax these next few days." Keith deftly switched gears, probing at the matter that was most important to him. "I tried on my tux last night. Glad to see it still fit."

"I left mine hanging in the truck," Brad admitted. "If anything, yours and mine should be baggy. I don't know about you, but the past few months… I can hardly eat. I'm nauseous all the time. I've lost ten pounds."

Keith drew back, taking in what he now recognized as a more svelte Brad. "Have you been to the doctor? That doesn't sound good."

Brad shook his head. "It's stress. If Carter and the board did that to you, they could do that to me. We spent over a decade finding the right product with the right name, the right production partner, the right pricing structure and sales pitch. You and me. We were the ones who didn't want to sell, the ones outvoted by Carter and the board. If I'm out next, what do I do? I'm clinging to this job like I'm on a crumbling mountain ledge. It's like my childhood all over again." Where his mother had battled addiction, often unsuccessfully, and lost custody of Brad.

"I understand." They came from two different family situations. Brad tried to hang on to what he had while Keith looked forward and closed doors behind him.

"I don't want to start all over again at thirty-five." Brad shook his head. "I don't want to be an entrepreneur. I want a fixed salary, great health care and a retirement package."

Keith wouldn't mind starting over, using his own money to fund a start-up and bet on himself.

And that was exactly why he and Tillie were a long-shot to work out. She was risk-averse when it came to money, to uncertainty, to betting on the future. And him.

"Just the person I want to see." Crystal maneuvered her golden palomino crosswise in front of Brad and Keith at the next narrowing of the trail. Her dress was fancier than Reese's but she'd been bouncing every time they galloped. She was an urban cowgirl, through and through. "Can we talk, Keith?"

The riders were more widespread now and there was a break between Brad and Keith and the riders behind them.

Brad stared at Keith. Keith stared at Brad. Neither one of them seemed to know why Crystal would want a word with Keith. Crystal had never done more than nod in Keith's direction to acknowledge his existence.

"I'll just ride on ahead," Brad said in a low voice before spurring his horse on.

Crystal circled her palomino around behind Keith, no doubt intending to take Brad's place.

Sable sidled sideways, ears flattened against his head. He disliked an unknown horse behind him.

"Your horse is as skittish as you are around folks," Crystal noted.

Up close, Crystal had an untouchable air about her. Not an unbeatable air, but a cold, remote one. Keith couldn't help but compare her to Tillie and find Crystal wanting. Tillie had a warm, approachable presence. An honest presence.

And in the face of her honesty about her marriage, I got hurt and ran. Again.

If a second chance with Tillie was possible, Keith had to do better emotionally and stand his ground. The same could be said for his relationship with Carter and Brad.

Sable was huffing and riding hard, hooves pounding a bouncy, uncharacteristic gait.

"You're your own worst enemy, boy." *Like me.* Keith shifted in his seat, applied pressure with his knees, and held the gelding to a tighter rein that said Sable was to obey.

"There's nothing like a retreat to foster business opportunities," Crystal said cryptically.

Sable finally settled into a steadier gait, ignoring a blackbird that swooped in front of them.

If only I could adjust my approach to life as easily.

Of course, Sable needed Keith to settle down. *What do I need?*

The memory of Tillie taking his hand came to mind, along with her reassuring smile.

"I'm going to cut right to the chase, Keith." Crystal spoke as if she was doing Keith a favor just talking to him. "I've been looking for an investment opportunity." Her butterfly lashes flickered up and down as she gave him an assessing look. "And I think I want you and that big brain of yours."

Keith didn't know whether to thank her or laugh her off. "Why would you want to invest in me?"

"Boone said you were cooking up ideas when you were handed your walking papers." Crystal's smile warmed.

I prefer Tillie's smile.

"I'm prepared to offer you an angel investment," Crystal went on. "I'll pay you a salary, along with those of whatever support staff you need—an engineer, a marketer—and office space, of course."

"Sounds like you want me and someone like Brad, and Carter." Keith didn't know how he felt about that, given what he'd learned today about their dysfunctional working relationship.

"No, darlin'. I only want you." Crystal stared down her nose at Keith, a difficult feat given her palomino was much smaller than Sable. "We can find replacements for the other two lickety-split."

Keith didn't know how he felt about that either.

Crystal laughed, very cartoon villainesque. "Don't look so surprised. You're the talent behind Sunny Y'all's success. I can back you on your next venture without the drag of Brad and Carter. Think about it and we'll talk more later." She kicked her horse and lurched forward, impractical dress rippling behind her like a supervillain's cape.

And Sable… Sable leaped forward, too, trying to make this a race.

Keith held him back, needing to process what had just happened.

I have an investor…if I want one.

Do I need one?

Keith wasn't sure.

He gave Sable a bit more rein, letting the gelding lengthen his stride now that Crystal was further ahead.

She wants me. Not Carter or Brad.

It was an ego boost. And even if he knew working with Crystal held no appeal, just for a moment, Keith felt flattered, validated, wanted.

CHAPTER TEN

AFTER AN HOUR on the trail, their tour guide called a halt next to a narrow stream that was sheltered from the westerly wind by a grove of tall oak trees.

Tillie dismounted and led Jam toward the line for the watering trough, glancing around with an eye toward trouble for Reese or the luncheon.

The resort had built hitching posts, a water trough and picnic tables in the glen. A small lunch had been set up, delivered by one of the wagons parked near one end of the line of hitching posts. A pair of resort workers were unloading an antique settee from the wagon. It was going to be used as a prop in the photos—Crystal's idea. Another worker manned a large grill. The smell of barbecued chicken filled the air.

Tillie's stomach growled.

"Make sure things run smooth, Matilda," Uncle Boone told Tillie when they were both looping their reins over the same hitching post after letting their horses drink water.

"Yes, sir." But first, Tillie needed to do something else.

Bixby was grazing a few feet away from the watering trough, his reins hanging loosely about his neck.

"Shay, what's the first rule of horseback riding?" Tillie's voice cut through the bridal party like a sharp knife through a chiffon wedding cake.

"Make sure your cinch is tight!" one of the groomsmen replied, eliciting a round of chuckles.

"Try not to bounce!" another groomsman replied before the laughter died down.

"Don't fall off!" Uncle Boone leaped into the fray.

"You're all wrong." Shay marched toward Bixby with a determined expression on her dear face. "The first rule is to make sure your horse can't run away."

"Spoken like a cowpoke whose horse has run away at least once," Keith quipped. "Best way to learn is to fail, Shay. Even if it's painful."

Tillie looked sharply at Keith. Was that a message to her? An invitation to try again after learning from their mistakes?

Their gazes connected, sparked. He mouthed one word, *"Sorry."*

Whatever the apology applied to, Tillie's cheeks began to heat.

"I wanted to see the creek first." Shay took hold of Bixby's reins and brought them over the pony's head. Then she led her mount over to the watering trough with her little nose in the air. "But the second rule of riding is to make sure your mount is watered and fed."

"I'm proud of you, Shay," Tillie told her.

The photographer called for the bridesmaids and flower girl Shay to join the bride near the stream where the antique settee had been positioned. Keith took over pony duty so Shay could join them. What followed was round after round of pictures. Soon the groom and his attendants were added to the mix. Then the parents. Then all of them.

"Why do we have to take so many pictures?" Shay griped. "It's not even the wedding yet."

More chuckling ensued.

"Reese wants to remember every happy part of this very special week," Tillie told her daughter.

Reese glanced at Tillie with an approving smile.

For a moment, Tillie was back in time, back in Clementine, back to her youth when she and Reese were best friends, not just cousins. Back to a time when Reese would never call Tillie an obligation.

But that moment passed. Pictures were snapped. Over and over. So many pictures that Tillie considered siding with Shay that too many were being taken. She was relieved when only the bride and groom were being posed. Except it was cold just standing around and the food service was waiting for the bride and groom to open the buffet.

Finally, the photographer was satisfied.

People were drifting toward the buffet table when Crystal stopped everyone in their tracks. "Wait. The groom needs to wade into the stream carrying the bride."

Carter frowned. Reese looked torn. The large bridal party seemed to hold its collective breath.

"Oh, come on. Come on." Crystal made a sweeping gesture from the happy couple to the stream. "Think about how unique this setting is, how romantic that pose is, how many likes it will generate on social media."

Carter's frowned deepened. Reese looked less torn.

"If it were my wedding, I'd do it," Crystal said authoritatively.

"What do you say, Carter?" Reese took his hand, drew him closer and smiled up at him with the face of an angel. "Everyone else can start to eat while we take this one…last…photo."

"Anything for you." Carter kissed Reese. Briefly. Sweetly.

The tension Tillie imagined in the bridal party seemed to deflate as the happy couple walked hand-in-hand toward the stream.

"Be careful in that crick," one of the resort workers cautioned. "The rocks are slippery."

"I've got this," Carter reassured him, sweeping Reese into his arms.

Tillie had to admit. Carter carrying his fiancée was a romantic image. She snuck a glance at Keith. Black cowboy hat, brown hair curling at the back of his neck, strong profile, sturdy shoulders, slight smile. His was a romantic image, too.

"Hang on, Romeo." Crystal scurried over to Reese and Carter. "We've got to make sure Reese's dress is draped just right." She tugged, tucked and fluffed Reese's long skirt. "There. Knock it out of the park, you two."

Most of the wedding party was lined up at the buffet table, backs to the last series of photos being taken for the day, including Shay and Gran.

But Tillie hung back, watching Carter wade out into the stream until the water neared the top of his cowboy boots, listening to the click-click-click-click of the photographer's camera.

"Shouldn't you move closer?" Keith said in a low voice, having come to stand next to Tillie without her noticing. "Just in case they stumble? It's your job to make sure nothing bad happens, right?"

Tillie shook her head, staring up into mischievous blue eyes. *All is forgiven.* "Take your sarcasm elsewhere. If they stumble, no one but Carter can keep them from—"

A scream rose in the air, startling several birds overhead. That was immediately followed by a series of splashes. And a ripple of gasps.

Keith ran forward before Tillie fully realized what had happened. He splashed into the stream and helped the sopping wet couple to their feet.

Carter was cussing, scrambling for their cowboy hats. Reese's face was white. And she was shivering. Keith helped them to the bank.

"You wanted noteworthy," the photographer quipped in his gravelly voice. "I've got the entire sequence on film." He chuckled. "I bet that will get lots of likes, right, Crystal?"

"Oh, shut up, Mike," Crystal sniped. "Show some compassion."

Tillie finally recovered enough to ask their tour guide, "Do you have a blanket, Daniel? Or a spare set of clothes?"

"I've got a hand towel," the cook offered, holding up a black towel he'd had tucked in his back pocket. "It's not much. But it's clean, haven't used it yet."

"Thank you. It'll help Reese dry her hair." Tillie hurried to the bank of the stream. "Here." She wrapped Reese's hair in the hand towel as best she could, then removed Reese's wet coat, replacing it with her own.

Keith took note of her actions and removed Carter's coat, offering him his lined jeans jacket. "It's not much."

"It's better than nothing," Carter told him. "Thanks."

"I'm sorry, Carter." Reese choked back a sob. "I knew we shouldn't have tried that."

"It'll make a great story for your grandkids." Tillie tried to make light of it. "But for now, we should get you back to the resort." Tillie guided an un-protesting Reese toward the horses. "Do you want to ride in the wagon? Or on Kimbrel?" Her flashy paint.

"I'll ride. Can you…" Reese stopped, lifting her wet, dragging hem. "Can you wring out my skirt?"

"Of course." Tillie got right to work.

"I'll ride back, too," Carter said, coming to stand next to Reese and pulling her close while Tillie did her best to wring the excess water from her skirt. "We don't want you catching cold."

"The four of us can go," Keith said, joining them. "Let the rest of them get fed."

Reese nodded, regaining some of her composure to call out, "Stay and have a good time, everybody."

"Not to worry, Tillie. I'll take care of Shay," Gran called to her.

"Don't worry, Mama," Shay shouted without missing a beat. "I'll take care of Gran."

"Shay is my hero," Reese whispered to Tillie. "She's perfect. You're so lucky to have her."

"I'm lucky to have you," Tillie whispered back, trying not to cry. "You never made me feel like…" *An obligation.* She couldn't say that. "Like I was less than."

"No one would dare do that to you on my watch," the old Clementine Reese said staunchly.

Tillie hugged her, every wet bit of her. How

could she not? This was the woman she'd originally taken on the role of maid of honor for, the
woman she'd go to battle for.

"Okay, ladies. We can talk on the ride back."
Carter mustered them toward their horses. He
tossed his and Reese's wet cowboy hats into the
back of a wagon.

The hungry wedding party called their quick
goodbyes.

In no time, the bride, groom, Keith and Tillie had mounted up and were headed back to
the resort. Tillie rode next to Reese, whose skirt
was twisted like a tail behind her, revealing her
legs clad in wet blue leggings. They walked their
horses through a tree-covered trail behind the
men. The wind swayed the branches above them.

"This is supposed to be the wedding of my
dreams," Reese said in a dejected voice. "If I'm
being honest, it's probably the wedding of Crystal's dreams."

"Tell me what you want to change and I'll do
it." Tillie would gladly put Crystal in her place.

"I… I can't." Reese hung her head, damp white-
blond hair stringy on either side of her face. "I
can't change anything. This is the kind of wedding Carter needs."

That was confusing. "I think Carter would have
been happy standing up with you in front of a
judge at the courthouse in Clementine. We can
change anything you want."

"It's not about what he or I *want*. It's what we *need* to do for his career." Reese snuck a glance at Tillie from between locks of wet hair. "I wanted to marry Carter right out of high school. I wanted to marry him when he graduated from college. I wanted to marry him when he returned to Clementine." Reese had stood by her man longer than anyone.

"I know you've waited a long time for this, Reese. You stuck by Carter since you were fourteen. But what does that have to do with your wedding? Or should I say the dream wedding you aren't allowing yourself to have."

Reese slowed her white and black horse nearly to a stop and lowered her voice. "Everything's been going downhill since the guys signed the agreement to consider a sale to Durant Ranch Products. According to Carter, every round of negotiations seems to take away something the guys wanted. At first, Durant offered for the entire portfolio of products. Now it's down to just two. Carter assumed they'd all be kept on after the sale but last I heard that was under discussion."

Jam swatted Tillie's leg with his tail, not pleased with the snail's pace she was imposing.

"Daddy's on the board of Sunny Y'all, but even he can't predict the outcome of this sale. And Crystal says—"

Tillie's jaw clenched at Crystal's name.

"—that Carter needs a strong social media presence to help him land a good job if this deal ends up with him unemployed."

Tillie was happy to poke holes in Crystal's opinion. "Carter has a strong track record bringing Sunny Y'all to a point where a larger company would want to buy it. His résumé speaks for itself. And you told me before that he'll get a handsome payout. It's not as if he'll need a job right away."

"Crystal says—"

"I'm not interested in anything Crystal says," Tillie cut her off.

Reese gave Tillie a wry smile. "*I believe* that anything associated with Carter needs to appear like he has the Midas touch. It's my way of supporting his career, whether Durant Ranch Products keeps him on or not."

"That explains your upgraded wardrobe, your indecision, the big name wedding photographer and the pricey, unusual wedding favors."

"All of it. Yes," Reese said miserably, shivering. "Do you hate me for turning into a bridezilla who only cares for appearances?"

"No." She understood Reese now. But before Tillie could say anymore, Carter called to them from the edge of the field.

"Get a move on, ladies."

"Coming." Reese gathered her reins and cued her horse into a trot. She wouldn't be able to talk until they reached the far side of the pasture.

Tillie eased Jam into a slow gallop, pondering

Reese's words. Her need to impress explained a lot. But did it mean she'd stolen her own wedding dress?

"YOU SHOULD RIDE with Reese," Keith told Carter when they reached the next grove of trees and had slowed their mounts to a walk. He glanced over his shoulder at the approaching women on their galloping horses. "She looks miserable."

Of course, Carter looked miserable, too. His shoulders were hunched, his features pinched. From the cold? Keith's lined jeans jacket was probably little consolation when Carter's clothes were drenched. Or was he dwelling on the fact that he'd dropped his bride in the creek?

"I don't think she wants to marry me," Carter confessed.

"That's not true," Keith said quickly. "And if you're worried about that, you need to talk to her more than ever."

Carter gave a curt nod, turning his horse around.

"Tillie, ride with me," Keith said, trying to ease the tension around the bride and groom.

"Sure." Tillie brought Jam to a smooth stop next to Keith.

They held their mounts back as Reese and Carter walked their paints beneath the canopy of trees.

Keith eased up on the reins, letting Sable walk forward. "Are you warm enough, Til?"

Keeping Jam even with Sable, Tillie reached over and grasped hold of his wrist with icy fingers. "Does that answer your question?"

"All I've got to offer you is the shirt off my back." And he'd give it to her if she'd accept.

Tillie withdrew her hand, chuckling. "Wouldn't that give rise to the impression we were getting back together?"

"Wouldn't want to give off that impression." Although he wouldn't mind a second shot, if things were different. If *he* were different.

Ahead of them, Reese and Carter held hands while riding.

"I never forgot you," Tillie said quietly. "When you left. I never forgot you."

Hope took root inside Keith.

"I was afraid to follow you to Dallas." She shook her head, gaze fixed ahead. "Moving... I have bad memories associated with moving. It signified financial failure for my family."

"And you work very hard at not failing financially."

A squirrel scampered up a nearby tree, scolding them as they passed.

Tillie stared at Keith, blue eyes filled with regret. "Since I saw you in the resort lobby, I've been wrestling with the idea that it takes two to fail at a relationship."

They rode in silence. Keith was tempted to reach for her hand, hoping his touch would reinforce the bridge they seemed to be building between each other, wishing he could banish the regret from her eyes.

"We've come this far in our professional lives because we didn't have to sacrifice for our relationship," Tillie continued. "And if I'm honest with myself, I'm still attracted to you."

"I sense an unspoken *but*."

She nodded, pressing her brown cowboy hat more firmly on her head as a gust blew past, sending the blond ends of her hair flying. "But maybe that's because our relationship is like an old pair of broken-in jeans. Comfortable but not appropriate for every occasion."

Keith shook his head instead of shouting, *"No!"* figuring that wouldn't go over well. He had to stay in the present. "Do you know what I wore to work every day at Sunny Y'all?"

"Ratty old blue jeans?" That elicited a smile from her.

"Yep. Even when the executives from Durant Ranch Products paid us visits."

Carter and Reese reached the edge of the next field and sent their white and black horses into a gallop.

Sable tossed his head, testing Keith's hold on the reins. The gelding wanted to run as well.

Keith patted Sable's black neck. "We're dancing around things, Til, instead of talking plainly.

There's still something between us. Something that is just waiting for—"

"Us to declare it officially over." Tillie sent Jam galloping across the field.

"—a second chance," Keith muttered, giving his gelding free rein, wishing he could give his heart the same.

CHAPTER ELEVEN

Tillie was tense by the time they reached the resort's barn. Keith wasn't seeing the writing on the wall. They may always have sparks between them but their lives were going in different directions. She couldn't dismount fast enough, not wanting to chat.

Reese groaned when she dismounted, letting Carter take her horse's reins. "That was a mistake."

"The picture in the stream?" Tillie asked, relinquishing Jam's reins to Keith without looking at him.

Reese shook her head as the men led the horses away. "Galloping back in wet clothes." She gingerly walked toward the path leading down to the lane and on to the cabins. "I might have a blister on my backside."

"Oh, honey." Tillie took her cousin's arm. "Let's get you out of these clothes and into a hot bath."

"Why is this happening to me?" Reese whined, fully entitled in Tillie's opinion. "If it's not one thing, it's another, all bad. Or it would be if Carter wasn't so kind and understanding. But everybody…everything…"

"Just say the word and I'll change everything to your liking," Tillie said, more than happy to be too busy for Keith's tempting presence. "Not everything needs to be photo perfect."

"I know. And I appreciate your offer," Reese said softly. "But I'm committed to trying to make it look that way."

A bird's shriek from a nearby bush had them both jumping, then stumbling. They reached for each other.

"I hate peacocks," Tillie muttered, glad they hadn't cartwheeled down the hill or fallen into a bramble.

"I hate weddings." Reese shivered.

Tillie took in her cousin's pinched expression. "You don't mean that."

But since Reese didn't answer, Tillie wasn't so sure.

"I'LL TAKE CARE of the horses, Carter." Keith reached for the pair of reins Carter was holding. "You look like an unhappy popsicle."

Despite looking damp and dejected, Carter didn't relinquish the reins of either painted mount to Keith. "I feel like one, too."

"I take it things didn't go so well with Reese," Keith guessed.

Carter shook his head. "I can't seem to connect

with her lately. It's more than pre-wedding jitters. I might be... I might be losing her."

"I hope that's not true," Keith said, meaning it. The more time he spent with Carter, the more he believed they could have some kind of relationship again. If they could get past the chip on Carter's shoulder and the grudge stuck in Keith's heart.

The two men led the four horses toward the open double doors of the lavish barn.

"We all need to take a beat." Carter sounded like he'd prefer his beat came with a set of dry clothes and a roaring fire. His voice shook. "Reese... Me... You."

"Was that why you wouldn't talk to me for months?" Keith pressed. "You needed to take a beat?" He lengthened his stride to enter the barn first, each step made with bug-crushing intensity. Even the well-trained stable hands took note, rushing forward as if he was the owner.

Keith handed Jam off to one of them, taking Sable to a spot near the tack room and looping his reins through a hook there.

"I've got to give it to this place. The staff is efficient." Keith was determined to be the better man but his patience was strained. He took a moment to stroke Sable's neck and try to find his center. "We were raised to take care of our own stock. I feel guilty letting those stable hands do what they're paid for."

"Wow." Carter gave the reins of Reese's mount

to the other stable hand, then brought his horse next to Keith's. "You hit the nail on the head."

"You've lost me." Keith hooked a stirrup over his saddle horn, then loosened the girth strap.

"You've never been able to see it," Carter said cryptically, unsaddling his horse at the same pace as Keith. "Our foster parents raised us to always take care of ourselves. If we were given a job or a responsibility, we saw it through. And often, you'd see it through without asking or accepting help."

Keith frowned, testing the truth of his words.

"That's the root of what happened after we agreed to negotiations for the sale," Carter went on. "You shut yourself off from everything and just kept plugging forward."

"Yeah. Well. I've recently realized I should have been more vocal about not wanting to sell." Keith hefted Sable's saddle and blanket off him, then headed for the tack room, more than ready to return to his cabin.

Carter did the same with his horse's silver-studded saddle and followed him into the tack room. "We should have talked things through more thoroughly. I know now that we wanted different things."

Keith hoped Carter and Reese didn't want different things out of their marriage. He separated the saddle from the pad and set his saddle on an empty metal stand.

Carter rattled around behind Keith at another

saddle stand. "I always thought we'd create a company and get bought out by a larger one eventually, and still keep our roles. But that's not how Durant Ranch Products wants to proceed. There's nothing to stop this sale going through, but it's likely none of our employees will be kept on, including me and Brad."

Oh, that stings Carter's ego, I bet. So much for Brad's pension fund.

Keith laid Sable's damp, sweaty saddle pad upside down on the saddle so that it could dry. And then he faced Carter, who was doing the same. "You knew this in December?"

"No." Carter nodded, looking uncomfortable, and not just because he was an unhappy popsicle. "Boone sat me down a few days before Christmas and had a no holds barred talk with me. He destroyed my...*our* dreams that day. He'd heard someone at Durant was of the opinion that our staff overhead was too high. We'd been trying to make our profit and loss statement look better at year end. Boone had heard you'd stopped one production line, lowering our output."

"And he decided I was expendable just to save the bottom line?"

"Yes." Carter shifted his feet. "Boone confirmed yesterday that when the final deal is signed all management personnel will be let go. I was going to tell Brad today."

"He'll be crushed." Keith tilted his hat back.

"How did we lose control of negotiations?" He didn't want to make that kind of mistake again.

Carter wiped a hand around the back of his neck. "Our investors have too much power. They're willing to take a lesser deal rather than have it fall through."

One of the stable hands came in with Reese's blingy saddle.

By mutual, unvoiced consent, Keith and Carter returned to their horses, exchanging bridles for halters, then brushing their horses down and picking their hooves clean.

Something struck Keith about Carter's speech and he couldn't shake it off. He rested his hands on Sable's back, watching his foster brother closely. "Carter, were you stressed about Boone's news because you didn't see this coming? Or because you weren't going to be some highly-paid CEO after the sale went through?"

"I'm not proud of this…but I'm not an orphan, like you." Carter's expression was drawn tight, his eyes sorrowful, his mouth tense. "My parents couldn't afford to keep me." It wasn't an answer. Except it was. Carter was driven by financial security, the same as Tillie.

"Yes, it's the title. But the salary is also important to me."

Keith felt as knocked off center as when he'd been competing in rodeo and been tossed about by a bareback bronc. He led Sable out to the walker where he and the other three horses could plod around in a circle and cool down. And Keith? He'd need some other outlet to ease the rolling in his gut and the throbbing in his temples.

"Say something." Carter brought his horse to the walker.

"You've been talking to the folks," Keith surmised, heading back toward the barn.

"I admit…" Carter nodded less briskly, frowning beside Keith. "They bent my ear after dinner last night. And I… I'm sorry we failed. I'm sorry I failed you. Can you forgive me?" Carter asked in a low voice, a vulnerable voice.

A tone of voice Keith recognized all too well.

"I can… I can try."

"YOU DON'T HAVE to come in with me," Reese said to Tillie as they neared her cabin.

"You don't have to be a trouper," Tillie told her compassionately, trying not to think about the cold and her lack of jacket. "You're tired, cold and chafing in parts. You're the bride. You need to be pampered."

And I want to see if you've got the missing wedding dress.

"I'm fine." Reese scurried toward her cabin, a mere twenty feet away. "I… I just need time alone."

"Is there something inside your cabin you don't want me to see?" Tillie tried not to judge or sound annoyed.

"No." Reese scoffed, but her eyes had a trapped look to them. "The place is a mess. I feel sorry for whoever came by to clean today. I changed clothes three times already. And you know how I get when I change clothes. I toss things around like I'm a bad free throw shooter."

"You know I don't care about that but…" Tillie was torn between respecting her cousin's wishes and overriding them. "If you won't let me in, at least let me go over to the lodge and get you something to eat. We still have dance practice to get through later."

"The dance…" Reese curled her fingers into the collar of Tillie's blue coat, the one she wore. "I know everyone hates the dance—"

"Everyone but Crystal," Tillie pointed out with an amazing lack of disdain.

"—but it'll be good for social media and for Carter."

"Weddings aren't meant to be milked for social media posts. They're supposed to be a reflection of the bride and groom's personality. Style." Tillie tried to call Reese out in a gentle, nurturing tone, one which pressured Reese to tell the truth about that wedding dress.

The whole truth and nothing but the truth.

But if she wanted Reese to tell the truth, maybe she needed to do the same and confess the wedding delivery hadn't been complete.

They reached the walkway to Reese's cabin.

While Tillie debated silently with herself, she knew that Reese had had a horrible day. After all the upsetting things Reese had gone through, Tillie shouldn't accuse her of stealing her own wedding dress.

But Tillie couldn't stop herself. "Your wedding dress is inside, isn't it?"

Reese's jaw dropped. And then she whispered, wide-eyed, "Is my wedding dress missing?"

Hers wasn't the reaction of a bride who'd stolen her own dress.

"No," Tillie hastened to reassure her. "The dresses were delivered on time this morning. No need to worry. I thought…your mother took it for safekeeping," Tillie lied. "No need to worry…"

Reese looked like she might cry. "What good advice. And yet, I'm going to worry until the sale of Sunny Y'all is final."

"While I'm going to worry until after we've performed the choreographed dance at the reception." And then Tillie would dance the night away and sleep through breakfast the next morning.

Reese seemed to gather herself as a gust of wind blew past. "Tillie, I know you think I'm making this wedding over-the-top for all the wrong reasons."

"Nope. No. I did not say that." Tillie was a bad liar. And she knew it. She turned and headed back toward the barn and the resort lodge, saying over her shoulder, "Don't jump to conclusions. I'm off to get a dry jacket. I'll bring you hot soup and French fries."

"They have sweet potato fries on the menu," Reese called after Tillie, sounding tearful.

"Even better." Tillie marched off without looking back. And then she stopped. Turned. Found Reese watching her. "No matter how the wedding turns out, Carter will still love you."

Reese's expression crumpled, as if she didn't believe it. She hurried into her cabin, closed the door behind her.

A peacock shrieked nearby, startling Tillie.

Unbidden, an image of Crystal came to mind. Crystal was always loud, dressed to be noticed, and assumed the world revolved around her. Like those peacocks.

Is that what Reese is becoming?

Tillie didn't know.

But she wondered...

Is that how Keith and I could make a go of it? If I changed and became the woman Keith needs me to be?

Tillie shook her head, marching up the hill with her arms wrapped around her to ward off the chill.

She had no idea how to be anything but herself. And six years ago, that hadn't been enough for Keith.

"WELL, LOOK WHO the cat dragged in." Woodburn set down his wrench in his A-frame fix-it shop and greeted Keith, looking like he was wearing the same coveralls and ratty tan jacket as the day Keith had arrived. "It's Mr. Thomas Edison, inventor of wonders."

Keith acknowledged the old man's greeting with a nod, still in a funk after talking to Carter. He shrugged deeper into the gray hoodie he'd retrieved from his cabin, seeking a distraction. "What are we working on today?"

"The water wheel motor installation." Woodburn frowned. "That can wait. What's bothering you, son?"

"Many things. My dreams. My next career move. My personal life." Family betrayals. "Who stole a package that was delivered here."

"That's quite a list you've got going on." Woodburn rummaged through a collection of metal tins on his workbench, opening one and reaching in. "What you need is a lollipop and a kind ear." He handed Keith a red sucker.

When Keith had left Carter, it had been a tossup as to what he'd do—go grab a beer or find something to challenge his brain and keep his mind off Carter's poor decisions. This seemed a better option.

Keith graciously accepted the old man's offer of a lollipop, unwrapped it and stuck it in his mouth. "Cherry. My favorite."

"You're already feeling better, aren't ya?" Woodburn chuckled, bringing two stools out from under his workbench. "Always works for me. Have a sit."

Keith graciously took a seat and removed the sucker from his mouth. "Are there security cameras anywhere on property?"

"Nope." Woodburn settled on his stool with a yellow lollipop. "What's gone missing?"

Keith tried to make light of it. "A dress." No sense in sending everyone into a tizzy by mentioning it was the bride's dress. "It was delivered this morning and signed for by someone claiming to be me."

"Ouch." Woodburn worked on his lollipop. "Wouldn't likely be one of our staff if the culprit signed as you."

Keith nodded, sucker in his mouth.

"You want me to ask if anyone saw anything?"

Keith nodded again.

"Consider it done. Now…" Woodburn leaned forward. "What's really bothering you?"

Keith glanced around the A-frame. "There's something peaceful about a workshop, isn't there?"

Woodburn smacked his lips. "If that's your way of telling me to mind my own business, that's a fine how-do-you-do when I gave you comfort."

"You mean this?" Keith held up his much-reduced sucker, smiling a little.

The old man nodded. "I do indeed."

Keith rubbed his forehead, tipping his cowboy

hat back in the process. He stared at the old man's wrinkled, trusting face.

What have I got to lose?

And so, he told him the saga of the past few years, of his mistakes, of his betrayals, of his heartbreak.

And then the old man gave it to him straight without pulling any punches, the way a cowboy from the Old West would have.

Giving Keith more to think about than he'd entered the fix-it shop with. And more to hope for, too.

CHAPTER TWELVE

"IS EVERYBODY READY to try this?" Reese stood on the dance floor of the wedding venue later that afternoon, directing the wedding party and family through dance rehearsal.

"I'm ready." Tillie raised her hand, trying to be perky and supportive, despite having second thoughts about Reese's innocence where the wedding dress was concerned. What other reason could Reese have for keeping Tillie out of her cabin?

Did Reese have super sexy lingerie laid out on the bed? Was she hiding an emergency stash of chocolate? But she kept coming back to the missing wedding dress. It hadn't been in Aunt Eleanor's room and she was the most likely suspect given she wanted Reese to wear her gown. It was just... Why would Reese steal her own wedding dress? It was a show-stopper and perfect for social media posts.

"I'm not ready to dance," Keith mumbled from next to Tillie, bringing her back to the present.

"All those with two left feet should be excused from this exercise."

Tillie faced Keith. He was easy on the eyes, and suitably distracting when she needed a distraction, like she did now. She waggled her finger at him. "What Reese wants, Reese gets. Even if it's a dance troupe that can barely remember the steps to the 'Electric Slide.'"

Keith tipped his black cowboy hat back. "No job should be worth humiliating your former boyfriend."

"It's not the job doing the humiliating," Tillie said firmly. "It's the dance. Now put on your big boy pants and help me out. Reese needs me."

And as soon as Tillie said those words, she knew they were true.

What did it matter what her cousin was hiding in her cabin? Reese deserved her support. It had been Reese who'd encouraged Tillie to study with Keith in high school. Reese who'd encouraged Tillie to apply for jobs that seemed out of her reach—the coffee shop shift manager, the restaurant manager, the store manager. It had been Reese who'd celebrated Tillie and Keith's first date. Reese whose shoulder Tillie cried on when Keith left town after proposing, when Shay was born prematurely, when Tillie decided to divorce Neil.

They'd had their rifts, as anyone close did. But they always made up. Because they loved each other.

"Get ready to dance, everybody," Tillie called out enthusiastically, the way supportive maids of honor did.

But others in the wedding party weren't ready to go.

Sophie Jean was asking for clarification about when she was supposed to enter the dance floor with Van. Jane was practicing the steps with Brad. And Crystal was directing the photographer as to the best angles to shoot from, presumably to capture Reese but Tillie wouldn't put it past the woman to want the best lighting and angles for herself.

Not that I'm going to let that upset me. Reese needs me.

Tillie glanced around the Ambling Horse Prairie Resort's wedding barn. It had never been a barn. It was new. And it was larger than most horse barns, had four-paned windows lining the sides lengthwise, a raised dais on one end in front of a dance floor, and a rollup door on the far end where trees and picnic tables provided guests with the chance to get some fresh air.

Tillie was longing for some fresh air. She wasn't a performer. When she went dancing, she went for her own enjoyment, mostly a two-step with a capable partner, like Keith. But Reese wanted them to do a choreographed version of the "Electric Slide." So, here they were. Trying to make her happy.

"Get ready." Reese fiddled with her cell phone, which she'd connected to the venue's speakers. "Remember. It's me and Carter. Then the bridal party. Then the rest of the family. And then you'll all exit except for the bride and groom."

The music started. Reese and Carter did the first two collections of steps together. They were good dancers but always had been.

The rest of the bridal party joined in, including Keith and Tillie. Not all of them had a good feel for the beat, particularly Keith. He was a decent dancer when he had a partner. But ask him to dance in a line solo? Keith was right. He had two left feet, and neither foot had rhythm.

"Grapevine right and stomp," he said under his breath. "Grapevine left and stomp. Back and back and forward and back. Whoa. Missed that turn."

He always missed the turn. Tillie felt sorry for him. "Now you're dancing. Keep it up."

On the fifth time through the steps, the rest of the family joined in, including Granny and Shay. Shay still wore her black tutu over her blue jeans. She was an enthusiastic dancer, tugging her tutu this way and that to emphasize where her hips should have been moving.

After executing the steps twice, everyone free-styled off the dance floor except the bride and groom. They kick-ball-changed into each other's arms, and then transitioned to a slow dance just as one song ended and a romantic ballad began.

"That was fantastic," Reese praised them, slipping out of Carter's embrace and applauding.

"Hey, what about my slow dance?" Carter eased her back into his arms. "I earned it."

Tillie glanced toward Keith, fighting a jolt of envy for the love Carter and Reese shared, fighting a feeling of love for Keith. It wasn't an easy fight. Keith was leading Shay in the two-step and Shay was loving it.

"Ho-hum." Crystal strutted onto the dance floor in a short blue dress and matching cowboy boots. "Nothing about this performance has *it*. If this were my wedding, I'd want to go bigger. Create something people will share because it's everything they wanted at their wedding but didn't have." She tossed her big, blond hair over one shoulder and smiled at the photographer.

Carter frowned. Reese looked indecisive. The rest of the bridal party was muttering about the lack of *it*.

Tillie couldn't blame them. What was *it*? She wasn't on social media enough to know.

"I think we were great," Tillie said supportively, smiling at Reese. "We had energy. We didn't trip over each other, not to mention that Reese liked it."

Everyone turned toward Reese. This was where Tillie's cousin should assert her authority and put her foot down. It was her wedding, not Crystal's.

Crickets…

"What do you suggest?" Reese asked Crystal.

Carter's shoulders slowly lowered. Clearly, he was disappointed.

"We need something spectacular like that lift from *Dirty Dancing*," Crystal began.

"I kind of wish someone would put Crystal in the basement, never mind a corner," Keith murmured in Tillie's ear.

She chuckled, reminded of Reese saying the same thing to her earlier. But Keith was too close, his breath too warm. Tillie nudged him backward. "That's not funny."

He snorted.

"What's not funny?" Shay demanded, coming to lean against Tillie's leg.

"Eggs," Keith said straight-faced. "Eggs aren't funny."

Shay stared at him suspiciously.

Crystal approached the bride and groom, a swagger to her step. "Carter, didn't you brag to me once that you used to do backflips when you scored a touchdown?"

"I might have." Carter scratched the back of his neck, looking uncertain. "That was a long time ago."

"Oh, but everyone loved it," Reese gushed. "*I* loved it. You used to do round-offs and back handsprings, too."

Carter stared at Reese for a moment before nodding. "I haven't done anything like that since high school."

"This is a disaster in the making," Keith murmured to Tillie.

"It's like riding a bike," Crystal assured Carter.

"Carter's gonna ride a bike to the wedding?" Shay asked, brightening. "I thought he was riding a horse? What kind of bike? A two-seater? I have a bike. It's pink and has tassels and a bell."

"That's nice, sweetie," Crystal said absently. "Now, if Carter tumbles to the far side of the dance floor and Reese runs over to do the lift—"

"In her wedding dress?" Tillie was starting to have a bad feeling about this, too. She tried to catch Reese's eye, to no avail.

"—we'll need something tricky for the rest of the wedding party to do." Crystal tapped a long, red fingernail against her lips. "Something surprising."

"If she suggests pole dancing, I'm outta here," Keith whispered to Tillie. "Are you with me?"

"In theory, yes. But we can't let Crystal hijack Reese's wedding more than she already has." Tillie took a deep breath, getting ready to step in if no one else said anything. More crickets.

Tillie turned to face a still-stumped Crystal. "I have an idea."

"Speak up," Crystal said impatiently, making the gimme sign with her hand.

"There's a reason the classics are the classics." Tillie purposefully talked in vague terms because she still had no idea what to propose that would wipe that worried look off Reese's face and make Crystal butt out.

"The Chicken Dance." Keith stepped beside Tillie. "If you're looking for something with more... *oomph*, it's the Chicken Dance. I hear anything retro is totally *in* these days." And if that wasn't bad enough, he proceeded to perform a portion of the crowd-pleasing group dance while singing. Off key.

And the crowd went...*silent*. They didn't even clap when Keith got to that part.

"Matilda," Uncle Boone growled, which Tillie translated to mean, *"Do something. Now!"*

"I think we should let Reese decide." Tillie crossed the dance floor and took her cousin's too cold hands. "We've got two more days of rehearsal. If you ask your father and the others to learn a new dance, something they don't know like the 'Electric Slide,' it might all fall apart once your backup dancers take the floor."

"She's got a point there," Crystal agreed, surprising everyone, especially Reese if her wide eyes were any indication.

And in another one of those moments where time stood still for Tillie, everything seemed to be back to normal—the bond between Tillie and Reese, Reese being a woman who fit in both in Dallas and back home in Clementine, Tillie and Keith in the friend zone.

But it was only a moment. In a blink, it was gone.

"That doesn't mean the bride and groom can't up their game after the group does the 'Electric Slide,'" Crystal said authoritatively. "What do you say, Reese? Are you up to it?"

"Sure. Let's just try it." Reese smiled. But it was a wobbly smile. "Carter and I will stay here with Crystal to figure something out. The rest of you can head back to your cabins to get ready for dinner."

And everyone agreed, even Tillie and Carter, because they all loved Reese and this was going to be her day.

Tillie only hoped it would be a good one.

"DID WE MISS HERCULES?" Shay plopped on one of the benches outside the wedding barn, pointing toward the fancy wagon the big brown draft horse pulled toward the resort cabins. "I can't see him but I hear his bells."

The jingle of bells grew ever fainter as the cart loaded with most of the bridal party disappeared around a corner about one hundred yards up the paved lane. Only Keith, Shay, Tillie and Velma remained at the building surrounded by prairie and a smattering of tall oaks.

Tillie and Velma were watching whatever was going on in the barn between Crystal, the bride and groom. Tillie and Velma were frowning.

"We can wait for the next wagon." Keith sat on

the bench next to Shay. The wood was colder than the air as the sun was rapidly fading.

"But Hercules is my favorite." Shay tugged off her pink cowboy hat, climbed into Keith's lap, and then set her hat on the toe of one of her pink cowboy boots. "You should always take a ride with your favorite." She laid her head on Keith's shoulder. So trusting.

Another part of the wall protecting his heart crumbled. Enough to risk love?

Quit thinking so much and trust your heart, Woodburn had told him earlier.

That pretty much summed up what the old man had to say about any situation Keith presented him with, personal or professional.

Should I try things with Tillie again?

Trust your heart, he'd said.

Should I forgive Carter? Should I try building another company with him again?

Trust your heart, he'd said.

Considering his foster parents would have answered yes to every question, Woodburn's advice sat better in Keith's gut. It allowed him to decide.

Inside the wedding venue, music played. Crystal's voice drifted out, indistinct other than her bossy tone.

Poor Carter.

Keith gave one lone chuckle.

Never thought I'd have sympathy for Carter ever again.

But something was happening here at the Ambling Horse Prairie Resort. Keith was beginning to accept things had been wrong with himself and Tillie, plus, at the company, between himself and the boys long before Durant Ranch Products made that offer.

Tillie and Velma joined Keith on the bench. Tillie wore a blue Ambling Horse Prairie Resort sweatshirt. Like Keith, she probably hadn't brought another coat.

Tillie looked at Shay, and then did a double take. "She's fast asleep."

"No." Keith tried to peer at the little girl's face. "Shay was just talking to me."

"That's how some kids roll," Tillie explained, smiling warmly at Keith. "I knew Shay was tired. She just needed a place to rest her head."

"What do I do now?" Keith tried not to move, not wanting to wake her.

"Lift her up and let's go." Velma stood and started down the road that would take them back to the cabins. "It's starting to get dark. If I sit here and wait for the next wagon, I'll fall asleep, just like Shay."

"And when we wake you up, you'll be just as cranky," Tillie predicted, still with that warm smile.

"That's an old lady's prerogative," Velma called over her shoulder. For a seasoned cowgirl, she was a fast walker, striding forward as the lights along the lane came on.

"Do you want me to take Shay?" Tillie held her hands out toward Keith.

"No. I've got her." It felt important to carry this precocious little person. Keith shifted Shay in his arms and got to his feet.

Shay's pink cowboy hat fell to the ground.

Tillie picked it up, dusting it off on her jeans pants leg. Then she removed Shay's thick glasses, tucking them in her hoodie pocket. "Let me know if she gets too heavy for you."

Keith scoffed. "I got this."

"Okay. Do you know what I don't have?" Tillie asked archly. "Reese's wedding dress. Did you have any luck with Brad? You rode with him a long time today."

"Brad is storing his tuxedo in his truck." Keith had found the truck earlier and looked inside to confirm. "He doesn't have a grudge against the bride or groom." Pending Carter's big reveal to Brad that he wouldn't have a job soon. That news might change things. "I don't think he did it. Did you find out why Reese didn't want us in her cabin this morning?"

"Nope. And she wouldn't let me in this afternoon either." Tillie looked unhappy about that. "She told me her room was a mess. She was pretty stressed out after the ride, so I didn't push it when I brought her lunch."

"Interesting." Keith adjusted Shay in his arms. Carrying a limp, sleeping child was like hefting a bag of loosely packed grain. As soon as he had a handle on one corner, another slid in a different direction. "Are you thinking what I'm thinking?"

"I hate when you ask me that." Tillie huffed. "But sure. I'll play along. You're thinking there's something in Reese's cabin she doesn't want us to see." Tillie shook her head, sending all that thick, blond hair undulating over her shoulders. "If there is, I'm not going to press it."

"But I can." Keith gave Tillie a winning smile. "I think we should go inside her cabin while she's working on new dance moves with Crystal." Easy enough given none of the cabins were locked.

Tillie bit her lip, considering. "That doesn't seem right."

"Neither does stealing the bride's wedding dress. Or writing my name on the receipt." He turned sideways to protect Shay from a building gust of wind that bent the prairie grass around them. "Even if it's the bride who did the stealing. Are you going to sleep like a baby tonight if we don't find it?"

"Not a chance." She looked mournful to admit that.

The wind died down.

"Then we should take a peek in her cabin." Keith returned to walking straight, smoothing Shay's hair. "All in the name of you sleeping better."

Tillie gave him a speculative look. "I'll think about it."

"Okay."

Velma was fast approaching the hill. Soon, she'd be disappearing around the bend in the road. Keith could no longer hear Crystal's voice from the wedding barn. With Shay asleep, he and Tillie were essentially alone.

Trust your heart.

Keith shifted Shay to his other shoulder, realizing he had an opportunity to air out a few topics. "I shouldn't have gotten my nose bent out of shape when you told me about your marriage. I'm sorry. If I made it sound like I was judging you, I didn't mean to." He spoke the words from his heart. "I was angry with myself for missing out when I walked away, for being so sensitive that I wouldn't listen to what you had to say after you said no."

Tillie blinked in surprise, her mouth forming a small, very kissable looking O. "Thank you."

Trust your heart.

"I don't think you meant to kiss me last night," he said and almost immediately regretted it.

Tillie's cheeks began to take on a deep red color.

Don't trust your heart that much.

The wind picked up as they ascended the curving hill. Shay murmured a complaint and snuggled closer.

Trust your heart.

"I think that kiss was a reflex," Keith said, reaching very deep for very thin straws. "You know, like when you hold a glass of water and you just take a drink because…" He paused. "Strike that. It just… It felt right to me. And I'm sure it felt right to you. And it made me realize—these last few days made me realize—that leaving you was a mistake. I hurt you. And maybe in your mind that's a scar that's healed but…" He blew out a breath, trying to read the subtleties in Tillie's expression in the gathering darkness. But that was like trying to read a doctor's scribbled handwriting on a prescription slip.

It didn't help that Tillie said nothing.

Keith trusted his heart and said, "We have unfinished business, you and I." If he hadn't been carrying her daughter, he'd have taken Tillie's hand and laced his fingers with hers.

She gave him a challenging look. "You're the one who famously looks toward the horizon. Why are you suddenly looking back?"

"Because I'm just now seeing things for what they are. Or were." If he hadn't been carrying her daughter, he'd have drawn her close and proven how unfinished their business was.

"It's too late for that." Tillie marched ahead while he adjusted the weight of Shay in his arms.

"Some of us take longer to figure out the difference between prepositions and conjunctions than others." He hoped she'd get the reference to their days as study buddies in high school.

She smiled.

That smile was like a ray of hope. And that ray grew inside of Keith like a clear dawn after one of Dallas' dark summer thunderstorms.

Somewhere ahead of them, someone laughed.

"But that doesn't mean we should start up again," Tillie said, bringing the thunderstorms rolling back over Keith's horizon.

"Til…"

"Keith…" Tillie batted Shay's hat against her thigh. "Things are more complicated now. My life… Your life… How would I explain you… this…us? And Shay…" She blew out a breath. "What if we don't work out again? Shay gets attached to people. You heard her this morning. You held my hand and she thought we were getting married. And if you disappeared again—"

"I'm not going anywhere." Now that he knew where he'd gone wrong, he wasn't going to let her go.

Shay squirmed, requiring a redistribution of her weight in his arms.

"Keith…" Tillie brushed a light hand over his shoulders as they walked around another curve in the lane.

Her touch made him ache with loneliness. He wanted her to stop so he could hold her with one arm and hold Shay in the other. He wanted to kiss her again. He wanted to kiss her every day as they grew old together.

But Tillie didn't stop. She kept walking and her hand dropped away. "Keith, the reality is that you're not going to Clementine."

Keith hadn't calculated post-wedding geography into this. "Is that a condition of our relationship?"

She nodded. "If a miracle occurs and Reese is happily married by Saturday night, I'll have a job in Clementine. And a house. Rent free. And Shay…" She hesitated before rushing on. "I have Shay to think of. And Gran."

This trusting his heart business was becoming increasingly painful. Keith pressed on anyway. "If it's about Shay's vision, there are great doctors in Dallas."

Tillie's steps became wooden. "I didn't tell you about her vision." Her words cracked like dropped chips of ice. "Is that what this conversation is about? Helping Shay?"

Her statement walloped into him like the time he'd been bowled over by a runaway horse. "This conversation is about you and me *and* Shay. This conversation is about how to stitch our lives together."

"It's about *if* we stitch them together." Tillie came to a stop on the lane, crossed her arms over her chest and faced him. Lights from a few cabins made her regret-filled expression clearer. "You're leaping ahead again, forgetting a few things in between."

"Right. Yes." He nodded continuously until he realized he was doing that.

"We're at a crossroads, Keith."

The nodding started again. Their conversation had suffered a serious derailment. "Yes, I know. I'm trying. Honestly."

"I should have kept walking." She pivoted, about to do just that.

He stopped her with a touch on her arm. "Why did you stop?"

"Because we're at Reese's cabin." Spoken like it was the most obvious answer.

"Oh." Keith glanced over at the west-facing cabin porch, which was catching the very last of the light of day. "Are we going in?"

The wind rustled the leaves in the nearby shrubbery.

"No." Tillie plunked Shay's pink hat on top of her brown one, then reached for her daughter, as if this was where they parted. "I wasn't sure before. But now… We're not snooping."

Keith took a step back, fearing that giving up Shay now would put an end to all discussion, derailed or otherwise. "And yet, you stopped here because you had mixed feelings. The same way you have mixed feelings about me."

"Yes. No." She scrunched her nose. "Do I have to answer?"

Something growled near them.

Keith realized that noise was coming from him. "Am I going too fast or too slow?" Frustration crept into his tone. "You may know the key to this conversation, Tillie. But I'm lost as to how to proceed short term." And he was afraid he'd be lost forever if she didn't give them a second chance.

"Keith…"

"Tillie…"

"Listen." She glanced back at the way they'd come, looking adorable with two hats atop her head. "Another wagon is coming. Reese and Carter could be on it. The jig may be up."

If he couldn't make headway talking about them, he'd try making headway with the missing wedding dress. "If I know Crystal, they'll be testing out lifts and cartwheels for hours yet." That woman had one speed and it was deliberate, one goal and it was hers.

Tillie shook her head.

"What happened to wanting a good night's sleep?"

Tillie sighed, possibly weakening.

The bells on a horse's harness were getting louder.

Keith moved toward the walk. "We'll just open the door and look for five seconds, and then close the door. If Reese is telling the truth, the place will look a mess. And if not, you'll discover what she's hiding from you. And by the time that wagon gets here, we'll be back on the lane."

"All right." Tillie started walking at a good clip. "Five seconds." She didn't wait for Keith to go first. She stormed the walk, nearly losing her balance when those three baby goats leaped out of the bushes and bounded around them like happy puppies.

"Hey, I'm not in there." That was Reese, appearing out of the gathering darkness ahead of the wagon. She jogged up to them. "I came back for a different pair of shoes. What do you need?"

Tillie turned slowly. "I was just…" She cast her thumb over her shoulder toward the cabin and looked to Keith for an assist.

"She needed the bathroom," Keith said, which he thought was perfect.

What woman refused restroom privileges to another woman?

"Yep, that's right." Tillie squirmed, playing along.

Reese breezed past Keith. "Sorry. That's where I'm headed." And then she zoomed right past Tillie.

"But…" Tillie watched her cousin scurry up the steps and inside. Then she turned to face Keith. "Don't they have bathrooms at the wedding barn?"

Her question was moot. They both knew they did.

"I told you this was a bad idea." Tillie took Shay from Keith's arms, leaving him feeling empty. She marched toward the lane, her silhouette outlined by that last gray moment before night officially fell. "From now on, let me handle this."

Keith stayed where he was, fighting this feeling that he'd done everything wrong. That he hadn't provided the right inputs or seen the right outcomes.

Shay lifted her head. "Mama?" Fear sharpened her voice. Her head twisted as if on a swivel stick. "*Mama!* Where are we? I can't see."

"I've got your glasses right here." Shay dug them out of her hoodie pocket with amazing speed, then put them on Shay. "The sun's gone down, pumpkin. Close your eyes. Give it a minute. Take a breath. Listen. You can hear the wagon bells."

A well-lit wagon came around the corner and up the lane. It had lanterns on the front and back.

Shay seemed to be staring at Keith, not to her right where the wagon was approaching. "I see it, Mama. I see it." Her panic was gone.

But the episode...

It wasn't the first time Keith had noticed something odd about Shay's vision. And the next time he asked about it, he wasn't going to let Tillie brush its importance aside.

Could be their futures depended on it.

CHAPTER THIRTEEN

Thursday, two days until the wedding

KEITH WAS AWAKENED in the morning by a sharp, rising scream, followed by several high-pitched yelps. A woman's voice.

Tillie.

Keith rolled out of bed, pulled on jeans and a T-shirt, grabbed his boots and bolted out to the front porch without his hoodie, listening.

Nothing.

The adrenaline was pumping, keeping the nose-chilling temperature from sending Keith scurrying back inside.

The sun was rising. If there was a storm coming tomorrow, there wasn't a cloud in the sky today. He tugged on his cowboy boots, listening.

The door to the cabin next to Keith opened. Carter stepped out, slipping into his boots. "Did you hear that scream?"

"Yeah." Keith nodded. "Do you know who it was?"

"No."

The two men strode down their respective cabin walkways to the narrow paved lane.

"Get out! *Out!*" That was Reese's voice, coming from across the road and a few cabins down.

They ran along the lane together, nearly tripping over scampering baby goats escaping from Reese's cabin.

Reese released a primal cry. *"And don't come back!"*

"What's wrong, babe?" Carter charged up the porch steps and gathered his fiancée into his arms.

"I woke up with those goats in my cabin and…" Reese angrily wiped at her tears. "They've chewed everything from my shoes to my makeup!" She released another primal sound, this time a moan. "We should have just got married at home in Clementine."

Carter had nothing to say to that and neither did Keith, who imagined they were all in agreement.

Tillie hurried up the cabin walk, clothes rumpled and blond hair uncombed. Despite that, she looked beautiful to Keith.

"Your things will be fine," Tillie promised. "We'll lend you or find you whatever you need. It won't be a problem, really."

"My wedding is jinxed," Reese whined, touching the bright red, swollen blemish on her chin, and then tightened her silk robe. "We should call the whole thing off."

When Tillie would have marched up the stairs

to join Carter and Reese on the porch, Keith waved her off. "Let's give them some space."

Tillie frowned. Then nodded.

"We're not canceling the wedding, babe." Carter turned Reese toward her door. "Come on. I'll make you a cup of coffee."

"No." Reese spun around, blocking his entry. "I need a moment alone." And then she stumbled inside, closing the door behind her.

The lock clicked into place.

Carter stood on the porch, back to Tillie and Keith. His chin dropped to his chest. His shoulders slumped. After a moment, Carter turned around, facing them with a solemn expression.

"I should talk to her," Tillie said, approaching the porch with purposeful steps.

"Please don't." Carter came down those stairs and put his hands on his hips. "It's wedding jitters. She'll be fine by breakfast."

Keith doubted it.

And so did Tillie, if her deepening frown was any indication.

"I'll walk you back to your cabin," Keith told her, indicating she should lead the way. "We'll see you at breakfast, Carter."

His foster brother gave Keith an odd look but trundled off toward his cabin.

"How did you sleep last night?" Keith asked Tillie. "Did you toss and turn? Worry about Reese's wedding dress?" Or Shay's vision?

"Do I look like I slept well?" Tillie pressed her fingertips to the bags under her eyes.

"You always look gorgeous to me." It was the truth. "We should get in Reese's cabin while she's at breakfast."

"No." Tillie tugged Keith along the lane, further away from Reese's cabin. "Reese made me a long list of items to take care of, including storing the dresses until the big day. She's touched base with me on most of the other things. But she hasn't asked about the dresses at all. I'm pretty sure she has her dress."

"Why would she do that? Do you think this is a cry for help?" Keith heard a rustling in the bushes alongside the lane and drew Tillie a safe distance away in case something flew out, like goats, chickens or shrieking peacocks. "Is she trying to back out of the wedding?"

"I don't think so." Tillie shrugged. "Let's give her time. She'll talk when she's ready."

"Speaking of talking…" Keith gave her what he hoped was an encouraging smile. "How about a cup of coffee?"

Tillie shook her head.

"A ride? An early breakfast?" He wanted time and privacy to talk about Shay's vision and their future.

Tillie shook her head again. "The wedding favors are supposed to be delivered this morning.

Besides, I need a shower, a toothbrush and clean clothes before I'm up to handling you."

"Darlin', I'm a kitten," he assured her, smile turning mischievous.

"I'm not buying that," Tillie called to him over her shoulder, hurrying back toward her cabin. "Even kittens have claws."

"WHAT'S GOING ON between you and my favorite cowboy?" Gran demanded at breakfast.

"Nothing." Tillie kept her head down and gaze on her omelet. "And by the way, you'll be watching Shay this morning when she comes down from her sugar crash."

Shay was sitting on the other side of Gran, eating blueberry pancakes and drinking hot chocolate and looking like the happiest child alive.

"What's one wrong breakfast in the scheme of things?" Gran wore a fancy straw hat with a turquoise band this morning. She fixed it at a jaunty slant before smiling at Tillie. "And you don't fool me. Something's going on between you and my favorite cowboy. He's been mooning at you all morning."

"Do you remember that one time you took me to the amusement park?" When Gran nodded, Tillie continued. "I convinced you to go on that roller coaster."

"Big mistake." Gran nodded. "I banged my shoulder on the corkscrew and lost my hat on the drop. I swore off roller coasters that day." She made an X with her hands. "Never again."

"And that's what it's like for me with Keith. He doesn't want to come back to Clementine and I'm not moving." She lowered her voice. "There's that job and all Shay's doctors."

"Tillie, you've always been careful with your steps." Gran fussed with the fringe of her white bangs. "But have you ever wondered if you're being too careful?"

Crystal tapped her water glass with her spoon. "Don't forget we're having a competition this morning. I made team uniforms and had them delivered to your cabins just now."

"That's nice of you to have done that." Reese gave Crystal the applause the bridesmaid obviously craved.

Gran leaned closer to Tillie. "What do you want to bet she's having the men dress up like cowboys from the Wild West, you young ladies like Annie Oakley, and the rest of us like townsfolk. I don't fancy wearing a petticoat and a bonnet."

"There you go again with your overactive imagination." But Tillie grinned at the thought. "If that's what Reese wants us to wear, we'll do it without complaint."

"Excuse me, miss." The cowboy concierge leaned close to Tillie's shoulder. "We received another delivery. The bride directed me to take the boxes to your cabin. But these are very large boxes. Can I leave them on your porch?"

Tillie assured him that was all right. When he left, she turned back to Gran. "That must be the wedding favors. Reese ordered these adorable little straw baskets at the last minute that each contain a tiny succulent. We need to attach the chocolate bells she bought originally."

"Do I like chocolate bells?" Shay leaned forward to ask, staring at Tillie from the corner of her eye, which was where her vision was strongest. She shoved her large glasses up her nose. "I bet I do."

"The chocolate bells are for the wedding guests," Tillie said firmly.

"I'll give you mine," Keith told Shay.

Shay grinned at Keith as if he hung the moon.

"Matilda, a word, please." Uncle Boone led Tillie out to the lobby. "I shouldn't have to tell you this, but Reese isn't happy."

"She's just stressed," Tillie rushed to explain. "Crystal has already taken care of most of the goat damage." New makeup in place, brand-new shoes borrowed from one of the other bridesmaids.

"These aren't the kind of wedding memories Reese wants to make." Uncle Boone puffed out his chest. "A good *manager* anticipates disaster and averts it." And with that, her uncle stomped off.

Tillie returned to the breakfast table and eased her sorrows by nursing her coffee and studying her cousin.

Reese smiled at everyone, her tone chipper, but every once in a while, her eye twitched. At this rate, she wouldn't be in any shape to go through with the wedding.

"Anything I can help you with today?" Keith asked, moving to sit next to Tillie when the rest of the bridesmaids left the table.

"We're gonna put bells on baskets," Shay piped up. She had a chocolate mustache and a syrup goatee.

Tillie pointed that out to Gran, who dipped her cloth napkin into her water glass and then set about cleaning Shay's face.

Tillie turned to Keith and was immediately caught by the compassion in his blue gaze.

"I'm on your team," he said softly. "I want to figure this out." He gestured back and forth between them. "A wise man once told me that you have to trust your heart to build the life of your dreams."

Tillie drew a pained breath. "Wise words, but—"

"Let's go put bells on baskets." Shay hopped down from her chair and rushed over to Keith. She wore a green sweater and blue jeans with her pink boots. But she'd paired that with a Roman soldier's skirt, something Tillie's brother had sent her last Christmas. She tugged Keith to his feet. "We'll take a ride with Hercules and Smidge. Then Mama will tell us what to do and we'll have to be nice when she changes her mind."

"Why do I feel like I've lost control?" Tillie took one last sip of her fabulous coffee and got to her feet, helping Gran to hers.

"Because you're falling in love again," Gran said unhelpfully. "And this time, you're taking Shay with you."

Tillie sighed. She was afraid Gran was right.

"WHAT?" TILLIE STOOD in the middle of the wagon as it rounded the corner nearest Cabin Twelve. *"Hey! Don't! Noooo!"* She grabbed hold of one of Keith's shoulders and tried to step over him to the wagon's edge. "Stop! There's a burro rooting around in Shay's wedding favors!"

"Tillie, hold up. You don't want to fall and break your leg," Keith told her, making sure she wasn't going to leap out over the side of the wagon before he turned his attention to her porch.

Sure enough, there were several large cardboard boxes that had been pawed at, exposing the contents.

The burro on the porch lifted his head without concern for the upset maid of honor arriving. He trampled on what looked like woven straw baskets the size of a baseball.

Smidge brought the wagon to a jolting stop. "Hey, Padre! Move on outta there!"

Tillie climbed over Keith and hopped down, charging forward and raising her arms. "No-no-no! Go away!"

A familiar trio of baby goats scrambled off the front porch and scampered across the road.

Padre clumped off the porch and trotted around the back, heading toward the swimming pool.

Tillie ran up the porch steps and gasped. She removed her cowboy hat and held it over her heart, as if paying tribute to the fallen. "They're ruined. They ruined two of the three boxes."

Keith joined Tillie on the porch, surveying the damage. It wasn't pretty. He took hold of Tillie's free hand.

The boxes had once been large cubes—three foot by three foot by three foot. The burro had gnawed from the top down. The baby goats had chewed through the sides of the boxes. There were strips of cardboard, scraps of straw and the odd spike of a succulent plant here, there and everywhere.

"Look at the bright side." Keith took her cowboy hat and put it back on her head. "They didn't wreck *all* of them."

"They wrecked enough." Tillie sounded like she might cry. "What am I going to tell Reese?"

Smidge joined them on the porch ahead of Velma and Shay, looking mournful. "They destroyed the whole lot?"

"No. They just destroyed a lot." Keith opened the door to Tillie's cabin. "Hey, we've got time, we'll figure this out. You should go inside, get a drink of water."

"Why?" Tillie shook her head, clumping her blond bangs to one side.

Keith guided her over the threshold. "Because Smidge and I are going to salvage what we can and I don't want you to get upset."

"Right." Tillie peered around him. "Gran? Shay? Come on inside and join me, please."

Velma and Shay had been hesitant to approach them on the porch. They came forward, holding hands, stopping at the threshold to take in the damage.

Shay bent, reaching for a plant basket, her movement rattling her plastic gladiator skirt. For once, her glasses were in place. "Can I have one?"

"Nope. Those aren't for us." Velma shooed Shay inside. "Let's see who's out by the pool."

"Okay but I want to look for a peacock or my goat babies." Shay skipped to the window.

Tillie hung her hat on a hook by the door, then fluffed her blond hair. "Is it too soon to wave a white flag? I can surrender to the wedding gods."

"Don't go giving up now, Til." Keith grabbed the kitchenette's tall trash bin, removed the white trash bag from it, then closed the cabin door and shifted into high gear. "Smidge, you better notify your local veterinarian that some of your stock might have eaten straw baskets and succulents." Each basket had a small note indicating what variety of plant it was. Keith handed the old man one of them. "Let's hope none of these are poisonous."

"On it." The old man scurried back to the wagon and called someone.

Keith quickly loaded damaged plants and straw baskets in the trash bin, not wanting Tillie to dwell on the carnage.

"The front desk is calling the vet." Smidge took in what Keith was doing, and then sprang into action, consolidating the good plants into the one gnarled box that was in the best shape.

The door opened a crack. Tillie peeked out. "How bad is it?"

Keith nudged the nearly full trash bin out of her line of sight. "We haven't counted. Can you go back inside and look out the other window with Shay?"

"Yes." She closed the door. And then opened it again almost immediately, all the way this time. Shay dawdled a few steps behind her, fingering one of the panels of that gladiator skirt. "No. I have to face this. For Reese." Tillie drew a deep breath before stepping out. "Oh, boy. That's more than half."

"I've heard succulents are hardy plants." Keith withstood her gathering tears. "Hard to kill, I mean. We might be able to salvage some baskets. See here." He pointed. "These were eaten at from the sides, most likely by the baby goats. They ate the baskets more than the plants."

"My bad, bad babies," Shay scowled. "They aren't all bad, you know, Mama."

"We know." Keith pointed to another box. "Now look at the box Padre dove into from the top. He seemed to be sucking out the plants more than the baskets."

"Not everyone will want a plant," Velma called from the rear window. "Some might prefer the chocolate bells."

"She's right," Smidge told them. "Can't tell you how many wedding favors go unclaimed."

"Do you save them?" Keith wondered aloud.

Tillie crossed her arms over her chest. "We're not going to hand out wedding favors that say congratulations Buster and Carmen. Or whatever other wedding favors have been left behind."

"Calm down." Keith loosened those knotted arms of hers, taking both her hands in his. "We have a shortage. I'm spit balling how to make up that shortage. Not all ideas are going to be ideal. Maybe there are plants or flowers here on the ranch we could use instead?"

"No can do, I'm afraid. Wrong time of year for that." Smidge rained on Keith's parade without even looking up from re-sorting the basket remains.

"We just won't tell Reese about this until the reception," Tillie murmured.

"Agreed." Keith was at his most chipper. "You know, I could repair some of these with a little ribbon and glue…if you can stand to brave the storage unit for ribbon, Til."

She shivered. "If I must."

"I wanna go get ribbon, too." Shay brightened, picking up one of the baskets in better shape. "I need to help make this pretty again 'cuz my goat babies were bad."

"That's very sweet of you." Tillie gave her daughter a side hug. "But there are bugs where the ribbon is stored."

Shay yelped and ran inside the cabin, shutting the door behind her.

"The way you two react to bugs begs the question…" Keith gave Tillie a mischievous smile. "What do you do when there's a spider in your house?"

"We scream for Gran." Tillie shivered again.

He had to stop himself from putting his arm around her and drawing her close. If he couldn't fix wedding favors, he could at least protect the maid of honor from creepy crawlies.

"I'll go with you to the storage unit," Keith said instead. "I promise to vanquish any and all bugs."

A familiar jingle of bells sounded in the distance.

"I'm awful sorry about this." Smidge climbed over and past the mess on the porch. "But I've got to move that wagon or we're going to gum up the works." He hurried down the stairs with their blessing and was soon setting off down the lane.

Another horse and wagon came around the

bend. The wagon carried the bride and groom, along with their parents.

By unspoken agreement, Keith and Tillie shoved and hid the debris, waving as they passed.

"Right. We'll get to work. Everything will be fine." And yet, Tillie didn't budge.

"What's wrong?" Keith tossed caution out the window and gently laid his arm across her shoulders.

Tillie turned into him, burying her face in his neck. "Nothing. I just need a hug."

Keith was more than happy to oblige.

CHAPTER FOURTEEN

"I'M THE BEST gluer in the whole wide world!" Shay cried, glue bottle in hand.

"Less bragging and more gluing," Keith told Shay indulgently.

If they weren't trying to save as many wedding favors as possible, Tillie's heart might have melted at the way Keith and Shay were bonding. She didn't have time to melt.

Shay, Keith, Tillie and Gran sat in a small conference room at the main lodge trying to rescue what plants and baskets they could. They'd skipped the wedding party's late morning ride.

Smidge had come back around the loop and helped them transport the remains. He'd also arranged this space for their repair efforts since their cabins didn't have a big enough flat surface. One of the servers had brought them coffee and water, and Shay was allowed a hot chocolate. The concierge had covered the long conference room table with a plastic red and white checkered tablecloth and produced some white glue, which Shay had immediately latched on to, claiming her role was to squeeze the bottle for everyone.

The resort staff was being extremely accommodating. If they hadn't been, Tillie might have had the meltdown she'd predicted Reese was headed toward.

After a little trial and error, and some back and forth between Tillie and Keith as to the best way to repair the straw weave, they'd determined that gently dabbing the broken straw into a smidgeon of glue and then working the ends together had the best chances of success. Frankly, it was a good thing Shay wanted to dispense glue. The repair work required more finesse than a toddler could muster.

"I'm not bragging. I'm just good." Shay squeezed a glob of glue on the tablecloth near Gran. "G-loo-oo!" She glanced around the table at the adults. "Mama needs more."

"Make hers a smiley face," Keith said without looking up. "Your mama needs more smiles."

"Coming right up." Shay scurried around the table. "Here you go, Mama," her daughter said happily. "One smiley face, coming right up."

Two big globs and a semi-smile soon graced the tablecloth to Tillie's left.

"How about you give me a smile?" Gran asked. And when Shay did, Gran kissed her cheek. "You're a good helper."

"The best!" Shay thrust the glue bottle into the air.

"Can you put plants in the baskets, pumpkin?" Tillie tried to make her request sound more like a suggestion. But they were in need of space and it would be more efficient for Shay to do it.

"No. I wanna stick with glue." Shay proceeded to make a glue trail around the perimeter of the table.

"Could be worse," Keith said softly.

"Let's not even talk about how," Tillie said back. It was a toss-up if the ruined wedding favors would sink her employment chances with Uncle Boone.

The door to the conference room swung open. A man and a woman paused there, taking in their work, as if waiting for someone to greet them.

"We heard there was a wedding favor emergency," the woman said as if feeling her way through an unaccustomed situation. She was a pretty brunette. But she wasn't wearing the standard brown check button-down the resort favored.

"We have a suggestion," the man said, curling his burly arm around his companion's waist. He looked vaguely familiar. But he wasn't wearing the resort's theme park cowboy uniform either.

"Oh." Recognition struck Tillie. "We've had so many resort employees pop in here that I thought you were two more bringing us something. But I recognize you." She gestured toward the man. "You ordered flowers the first morning I was here."

He nodded.

"I'm Lois and this is Joshua. We have a suggestion." The woman glowed. "If you're open to hearing it."

Tillie exchanged looks with Keith and Gran. They both nodded.

"At this point, we're open to anything," Tillie told them.

"Well…" Joshua came to stand next to the table, scanning their work. He had a broad chin and broader shoulders. "I'm a blacksmith and I spend the few days before and after this event shoeing the ranch horses. I have a lot of used horseshoes."

"Tell them the meaning of a horseshoe to a wedding," Lois prompted. Her brown hair had a purple streak in it.

"I'm getting to that," Joshua said with an indulgent smile that told Tillie he was well and truly smitten by Lois. "You all probably know that a horseshoe is a symbol of good luck. But where I come from, giving a horseshoe is a symbol of everlasting friendship."

Gran raised her brows at this.

Shay seemed to be mouthing the word *everlasting*.

"Anyway, when I heard you were short on wedding favors, I thought I'd offer some to help round out your numbers. And Lois—"

"I'm an artist," Lois interjected. "I brought my paints here for one of our ice breaker sessions but

I thought I could paint them. The horseshoes, I mean."

Shay gasped. "I could paint them, too. I'm a good painter. Especially with finger paints."

As much as Tillie wanted Shay to help, she needed sophisticated looking favors.

"Finger painting can be striking," Lois said kindly. "As long as you don't mix all the colors to black."

Shay tilted her head, considering this limitation.

"I think it's a great idea." Keith flashed his easy-going smile at Tillie. "And Tillie can add some elegant ribbon to the horseshoes."

"Not to mention, we can play horseshoes during the reception," Gran added with a nod. "Stellar idea. Joshua and Lois are lifesavers."

Tillie agreed, getting to her feet to hug them. "I don't know how many horseshoes you have, Joshua, or how many you can paint by Saturday morning, Lois. But it looks like we're short more than one hundred."

The couple was certain they could provide sixty. They left shortly thereafter, holding hands.

"I don't know if this is good or bad news but…" Keith set his phone down. "The ice storm isn't headed this way. It's turned further east of Dallas." And they were to the west.

"I say that's good news." Gran set a finished basket on the table. "Considering our outside activities."

"But Gran, if there was an ice storm, I bet a lot of guests wouldn't show up." Tillie was on the same page with Keith. "An ice storm means we wouldn't have outdoor activities but we also wouldn't be short wedding favors."

"Exactly." Keith picked up a broken basket, turning it around and testing the loose straw ends. He was meticulous with his repair work.

Tillie was happy to see how few baskets they had left to fix. "I feel like I need to be acknowledged for not having a meltdown this morning."

"Is a meltdown like glue monster fingers?" Shay had dipped her fingers into the glue globs— all ten of them.

"Glue monster fingers *give* mamas meltdowns." Tillie rushed to wipe Shay's fingers clean.

"Tillie, you're the gold medal winner in the maid of honor category," Keith teased, his blue eyes dancing. "We're just part of your team."

"And that's why you are my favorite cowboy," Gran told him.

And for once, Tillie didn't feel as if she should lay down the law and insist they weren't a couple. Keith was her person. He probably always had been. He cheered her up and cheered her on. He pitched in when needed. She'd loved him six years ago and she loved him today. And since they wouldn't be seeing much of each other after this week, the idea made her melancholy.

"Speaking of hero support..." Tillie set the glue

in the middle of the table and out of Shay's reach. "We've got to get that ribbon to spruce up these baskets and the horse shoes. It needs to be the right width and color."

Keith nodded. "As soon as we're finished here, we'll get the ribbon from the bug-infested storage unit."

"Bugs!" Shay shrieked, then threw her hands in the air and ran around the conference room. "I'm not helping. I'm not helping."

Thirty minutes later, Gran and Shay headed for the restaurant while Tillie and Keith wound their way toward the back of the property, armed with keys to the shipping container. They each walked along the path with their hands in their hoodie pockets, not having received their jackets back from Reese and Carter.

Tillie felt self-conscious, as if they should be holding hands or talking up a storm. She tossed out a possible topic of conversation. "Our glue session went better than I expected."

"Agreed. We saved a lot more straw baskets than I estimated." Keith paused to watch one gray squirrel chase another around the thick trunk of a tree. "And that was really generous of Joshua and Lois to pitch in with horseshoes. But we're still short."

Tillie waited for Keith to start walking again. "We could take Gran's advice and give some guests a choice of chocolate bells, plant baskets or horseshoes. Then we'd have plenty for all."

This is not the conversation I want to have with Keith.

Tillie wanted to talk about the future...the immediate future. Could Keith return to Clementine while he planned his next move? Was that too much to ask at this stage? Tillie didn't know.

They reached the shipping container.

Tillie drew a deep breath as she undid the padlock. "Let's open the doors wide to give all the critters plenty of time to flee."

"They're more likely to crouch down in a crevice and watch." Keith wasn't teasing.

Tillie nudged his shoulder. "You really know how to rub it in, don't you? What happened to my teasing, supportive team member?"

He shrugged, not playing along. "I don't know. For some reason, on the walk over it felt as if things got real between us."

Tillie nodded. "I felt that, too. But..." She gestured toward the shelves lining the walls of the shipping container, hand brushing into a clingy strand of spider silk. Shuddering, she brushed it on her jeans. "We've got to get through this wedding first."

"If only that was the biggest obstacle we face," Keith murmured.

They opened the doors wide and stepped inside.

Immediately, hissing began, accented by a distinctive rattle.

"Snake!" They both leaped back outside, eyes wide.

Silence.

Tillie closed the door on her side of the unit. "What are you waiting for? Close the door!" She had visions of that rattlesnake stalking them.

Keith thrust out his jaw. "Tillie… We need that ribbon."

"We don't need the ribbon that bad." She placed her hands on his shoulders, giving him a little shake. "I was willing to suck up my fear of creepy crawlies for Reese." She gestured toward the squished scorpion several feet inside. "But not snakes." Never snakes.

A bird cackled at them in the branches above.

I'll laugh about this, too. Someday.

"Where's the ribbon?" Keith had a determined look in his blue eyes. He lowered his hat brim, cowboy code for *I mean business*.

"When I was here before, it was about halfway back is a clear plastic storage box on the left. But you're not going in there. Rattlers are unpredictable." Tillie's heart was pounding but not in the *ka-thump* for Keith kind of way. She was afraid. Tillie grabbed onto his arm. "I don't even know where the nearest hospital is. Don't go in there."

Keith drew her into his arms for a tender hug.

A tender hug, not a last soul-seeking hug before a person faced certain doom.

Tille shrugged free of his embrace, angry at him. "How can you go in there and not be afraid?"

"Oh, I'm plenty afraid." Keith's words were at odds with that mischievous grin, those sparkling blue eyes, that hero stance. "Do you know what snakes don't like more than cold?"

"If this is an academic question, I didn't store that fact in my brain during my school years." Unlike him keeping track of what she wanted to name her children. "And you *can't* go back in there."

Keith tsked, as if to say he certainly could. "Snakes avoid being trampled or run over. I'm going to step in there and listen to where he is. And then I'm going to stomp around near the doors in the hopes that snake thinks he might be crushed if he doesn't skedaddle."

Tillie washed her hands over her cheeks. "And if he's within striking distance? If he's territorial?"

"I'll run. I promise." And then he kissed her briefly—hard and deep. Before stepping into the shipping container.

Tillie froze. Was that hissing? A rattle? Heart in her throat, she peered into the shipping container unable to place the now subtle sound.

Keith stomped about, heavy footfalls reverberating through the metal container. And then he stopped abruptly, listening.

There was no hissing. No rattle. No rustling noise indicating movement.

"Yep, he's gone!" Keith glanced at Tillie but his head was cocked as if he was still listening.

"*Where* would he have gone? We didn't see him go past us!"

"He probably came in through a mouse or rat hole." Keith stomped around some more. "He'd probably go out the same way."

Tillie inched her way to the right of the shipping container, glancing along the packed ground. Nothing moved on that side. She moved to the left of the unit, glancing along the scraggly shrubs next to the metal walls. Nothing moved to that side either. And when she returned to the doorway, Keith had gone deeper inside.

"Keith…" She hugged herself tight to keep from shouting at him to run back out.

He grabbed the plastic container filled with ribbon and sprinted out to join her, laughing, gosh darn him.

Tillie slammed the door shut and locked everything up tight. "Let's get out of here."

"You don't have to tell me twice." Keith set off at a ground-eating pace. And when they'd gone forty or fifty feet, he stopped and set the ribbon container down. "We did it."

"You did it." Adrenaline made Tillie's knees week and her laughter sound maniacal. "Thank you. Thank you very much."

"I have a different thank-you in mind." And without further ado, Keith kissed her.

It was a long kiss. A slow kiss. A kiss that made her forget about creepy crawlies and territorial snakes.

KEITH HELD TILLIE'S hand as they walked back to the resort lodge, the ribbon storage box tucked beneath one arm.

Kissing Tillie was great but he knew he had to make a stronger emotional connection if he was going to overcome her objections to starting over. And they had to follow their hearts when it came to where and when that new beginning would take place.

"But first… Can you tell me about Shay?"

"Shay?" Tillie veered away from him, as if instinctually trying to put her guard up. But she didn't let go of his hand. "What about Shay?"

"Whatever you feel comfortable telling me." He purposefully didn't look at Tillie, continuing to mosey down the path as if they didn't have a wedding dress to find or wedding favors to save. As if the wind wasn't nippy and the sun blocked by a canopy of oak trees.

"Shay…" Tillie sounded as if she didn't know what to say. "She was…premature. Ten weeks." Tillie started slowly, but Keith didn't care. She was talking, which was a win in itself. "She was

so small. Barely more than skin and bones and...
Well... Neil had a hard time with it."

Keith didn't like the sound of this.

"Neil was glass half-empty." Tillie didn't say
anything for what felt like a long time. "I needed
him to be glass half-full."

Keith wondered if that was when her marriage
had fallen apart. But now wasn't the time for that
question.

The dam had broken open and Tillie's tale was
spinning out. "I spent most of my maternity leave
sitting next to a bassinet in the neonatal intensive
care unit, talking and singing to her, resting my
fingers beneath her tiny hands or next to her delicate feet." She cleared her throat, smiling a little. "Preemies have sensitive skin, so you aren't
supposed to stroke them. But they're supposed to
thrive with touch and communication. It was a
long six weeks later, when I finally got to hold her.
Even then, I was terrified I'd drop her. And I know
it was too early but I could swear she looked up
at me and smiled." Tillie's smile seemed fragile.

The wind gusted past. A pair of small birds
flew past, paths intertwining.

"Lots of preemies have challenges," Keith said
gently.

"Oh, Shay is fine." Tillie didn't sell that line any
more than she'd been able to on the morning the
wedding dresses had gone missing. "Obviously,
her vision isn't 20/20."

Keith let that statement sit between them.

"This is where you want me to tell you why I'm so touchy about her vision." Tillie kicked a rock down the path. "When she was two years old, she started bumping into things. At first, I thought it was just her exuberance toward life. She hardly ever walks if she can run. But it got worse, not better. Six months and a back breaking amount of medical fees later, a specialist told us she has Stargardt disease." Tillie came to an unexpected halt, turning to face Keith. "It came on sooner than most diagnosed cases which isn't good. For now, she has a black hole in the center of her vision."

"Which is why she cocks her head to look at people." The creative, problem-solving part of Keith that had been dormant since December perked up.

"She adjusts her head all the time." Tillie nodded. "And she also has trouble seeing in dim light."

"Like last night at dusk." Again, he was intrigued.

Again, Tillie nodded. "But the doctors can't predict if this is as far as her vision deteriorates or if she'll go completely blind." She choked on the last word.

Keith set down the box of ribbon and wrapped his arms around Tillie. How could he not? As a parent, she must have been devastated. He wasn't Shay's father and he had tears in his eyes.

"I want Shay to see and experience everything before things get too bad," she said into his chest.

"Hence the importance of that job with Boone." Things were making sense now.

Tillie nodded. "And now you know."

Keith held her at arm's length. "Know what?"

Tillie's blue eyes shone with tears. "Why my responsibilities will influence where I live and work. Because Shay will always be my number one priority over everyone else I love."

And by everyone else, he assumed she meant him.

The cowboy no one wanted.

CHAPTER FIFTEEN

"*I NEVER THOUGHT* I'd say this?" Tillie held up a pink T-shirt and ball cap imprinted with the words Team Bride. "But I'm disappointed in Crystal's surprise uniforms. This is the best she could do? T-shirts and ball caps? And they're pink. Aren't we supposed to wear green today?"

"Surprise," Gran deadpanned. "I didn't notice them earlier when we were dealing with the wedding favor fiasco. But look. You also got back the blue coat you loaned Reese." Gran shook out her olive green T-shirt with the words Team Over The Hill on it. "I thought this was a hoity-toity wedding. But now I'm on Team Retired."

Tillie choked back a laugh. "Maybe the goats ate Crystal's original uniforms and she had to scramble for these."

"Is that true?" Shay piped up. She'd donned an olive green ball cap and T-shirt the same color as Gran's but hers said Just Getting Started instead of Over The Hill. "Did my babies eat something else?"

"I don't know." But it would explain why flamboyant Crystal had provided them with plain uniforms.

"You don't hate my baby goats for eating the wedding favors, do you?" Shay tilted her head to one side, presumably looking at Tillie using her peripheral vision.

"No, pumpkin. Even if we hadn't managed to salvage them, I wouldn't hate your baby goats." At least, Tillie had ribbon to decorate the straw succulent baskets with tonight when she had some free time. She still couldn't believe what Keith had done for her—braving a rattlesnake. If that wasn't love…

Tillie shook the thought away. When she'd told Keith about Shay and how her daughter would always be her first priority, he'd gotten quiet and she'd thought the worst. Not every man could love a child that wasn't theirs to the moon and back. They hadn't said much the rest of the way to the lodge. And then, they'd joined Gran and Shay for lunch where he'd talked mostly to them rather than her.

It's for the best.

Tillie didn't want to be the woman who influenced Keith's choices about his future, which was essentially what she'd told him he had to do to be with her—come back to Clementine.

"My shirt is boring," Shay complained, scratching beneath the olive green cotton. "Can I wear my gladiator skirt over my blue jeans?"

"I don't see why not." Gran frowned at her uniform. "No sense looking like everyone else."

Shay perked up. "I hear a wagon." She ran to the cabin door, setting her ball cap on her blond head and forgetting all about her gladiator skirt. "I see Hercules!" She ran down the walk to the lane, flagging down their ride.

Tillie grabbed their jackets and followed.

A few minutes later, Gran emerged from the cabin with her Team Over the Hill uniform on, a testy look in her eyes.

Tillie helped her up and in. "You look ready to have some fun."

"This is the longest week of my life," Gran muttered.

And then, none of them spoke until they reached the competition area on the far side of the wedding barn. There was a trap shooting pad, a pair of horseshoe pits and a putting green.

Smidge pulled Hercules off the lane. "I'm a scorekeeper for this event. My brother Woodburn is master of ceremonies."

"I'm gonna be a winner," Shay announced excitedly. "I hope Crystal brought medals and trophies."

"Not likely," Gran muttered.

Tillie shushed her.

Smidge climbed down, lowered the exit stairs, then helped the Powell ladies to the ground. "In my day, winning wasn't everything."

"But it's what I do best," Shay said staunchly, heedless of her glasses drifting down her nose. She followed the cart driver toward the gathering crowd. "Smidge, can you tell me your story?"

There were others from the wedding party on the grounds. The photographer was already setting up poses with Carter and Reese.

Crystal waved Tillie over. She wore a pink jeans jacket over her pink Team Bride T-shirt and white slacks. "Have you noticed Reese's mood? She doesn't seem like a happy, blushing bride."

Tillie was surprised Crystal had noticed. "The stress is getting to her."

"I tried cheering her up earlier," Crystal admitted, frowning in the direction of Reese. "She snapped at me."

Bravo, Reese.

But Tillie worked her expression into one of sympathy. "As acting wedding planner—" *otherwise known as staff*"—and the only family member in the wedding party, I'll try my best to cheer Reese up. We might give the photographer the afternoon off, just to give Reese some breathing room."

"That's a good idea." Crystal's gaze sharpened. "You gave Tillie your jacket yesterday after Carter dropped her in the creek. You'd do anything for Reese, wouldn't you?"

"Just about." Tillie nodded. "You?"

"Just about." Crystal seemed to come to a decision. "I'd like to be friends."

"Why?" Tillie blurted because this had come out of the blue and she had no interest in forming a friendship with Crystal.

The other bridesmaids turned their way.

"Because you care about Reese and you're important to her." Crystal took Tillie's outburst in stride. She even smiled. "I thought you might be siding with Eleanor, pressuring Reese to wear her vintage wedding dress."

"Nope. Not me. I just want Reese to be happy." Tillie held out the front of her T-shirt. "Team Bride all the way. No snark. No putting anyone down."

Crystal's smile widened. And what was shocking was that it looked genuine. "Sometimes I can get prickly when defending my friends or when I'm going after what I want. I think you and I got off on the wrong foot." She spread her arms. "Hug, girlfriend."

Girlfriend? I didn't have Crystal accepting me on my wedding bingo card.

Tillie didn't think they'd progressed as far as friendship but she submitted to the hug, not wanting to rock the boat. And for her troubles, she earned a heartfelt smile from Reese while Crystal went over to Mike, the photographer, and told him to take time off.

An old man with an unsteady gait gathered the wedding party around. "I'm Woodburn. For this afternoon's competition, we're going to have three stations—trap shooting, horseshoes and a putting contest. Team Bride will start with the trap shoot." The bride and bridesmaids. "Team Groom will start at the horseshoe pit." The groom and his groomsmen. "And Team Over the Hill will start at the putting green." Parents of the bride, Gran and Shay. "You'll score a point for your team with every pigeon shot, every ringer made and every putt sunk on one swing. You each have ten tries at each station."

Smidge handed out clipboards for each team to record their scores. His spry steps contrasted his brother's stilted ones.

"Am I gonna shoot a real gun?" Shay asked, blue eyes large behind her big, round glasses.

"No," a chorus of people chimed in, the loudest of which was Tillie.

"I have a Nerf gun and a target set aside for those who won't be shooting live ammunition." Woodburn spoke to Shay although his words seemed to apply to anyone who didn't want to take down a clay pigeon.

"Have you shot trap before?" Tillie asked Reese.

"No. And I've never wanted to." Reese shrugged. "But Carter thought it would be fun. So I'll give it a try."

"It's just like golf," Crystal said casually.

Team Bride all looked at her as if she'd recited a long, confusing algebraic equation.

Crystal started to smirk, then caught Tillie's eye and headshake. She softened her expression. "I mean, it's one of those activities you can combine with business. Golf, trap shooting, handball. My daddy is convinced that any time you can get someone away from a conference room, you have a higher chance of getting a hard deal done."

Team Bride blinked as if this was even more confusing.

"Ah." Reese nodded, smile growing. "Like a horseback ride. My mother used to say that was where you could really get to know a beau."

"Oh…" Jane, Sophie Jean and Tillie were finally on board with Crystal's words of wisdom.

"Come on." Crystal tugged down the brim of her pink ball cap. "We need to get our shotguns and shells. Follow me." She led them to a small building next to a bit of pavement with lines drawn on it like a fan. "This is going to be fun."

And surprisingly, Tillie believed her.

Forty-five minutes, five destroyed clay pigeons and several rounds of laughter later, Team Bride was done with their round of trap shooting.

Reese gave Tillie a high five. "That was fun."

Tillie hugged her. "I'm glad to see you're feeling better."

"Things are looking up, aren't they?" Reese fairly glowed. "The weather is cooperating. The wedding favors were delivered. We had a good ride this morning—that you missed, by the way."

Reese glanced toward the men who were finishing up horseshoes. "How do the favors look?"

"Good. So cute you could eat them up." Hardy-har. Tillie felt hot in her blue jacket, uncomfortable lying to her cousin.

Reese's smile broadened. "I canceled the scavenger hunt tomorrow. We're going to have a spa day while the guys have a poker tournament in the lobby."

Tillie hugged her again, laughing. "Who suggested this?"

"Keith." Reese grinned. "Last night at karaoke. You missed that, too."

"Nobody wants to hear me sing into a microphone." Tillie lacked the confidence. "But I'm glad you changed this up. You deserve a spa day."

Reese's laughter filled the crisp air. "Me? I think *you* deserve a spa day. You've been doing all the runaround to make my day special."

If you only knew.

"Okay. I won't argue." Tillie pulled her hair off her back and over one shoulder.

Reese fussed with Tillie's hair. "And don't argue with me about you getting back together with Keith either. I think you should. He's changed. And I worry about him. He lives too much in his head and now with Carter marrying me and the business being sold, he's alone and adrift."

Tillie let that comment slide along the same path her heart was taking—toward the wayside. She'd put him off by saying Shay came first but she wasn't going to admit that to Reese. Her cousin had enough to worry about.

"I sunk a putt, Mama!" Shay ran up to Tillie.

She looked like she was having a great time.

And despite an uncertain future, Tillie vowed to do the same.

"THEY SAY THIS is a team competition but we know better, don't we, boys?" Carter stood on the fake turf that made up the putting green. His black ball cap visor sat over his sunglasses. "We're competing against each other."

"Mano a mano," Brad said hollowly, as if tired of being cheerful. "What are the stakes?"

"Loser treats the other four to a round of golf," Carter said, which was their usual bet.

Woodburn joined them on the green. Instead of his fix-it-shop uniform of faded overalls, today he wore crisp blue jeans, a gray sweater and a respectable, red puffy jacket. "Life isn't a competition. Life is about doing yourself proud, making lasting relationships and finding your joy."

Carter smiled indulgently. "Sounds like you've been talking to our parents."

"Or just Dad," Keith murmured, even though he suspected Woodburn's words were his own.

"Dad is a good guess." Brad smiled. "Did our father catch you in the barn, Woodburn? That's where he used to talk to us about life's lessons."

"Actually, I just met your father." Woodburn tugged down the brim of his straw cowboy hat. "Wise man. He told me he raised over thirty foster boys. Isn't that somethin'. And you all make him proud. Every day." The old man moseyed off toward the horseshoe pit.

Keith felt everyone's eyes upon him the way they had been the day they'd arrived. He didn't like it. "We should putt."

"Wait." Carter removed his ball cap, then held it over his heart. "I have something to say. To everyone."

The groomsmen shifted their feet, looking away. Brad looked pale, as if expecting bad news.

"I failed you," Carter began slowly. "All of you. We won't have jobs when the final sale goes through."

Brad's gaze darted to Keith, who slung an arm over his shoulder with a whispered, "It's going to be all right." He didn't know how he'd make it so, but he was suddenly determined to try. Just like he was suddenly determined to give a relationship with Tillie a second go-round.

Granted, her confession that Shay would always come first had hit him wrong, like the time after his parents died when his uncle had said he couldn't afford to keep him. And during that reopening of his old wound, he'd had a moment, however brief, where he'd wondered if he could do the same for Shay—putting her first above all others, including himself. After all, she wasn't his flesh and blood. And even though he'd rejected that thought almost immediately, he'd learned enough about himself this week to question what that hesitation meant.

Can I love Shay as if she's my own? Keith thought so.

Can I be a work with Clementine as my home base? Keith knew that would be tricky.

Carter picked up his apology where he'd left off. "I should have been a better negotiator, a better brother, a better example of the way we were raised." He put his cap back on, frowning fiercely. "I've been carrying a feeling of doom around since December. It gets worse every time there's a new round of negotiations. And I just wanted to say that I love you all and appreciate you standing by me."

"I think we need a good lawyer," Keith said, struck by an idea.

"To sue me?" Carter dropped back a step, a hurt look in his eyes.

Keith shook his head, holding Carter's gaze. "We need a better contract lawyer than the one we have on retainer."

"Are you saying we should scrap their latest offer and redraw new terms?" Brad scratched his head. "Can we do that?"

"I'm not a lawyer but I don't see why we can't redraft the contract. Isn't that what we've been doing all along?" Keith's mind started working double-time, listing things he wanted to bring back to the negotiating table, things he hadn't thought of before.

"What if the deal falls apart?" Carter asked, voice nearly a whisper.

Keith shrugged. "I'd imagine you'd have to pay back the earnest money they gave Sunny Y'all when they first approached us. But you'd all still have your jobs."

"That's something," Brad said quietly.

Luther and Van nodded. Since Carter's earlier announcement about them losing their jobs, they'd probably been calculating what their share of the sale would be and how long they could pay their mortgage if they couldn't find work right away.

None of the men looked Keith in the eye.

So, he kept talking. "When we were teenagers living on the Done Roamin' Ranch, I knew that whatever I told you that was bothering me, you'd give it perspective. You'd help me laugh at myself, or pick me up, even get angry with me. But whatever happened back then, you'd be honest with me. In the past year, the people who invested in us steered us on a course they wanted—a sale to earn a return on their investment in one lump sum. But is that what *we* wanted? Is that best for us?" Keith shrugged. "Honestly, I don't know. But I have a feeling it's not."

The men nodded slowly, as if they didn't either. Even Carter. Brad placed a hand on Keith's shoulder. A moment later, Carter came over and did the same. And then they were joined by Van and Luther.

A sense of peace settled in Keith's chest.

"Hey," Boone called from the trap court. "We're nearly done shooting and you guys haven't even started putting."

"We're getting there," Carter called back. And then he faced Keith. "We're getting where we need to be."

"OH, KEITH?" Crystal held him back when the competition was over and the winners had been announced—Team Over the Hill won the event, having trounced everyone on the trap shooting portion. "If you have time tonight, I'd like to hear your ideas for something new you've invented or would like to invent."

"Not tonight." If Keith was being honest, not ever.

"Why? Is it because you're getting chummy with the boys again? You don't need them." Crystal laughed. "Or do you think Tillie would be jealous?"

Something sharp filled Keith's chest, skittering out through his veins. He clenched and unclenched his fingers, trying to dispel it.

"To tell you the truth, Crystal, I can only be an extrovert for so long. And then I need to recharge my batteries with peace and quiet." That much was true. And so was the strength of an idea forming in Keith's head: *I want to be in charge of my own destiny.*

"Someplace quiet, then." Crystal wasn't giving up. "My cabin. This deal could be beneficial to both of us." Crystal touched Keith's arm, making him frown. She wasn't exactly coming on to him but she wasn't exactly not.

Ahead of them, Tillie sat in one of the wagons and she was watching.

"You know, Crystal. I'm not convinced I want to do a deal with you."

"What?" Crystal's laugh turned into that harsh, villainous one. "I'll let you think on that a bit longer, Keith. You can't pass up what I have to offer."

"But I think I can." And for once, he believed those words, believed in himself. And with that epiphany, he realized something else. He'd hesitated with Tillie earlier because he lacked confidence in himself as a dad. That was something he'd never done before.

But this week, he was changing. He wanted to tell Tillie why he'd gone silent during their walk back from the snake skirmish in the storage container.

But when he glanced up, Tillie and the wagon had left.

CHAPTER SIXTEEN

Friday, one day until the wedding

"TILLIE! TILLIE!" Someone pounded on Tillie's cabin door.

Tillie cracked her eyes open and sat up. It was dark. And quiet. She felt as if she hadn't logged enough sleep. And she couldn't remember why she'd woken up in the first place. No one was knocking. Had she dreamt it?

Gran snored quietly in her bed. Shay tossed fitfully before quieting.

"Tillie!" Reese's voice. Followed by a soft knocking on the cabin door.

Tillie rolled out of bed and stumbled to the door. "Reese?"

Her cousin stood on the front porch in a yellow tank top, black jacket, baggy gray sweats and red fuzzy slippers. Her white-blond hair was in a messy ponytail. She darted inside and then slipped inside the bathroom, turning on the light and gesturing Tillie to follow her.

Tillie closed the front door and joined Reese

in the bathroom, shutting the door behind her. "What time is it? What happened?" she whispered. "What's wrong?"

Reese's cheeks were streaked with tears. "It's after five. I got up to get a drink of water and I saw this." She pulled aside her tank top to reveal a bruise where her right arm met her right shoulder. It was deep red and a rectangular shape, like that of the butt of a shotgun. "I think it's from the recoil of the gun." Her brave expression began to crumble.

Tillie hugged her. "It'll be all right."

Reese eased out of her embrace, looking like she might cry. "My complexion…" She gently touched her receding zit. "My hair…" She touched the shorter ends. "My backside…" She patted her bum. "And now this…" She pointed to the recoil bruise. "What am I going to do?"

Tillie gathered her cousin's hands in her own. "You're going to marry Carter on Saturday. He loves you and he doesn't care about any of this."

"But what about Carter's *perfect image*—" Reese surrounded the phrase in air quotes "—on social media. I have a strapless wedding gown. It'll look like I've been sabotaged by my makeup artist. Or worse."

Uh-oh.

Tillie gave Reese's hands a gentle shake. "I've never liked those picture perfect posts on social media. What does it say about someone? That they're capable? Or that they spend too much time looking in the mirror."

Reese's gaze strayed to the mirror. Her lower lip trembled.

Tillie rushed on. "Maybe you should post something people can relate to—the triumph of true love despite all these accidents."

Reese tugged her hands free, frown coming too quickly. "Like the pictures Mike took when we stumbled and fell into the creek? How are they going to help Carter?"

"Well…" Tillie tried to think fast. "Maybe instead of framing him in an aspirational light, they'll make potential employers see him as human and relatable."

"As comedic relief." Reese wiped at her eyes and stared at the ceiling. Her hand crept to the neckline of her yellow tank top. "I feel like there's a very large bull sitting on my chest and he won't move."

"Let's try to think of something positive." Because Reese was scaring her now. "There's one more day until the wedding."

"What more can go wrong?" Reese rolled her eyes. "Don't tempt fate."

"Fate." Tillie scoffed. "Who needs fate when we're going to have a spa day?" She laid her hands on Reese's shoulders. "Take a deep breath and think about that. A spa day. They probably have some kind of treatment to get the blood flowing in bruises. There'll be massages." She kneaded Reese's shoulders, pleased that her eyes drifted closed. "Facials. Mani-pedis. And plenty of time to just sit and relax."

"It sounds perfect."

Someone knocked on the bathroom door.

Reese tensed, eyes flying open. She gathered the ends of her jacket, covering any hint of the bruise.

"Tillie?" Gran opened the door a crack. "Are you going to be long?" She spotted Reese and opened the door wider. "Oh, hello, Reese. I thought Tillie was talking to herself."

"Why would I be talking to myself?" Tillie shook her head.

"Because you've been trying to talk yourself out of starting up with Keith again." Gran leaned against the doorjamb. "And even these old eyes can see that you should quiet that voice in your head and follow your heart. That's why I thought you were in here arguing with yourself in the mirror."

Reese and Tillie exchanged glances. And then they laughed because they'd each had talks to themselves in the mirror at various points in their lives and Gran knew it, having hosted many a sleepover when they were growing up.

"If you're through…" Gran gestured toward the commode.

Tillie escorted Reese to the door. "Try to get

some sleep. Everything is going to be just fine. I promise."

Reese chuckled as she shuffled down the stairs. "No one can promise that."

"One more day," Tillie called after her instead of arguing.

TILLIE AND REESE skipped breakfast.

Reese didn't want to see anyone in the bridal party. Well, except for her bridesmaids. But only when they were fully ensconced in the spa.

"What do you think, Crystal?" Reese asked while they sat sweating out toxins in the sauna and drinking mimosas. The bride looked calmer than she had at five in the morning. "Can you cover this up?"

"I told her you could." Tillie threw a big hint-hint into her tone.

Come on, Crystal.

Crystal studied Tillie a moment before answering, reminding her of that moment yesterday afternoon when Crystal had stopped Keith to talk and Keith had seemed to look over at Tillie with guilt in his expression.

Had they dated in the past six years? Flirted? Tillie couldn't give that expression on Keith's face context.

"Your dress is strapless, so it'll be a disaster to cake your armpit and above it with makeup." Crystal tilted her head as she regarded Reese. "But there's this new spray tan product and I'm told they use it at this spa. It's guaranteed not to rub off. That could work."

"Spray tan..." Reese sipped her mimosa. "I don't know. I've never done that before. Have you tried it, Crystal?"

"No. But I will if you will. No need to make a decision right now." Crystal sprawled across a sauna bench. "We've got all day."

"What do you think?" Reese asked Tillie.

Tillie leaned closer, and whispered, "I think your mother's wedding dress would cover it nicely."

"Vintage will do in a pinch. But it lacks...something." Crystal had supersonic hearing and an apparent dislike of Aunt Eleanor's wedding dress.

"The ability to pivot is a well-respected skill," Tillie said in a louder voice. "And it makes for a good story on social media."

"I know the perfect hairstyle to complement your mother's dress," Sophie Jean said kindly.

"And those calla lilies are just as retro as your dress," Jane pointed out.

Tillie could have hugged them. She made a mental note to do so later.

Full body massages were next with Tillie and Reese up first. Tillie hadn't realized she'd been carrying so much tension in her neck. When they were done, they had a light lunch while waiting for the others to have their massages.

"I owe you an apology." Reese nibbled on a cucumber sandwich. Her hair was slicked back with a hair treatment meant to soften her curls. "Crystal has been…well, she was being Crystal-y for most of the week. And I said something I regret to her. It's been nagging at me ever since."

Tillie munched on a carrot, curious. She pushed up the wide sleeves of her white terrycloth robe.

"I told Crystal I chose you as my maid of honor because my parents expected me to." Reese grimaced. "I told her I was obligated to choose you. That couldn't be farther from the truth. I'm sorry."

Tillie took Reese's hand and gave it an affectionate squeeze. "That's okay. Before we got here, I called you a bridezilla because you couldn't make a decision about anything. I didn't understand that you were making decisions to promote Carter." She still didn't agree with that. "I'm sorry I thought of you that way. But now we're even."

"You have a way of grounding me." Reese reached for her mimosa. "Can't you move to Dallas?"

"Nope. You know me. I'm a Clementine girl."

Keith's handsome face came to mind. That mischievous smile. That sparkle to his blue eyes.

That silence after I told him Shay was my top priority.

"You were right, Tillie." Reese sighed. "Nothing can go wrong today."

Tillie hoped so. So much that she crossed her fingers.

Not long after, they were joined by the others. Mani-pedis were up next. That was followed by facials. And then they were placed in a quiet room where they were supposed to lie back in their chair and enjoy the silence.

But Crystal hadn't gotten that memo. "Reese, we need to spray tan."

Tillie shushed her. No spray tan meant Reese would wear her mother's wedding dress.

"If you want to wear that gorgeous dress without looking like Shay finger painted your shoulder, we need to get your glow on." Crystal got to her feet and came to stand in front of Reese. "Satisfaction guaranteed."

"I don't know." Reese reached across the divide between her lounger and Tillie's, taking her hand. "Do I need to pretend I'm perfect?"

"You are perfect," Crystal said unexpectedly. She rarely passed out compliments. "*We're* all perfect. But you'll look lovely in your pictures with a tan, Reese. You know it's true."

"What do you think, guys?" Reese asked her attendants.

"I'm a no," Jane said, which wasn't surprising given her no-nonsense character.

"I'm a yes if it'll make you feel better," Sophie Jean chimed in.

Reese turned to Tillie.

Intuitively, Tillie knew Reese wanted that spray tan to cover up her shotgun recoil bruise. But she just couldn't go along with it. She shook her head.

"It's a tie," Reese said quietly.

"But you're the tie-breaker," Crystal pointed out. She gently pulled the collar of Reese's robe to one side, revealing that colorful bruise. "I bet you'll tuck that shotgun tight to your shoulder the next time you shoot, the same way we did."

None of the rest of them had a bruise like Reese's.

"Okay." Reese got to her bare feet. "I'm going to get my glow on."

"That's my girl." Crystal sashayed out the door with Reese, arm in arm.

Tillie sent up a silent prayer that the spray tan worked the way Reese wanted it to.

"Matilda, where is Reese?"

They were waiting for the bride to start dance rehearsal and Tillie didn't seem to know how to answer her uncle's intense demand.

Keith moved closer to her. Tillie had been avoiding him, moving through the wedding party and checking on everyone. But now… The bride was late and tempers were beginning to flare.

"She's not answering her phone." Carter stared at his cell phone as if willing it to ring with a call from Reese.

They'd been at the wedding barn waiting to rehearse their wedding dance for the past half hour. No Reese. No Crystal.

"Is Aunt Reese lost?" Shay pushed her glasses up her nose, then took Keith's hand. She wore a thick brown sweater, and her gladiator skirt over beige leggings. She was the only one still sticking to the color dress code for today. "Did Aunt Reese take a walk in the pasture alone? Mama says I'm not supposed to walk anywhere alone. Did she drive somewhere? Or ride her horse? Sometimes Gran takes me for ice cream when I'm supposed to be in the bath."

"Shay." Gran came up behind her and leaned close to her ear. "Our ice cream runs are supposed to be our secret."

"Sorry, Gran." Shay tugged Keith's hand. "But maybe Aunt Reese needed an ice cream."

"She's just late," Tillie said, chin up.

"Matilda, call the main lodge and ask if my vehicle is still in the lot." Boone paced the dance floor, a bull unhappy to be corralled. "I wasn't sure Reese was going to go through with the wedding. She may have taken it."

"She's going through with the wedding," Tillie said firmly.

"When you call the main lodge, Tillie, ask if my truck is still there, too," Carter added, worry furrowing his brow.

"I'm telling you, Reese isn't a runaway bride,"

Tillie insisted, staring them all down. Her gaze landed on Keith. "Reese loves Carter."

"Reese isn't a runaway bride," Keith dutifully repeated. "She loves Carter."

"This is all your fault," Crystal's voice carried from the wedding barn's entrance. She'd walked through the door but had turned to throw her accusation at someone behind her.

Reese?

"My fault?" Reese sounded panicked. "It was your idea. *Get your glow on.*"

The two women crossed the threshold and turned to face the group.

Oh no.

Air rushed out of Tillie's lungs in a rush because…of all the mishaps that had occurred this week, this was the worst.

"Did I mix the spray tan lotion?" Crystal continued to gripe. "Did I set the timer wrong? Was I the new employee at the spa? The answer is always no."

The group stared at them, mouths open, speechless.

Reese and Crystal were orange. As orange as Oompa Loompas.

Tillie moved slowly toward them, unable to think of one fix. The job for Uncle Boone… She hadn't really thought about it much in the past twenty-four hours, being distracted by thoughts of Keith.

But now…this…

The bride is orange. There's no way Uncle Boone will hire me because there isn't going to be a wedding.

"Reese?" Aunt Eleanor walked forward to meet her daughter but even she seemed at a loss for words.

"Mom." Reese rushed forward on a sob, throwing herself into her mother's arms. Not only was she orange but her hair looked as if she'd dumped a bottle of olive oil on it.

Reese lifted her head, saw Tillie and transferred her orange self into Tillie's arms.

"We'll fix this," Tillie murmured, although she had no idea how. "Everything is going to be fine."

"Did Aunt Reese and Crystal take a bath in orange juice?" Shay asked, approaching the two women with her head tilted to one side. "Or orange popsicles? Orange popsicles turn my tongue orange like that. But they're orange all over. Can I take a bath in orange juice?"

"I wouldn't recommend it," Crystal said in a defeated voice.

"Honey." Carter hugged Reese. "What happened?"

Reese began to cry, burying her orange face in Carter's chest.

"I admit, this looks bad." Crystal held up her orange hands. "It takes a week to wear off. We tried showering. We tried tomato juice baths. Then vinegar baths."

"That explains the smell of Easter eggs," Keith said softly.

Tillie considered whapping him with her cowboy hat.

"I smell, too?" Reese cried harder. "And it's not even Easter."

Aunt Eleanor touched Reese's greasy hair, as if she might be able to diagnose and fix one thing about her orange-skinned daughter.

"Sophie Jean." Tillie caught the beautician's eye and then pointed toward Reese's hair.

She rushed forward.

"This is all your fault." Boone stomped over to Tillie. "You were supposed to make Reese's dream wedding a reality. But now it's a nightmare."

"You can't blame Tillie," Crystal said, surprising Tillie by coming to her defense. "She's been the steadiest one among us, other than her infatuation with Keith."

Shay moved closer to Tillie, tugging Keith along with her.

Keith gave Tillie a hearty smile, one that would have lifted her spirits if not for the wedding she was supposed to save falling apart around her.

No way could Reese walk down the aisle looking as bright as an orange Skittle.

"That's right, Daddy." Reese lifted her head and stared down her father from the safety of

Carter's arms. "Tillie didn't want me to change everything at the last minute. She picked up the slack of the wedding planner without complaint. She tried to talk some sense into me when I went full-on bridezilla in my quest to make Carter look good to potential employers by posting perfect pictures on social media. And she voted against the spray tan."

"A good manager anticipates worst-case scenarios," Uncle Boone said in that booming, superior voice of his.

I really don't want to work for him.

But no way was Tillie telling him that.

"Not even a professional wedding planner could have anticipated the worst-case scenarios that happened this week," Keith said, earning a grateful smile from Tillie.

"Why does Uncle Boone keep yelling at you, Mama?" Shay frowned. "What's his story?"

Tears collected in Tillie's eyes. She hadn't expected so many people to rise to her defense.

"Is that true, Reese?" Carter asked softly, rubbing Reese's back. "Was all this amped up production of our wedding your way of helping me if I lost my job?"

Reese nodded, face still buried in Carter's chest. "Social media can be really powerful. It's part of the job screening process and says a lot about your character."

Carter frowned sharply, as if Reese had struck

a nerve. "You didn't need to do that." After everything Reese had done and the reasons she'd done them, that statement was a mistake.

Reese flinched.

"This is our wedding," Carter continued. "Not a promotional opportunity. And staged wedding photos aren't going to help me get a job. I'm not a house you're trying to sell. You can't spruce me up to hide my flaws."

Reese stumbled back. "Am I a joke to you?"

"No." Too late, Carter seemed to realize he'd prodded a sensitive topic, just as Reese had to him. "No. I meant that—"

"I don't think Aunt Reese should marry Carter," Shay jumped in. "He doesn't smile right. And besides, I don't think he likes her being orange."

No-no-no.

Before Tillie could intervene, Reese got that feisty gleam in her eye, the one she'd had before Griff Malone dared her to ride a bronc bareback in high school.

"You're right, Shay." Reese raised her voice. "Carter isn't looking at me like he'll love me forever and always, no matter what foolish thing I do or how orange I get."

"Here we go," Uncle Boone muttered, giving Tillie a dark look.

"Hey, I never said that, exactly," Carter protested.

"Reese? Carter?" Tillie moved in, mediation

on her mind. "I think we're forgetting something important here."

"No. We're learning something important here." Reese brushed the tears off her orange cheeks. "Carter is no good at relationships." She flung her arm out, pointing at Keith. "He wouldn't stand up and protect Keith when Daddy said Sunny Y'all's sale would be easier without him." Reese stared at Carter and began to sob. "I fell in love with you when we were kids, Carter. And I waited for you to find the right time to finally get married. I waited and tried to find ways to help you feel better about yourself. And I think I waited so long and tried so hard that I don't know who I am anymore. I certainly don't know who you are."

"We should all just take a breath," Tillie inserted.

"No." Reese sobbed again, managing to choke out. "The wedding is off!" She turned and fled.

"Matilda!" Boone growled Tillie's name.

"Shut up, Boone," Carter said, standing with his eyes closed and his hands clenched as if he couldn't stand to see Reese run out of his life.

Tillie took a deep breath and tried to project calm. "We're all interested in Reese's happiness. But she's in a vulnerable place right now. Dance practice is obviously canceled."

"Oh, I can run dance rehearsal," Crystal countered. "Trust me. They need all the practice they can get."

"Not if there's no wedding," Carter said through gritted teeth.

"The point is…" Tillie said firmly, giving Crystal a hard smile. "That Reese has been living two roles—the Clementine woman who loves Carter and the Dallas woman who stands by her man." She turned toward the groom. "If you truly love her, Carter, both sides of her, you'll need to do something truly grand to convince her to marry you tomorrow."

"She can't get married tomorrow," Aunt Eleanor said breathlessly. "She's *orange*."

"She makes a pretty orange," Shay said, earning a hug from Gran. "And I love her forever and always, no matter what color she is."

"From the mouths of babes," Keith murmured.

That was the last thing Tillie heard before she ran after Reese.

CHAPTER SEVENTEEN

"REESE?" TILLIE MARCHED up the front steps, opened Reese's cabin door and—stopped cold.

The room was immaculate. But hanging from the curtain rod over the rear window were two wedding dresses.

Before she had a chance to process the meaning of her find, three baby goats bounded past her, like happy bunnies on a carpet of fresh grass.

"No. No-no-no." Tillie ran in after them. "Shoo. Shoo." The last thing she needed was goats to eat either of Reese's wedding dresses on the off chance that the nuptials proceeded as scheduled.

The baby goats took evasive maneuvers, jumping onto the bed when Tillie tried to herd them all in one direction and darting behind Tillie when she had them moving toward the door.

"What's going on?" Reese stood in the open doorway, just as orange and sad as she'd been when she ran away from Carter earlier. "How did those devil-spawn get in here?"

"I opened the door and they took advantage of

me." Tillie spotted an open box of Holly Explorers cookies. She grabbed the box and shook it. It made a crinkly noise.

The three goats paused, and turned her way, sniffing the air. And then, as one, they took a tentative step toward her.

Like velociraptors on the hunt.

Tillie was banking on that anyway. She moved slowly toward the door, reaching in the bag for a cookie. "Step clear of the door, Reese."

Reese backed into the bathroom.

The goats were still stalking Tillie, walking slowly, noses raised and sniffing. But Tillie knew that wouldn't last.

"Come on, babies." Tillie reached the door. "Come and get your cookies." And then she tossed the cookie and the box out into the yard.

The trio of troublemakers scampered out the door.

And Tillie shut it behind them, sliding the lock in place. The sound of scrabbling hooves and tussles over cookie bags quickly receded.

There was a moment of silence where neither Tillie nor Reese moved.

And then Reese gave a little hiccup-sob. And Tillie turned to give her a hug, which seemed to turn on a waterwork of tears on both their parts.

When they were both cried out, when their tears were dried and noses blown and they'd drank a full glass of water, Reese stared at Tillie and admitted, "It's all my fault."

Tillie allowed herself a small smile, thinking of Keith. "I've been hearing that a lot lately. Self-blame, that is. But I have news for you. It takes two to tango their way into an engagement and two to have the courage to say I do."

Reese bit her lip, looking like she was going to fall apart again.

"Why do you have two wedding dresses, Reese?" Tillie thought they should back up a bit before tackling the heavy issues. "Did you sign for the delivery? In Keith's name? With a little heart over the *i*?"

"Yes. And after Shay sold me cookies, I sent Crystal on an errand so I could plant the bridesmaid dresses in Keith's cabin." Reese sank onto her bed. She covered her orange face with her orange hands. "What is happening to me?"

"That's exactly what we've all been wondering." Tillie sat next to Reese and gave her a hug. "If you want to talk about it, we can figure it out."

"Why? It's all over." Reese's voice was muffled. "Sunny Y'all will be sold. Carter can't stand the sight of me. My parents think I've gone off the deep end. And…" She raised her head, staring at her hands, much the way Crystal had in the wedding barn earlier—in disbelief. "They're not wrong."

"Hey." Tillie gave her cousin a side hug, rubbing her arm consolingly. "We had some good times this week, you and me. We made some awesome memories."

"Like me stealing my own wedding dress so I wouldn't have to choose which one to wear until the last minute?" Reese tried to laugh. "Or you kissing Keith because you never fully got over him?"

Tillie sat back to give Reese a shocked stare. "I never told you about kissing Keith." She very carefully did not pursue the topic of still loving Keith.

Reese did laugh this time. "You didn't have to tell me. I recognized the way you looked at him. And Crystal did, too."

So much for thinking only Gran suspected her feelings for Keith had recharged. "You know what I'll always remember about this week? You buying cookies from Shay."

"That was sweet," Reese agreed.

"And Shay telling you how beautiful you were on horseback in your blue dress." Tillie was relying on Keith's lip-reading technique for those memories. "And you telling her how pretty she was in her blue jeans and black tutu."

"Shay telling you she'd watch out for your Gran as we left the picnic," Reese added.

"Shay telling everyone that you were a beautiful orange shade."

"I love her so much," Reese whispered. "What else did that lovebug do this week?"

"She asked Keith if he was going to marry me," Tillie admitted.

Reese jerked sideways, facing Tillie. "Is he going to marry you?"

Tillie shrugged. "Don't be like him, Reese. You're jumping ahead of all the things that have to fall into place first."

"Well…" It was Reese's arm that came around Tillie's shoulder this time. "If you do get engaged, your wedding can't be any worse than mine."

"Are we having a wedding tomorrow?" Tillie asked softly.

"I say yes, but what will Carter say?" Reese's voice was very small. She didn't believe in Carter anymore.

"He'll come through," Tillie said with conviction. She had a feeling Keith would help Carter find his way. "And when he does, you'll have to decide which wedding dress to wear."

"You want me to walk down the aisle tomorrow? Seriously?" Reese held up her orange hand. "Have you seen the color of my skin?"

"Nope." Tillie stuck her nose in the air. "Love is color blind."

"DID SOMEONE UPLOAD malware in your head?" Keith demanded of Carter, pacing in front of him, hat brim pulled low. "How could you say those things to Reese? She's been nothing but supportive of you—of us—for years."

Carter sat on the small stage in the wedding barn turning his cowboy hat slowly in his hand. He looked defeated, from the dullness of his short blond hair to the way his shoulders slumped.

Brad sat on a chair a few feet away, arms crossed over his chest, glasses pushed so far up the bridge of his nose that the lenses had to be resting against his forehead. He'd tipped his cowboy hat back so far that a strong breeze would knock it off his head.

The rest of the wedding party had left them. The sun had set. And there was a chill air of gloom hanging over them.

"I'm a sham," Carter admitted, staring blankly at a spot on the wall. "The suits… My title as CEO… It's all for show. I have no idea what I'm doing when I'm not selling. Run a company? I'm in over my head, acting my way through it. And yet, when my fiancée tries to position me as a success on social media, I get my nose bent out of joint."

It was the first time he'd spoken since Tillie had left. Carter hadn't argued while Boone tore into him, railing about expenses, appearances and the years he'd strung Reese along. He'd said not a word when Eleanor expressed her keen disappointment in the way Carter had broken her little girl's heart. Not a whisper when their foster parents tried to talk to him about courage, love and honor.

Keith decided to remind him of their upbringing now. "You love Reese. And when she tried to perpetuate the image of who you've been trying to be, somewhere deep down inside, you must have realized how unauthentic you've been."

Carter blinked, gaze shifting to Keith.

"It was an honorable thing to do…in theory," Brad said quietly. "And sometimes, the hardest thing to do is the most honorable."

"Your delivery was all wrong," Keith added, trying to lighten the mood.

"And your timing was the worst," Brad said, grinning.

"Quoting Mom and Dad. Teasing me. After what just happened… Why you two put up with me…" Carter slipped his cowboy hat back on and shook his head. "Why Reese puts up with me…" And just like that, Carter was back to being forlorn.

"Hey, it wasn't all one-sided. You were the only reason we had any sales at first," Brad said quietly. "Remember the automatic nail buffer?"

"Insert your finger into a pencil-sharpener-like device to smooth the surface of your nails?" Carter scoffed. "How could I forget?"

"We sold a thousand units to salons in the south." Keith latched onto the tale, if only because it had reached Carter somehow. "You wrote the best product copy. *Why waste time buffing when you can get right to the point?*"

"That product could have been our Chia Pet," Brad lamented. "If only our manufacturer hadn't shut down just as we picked up momentum."

"A product failure but not your fault, Carter." Keith sat next to Carter on the edge of the stage. "Oh, and what about earring earphones? Fashion combined with function. How many units of that did we move before Covid hit?"

"Five thousand. It was a low profit margin but a winner." Brad smiled. "Easy as pie to produce."

Carter chuckled. "Better for your long-term hearing than headphones." That had been his sales pitch. They'd sold them to budget fashion chains for the holidays.

"Somewhere along the line, we lost…*it*." Yes, Keith used a term that Crystal had applied to Reese and Carter's wedding reception dance. But it seemed appropriate here. "Carter, you got caught up in status. I was living too far into the future. And Brad… I don't know what happened to you, man."

"I got a huge mortgage, miscalculated a little," he lamented. "I'm over-extended."

"That'll make you risk-averse." Keith thought about Tillie. He loved her. Heart as big as the Oklahoma plains. Brain focused on results and the bottom line. Maybe she wasn't the most risk-averse person he knew. Maybe it was Brad. And then he thought about Shay. She was the most precocious person he knew. He was certain he could love her as deeply and fiercely as if she were his own.

"What we have here…" Carter assembled what almost seemed like a smile "…is a total breakdown. We stopped communicating. We lost our way. On both a personal and a professional level. And now…"

"We've hit rock bottom," Brad said.

Keith shook his head. "I don't think we've hit rock bottom."

"You think it can get worse than this?" Carter removed his cowboy hat and swatted Keith with it.

"Hey!" Keith protested, although he was heartened by Carter's comeback. "I should have said rock bottom is when that sale happens to Durant Ranch Products and Sunny Y'all is no more."

They all fell into silence.

If I could do it all over again, I would do things a lot differently.

"But…" Keith slapped his palms on his thighs. "We'll deal with rock bottom when the time comes. Right now, we have a different situation to address—Carter's love life."

Carter shook his head. "You can't Einstein my way out of this, Keith. I said things… I was insensitive."

"You were hurt," Brad allowed. "Lashing out."

Carter rubbed the back of his neck. "I could have said things long ago."

"You thought Reese wanted to do all those galas

and yacht trips and dress like Crystal because she liked it." Keith patted Carter on the back. "It's understandable if you didn't clear the air. But the only thing that matters now is…do you love her?"

"Yes."

"Do you want to spend the rest of your life with her?" Brad asked.

"Yes." Carter sighed heavily. "But what can I possibly do to prove to Reese that I love her? She's never going to speak to me again."

"Oh, I think she will," Keith said, starting to smile.

Because he had a plan.

CHAPTER EIGHTEEN

"WE HAVEN'T HAD a sleepover in decades," Reese told Tillie the next morning. She sounded more like herself...even if she didn't look like herself. "I'd like to say it was fun but—"

"It was fun." Tillie stretched in bed, yawning.

She'd left Shay with Gran. She and Reese had dinner delivered. Then they'd had dessert delivered. And now, Tillie wondered if they were going to have breakfast delivered.

"When did you get up, Reese? And why didn't you wake me?"

"I rolled out of bed around an hour ago and tried to scrub this color off my skin." Reese heaved a sigh. "The good news is that I can't see the recoil bruise on my shoulder. The bad news is that I'm still orange and not getting married today."

Tillie rolled over on her side, smiling and staring at Reese. "What did Debbie Downer do with my favorite cousin? Swallow her whole?"

"Is Debbie a slight woman with a big appetite and orange skin?"

"Yep." Tillie grinned. "I'd like the real Reese to come out now. Cough her up, Ms. Downer."

Reese plopped on the bed, drawing her knees up to her chest. "How long do you think it'll be before they start knocking on my door?"

"Who?" Tillie stretched once more. She'd slept in a borrowed nightgown of Reese's. And given it had been the best sleep since she'd arrived at the Ambling Horse Prairie Resort, Tillie felt guilty.

"Everyone is going to be knocking on my door." Reese reached over and pushed Tillie's shoulder. "My parents… Your Gran and Shay… *Carter.*"

"You think Carter is coming?" Tillie chuckled, relieved that Reese wasn't freaking out about that possibility. "You want him to come around, don't you?"

"It wasn't his finest moment but yes. I want to see him because…" Reese floundered. "I wasn't nice to him. Or maybe it was Daddy who wasn't nice to him. But before… All this time… I thought I was part of his team but I was really just doing my own thing."

"You were supportive." Tillie yawned.

"Til!" Reese sat up and poked Tillie's arm once more. "You're yawning. I was a bridezilla or a fiancée-illa. I don't know how to fix this. Where is my pep talk?"

"You're doing fine on your own." Tillie yawned again. "Do you know how to work the coffee machine?"

"Well, duh. It comes with instructions." Reese crossed her arms over her chest. "And weren't you a coffee barista? You should know how to make coffee."

"I know but I never worked that machine and I kind of like it when other folks make me a cup of morning Joe." She pouted. *"Please."*

"Oh, all right." Reese went into the kitchenette and set the coffee machine to work.

Meanwhile, Tillie rolled over and pulled the covers over her head. She couldn't remember the last time she'd slept in.

Of course, as soon as she tried to go back to sleep a peacock shrieked outside the cabin, which made Tillie think of Shay, which reminded her of Shay reaching for Keith's hand at the wedding barn yesterday. And Keith sticking up for her to Boone. And the way his hand wrapped around hers just the way she liked it. And how well and thoroughly he kissed her.

Gran was right. He's a keeper.

The realization was like a thunderbolt. As if a bucket of cold water had been dumped over her head and she was suddenly looking at a new reality. And so, now. Tillie was wide awake.

It probably didn't help that Reese was banging around the coffee machine. "You'd think I'd be the one getting pampered, this being my almost-wedding day and all."

"If I treat you with kid gloves, you're only going to get upset all over again."

"You're probably right about that."

Steps pounded up the stairs outside.

Reese scurried back to the bed. "Someone's coming."

Obviously. "Who?"

"How would I know?" Reese trotted around the bed to Tillie's side and gave her a good shake. "Why aren't you getting out of bed?"

"Because if you don't face whoever that is now, you're going to move back to Clementine to the room you grew up in and you're going to regret losing Carter for the rest of your life." Tillie knew Reese better than she knew herself. Her cousin loved Carter and wanted nothing more than to work things out. She would have regrets if she hid from everyone.

Reese didn't budge from the bedside. "But…"

There was a knock at the door and a tentative "Reese?"

"That's Carter." Reese shook Tillie once more. "Come on. Get up. I need you."

Tillie rolled onto her back, flung the covers off her face and grabbed onto one of Reese's orange hands. "You don't need me. You know what to do." She hoped anyway.

"Do I?" Reese stared at the two wedding dresses hanging on her curtain rod.

"Reese? Honey?"

Reese's head snapped around toward the door. "Honey? I'm still his honey?" Reese walked with purpose to the front door. Unlocked it. Opened it. And stared. "Oh. My. Word."

Tillie bolted out of bed and ran in for support.

Carter grinned sheepishly at Reese, probably not even seeing Tillie. He shrugged. "I wanted to make a grand gesture that said I love you."

CHAPTER NINETEEN

The wedding

"ALL RIGHT, ladies and gentlemen, boys and girls, let's welcome Mr. and Mrs. Carter Trombley to the dance floor!"

Tillie clapped her hands and let out a whoop-whoop as the happy couple started the steps to the "Electric Slide." Reese had decided to wear her mother's wedding dress and style her hair in a romantic bun.

The wedding guests were decked out as their invitation suggested—in black, white or red attire. The wedding barn was decorated in a charming country style. Someone had recently added an enchanting water wheel outfitted with silver trays that were now filled with a variety of wedding favors—succulent baskets, chocolate bells and friendship horseshoes.

Now that the ceremony was over and the wedding license signed, Tillie was able to breathe easier and enjoy herself. All she had to do was complete the group wedding dance, and then she could relax.

"You know Carter's grand gesture was my idea, right?" Keith's voice eased into Tillie's ear, his breath warm as it flowed over her neck. "The wedding wouldn't have happened without me."

Tillie rolled her eyes. "Okay, all right. The grand gesture was your idea." They'd been having a back-and-forth about this all afternoon. "But banning all photography and cell phones was my idea. There's no way they would have gotten married if anyone and everyone could take their picture."

Not when Carter had gotten the same orange spray tan as Reese.

Oh, that had won over Reese, all right. Add to that Carter's suggestion that they take her fancy wedding dress and his tuxedo with them on their Caribbean honeymoon, and the problem of wedding pictures for the grandkids was solved.

And even though Reese was over the moon with happiness, Tillie didn't believe she'd pulled off what she'd meant to when she arrived five days ago. Was this really a happy ending? Was Uncle Boone going to offer her the job? He hadn't said.

But now wasn't the time for woolgathering.

Tillie grabbed Keith's hand. "Come on. This is our cue."

Keith grimaced. But he danced his way out there, looking like a candidate for a Western

James Bond in his black tuxedo and black cowboy hat.

"Turn," she told him, guiding him through the part he never seemed to get right.

And maybe she held on to Keith's hand a little too tightly and a little too long. But Tillie knew this was their last night together. Keith had had all afternoon to talk to her. And he'd done nothing more than gently flirt. He knew, just as she did, that this was the definitive end to their unfinished business.

"Turn," Tillie told Keith again.

The rest of the bridal party joined them on the dance floor.

"You look awfully pretty tonight, Til," Keith said, blue eyes showing his appreciation.

"I bet you're required to say that, given you're hero support to the maid of honor." She couldn't quite hold back a grin. "Turn."

"I'm required to say the pretty part." His grin was devilish. "But I added the *awfully* adverb because I'm smitten."

He's smitten? How many of those whiskey punch drinks did he have? "Turn."

The parents of the bride and groom came sliding in, along with Gran and Shay. Everyone who'd been here all week was on the dance floor, even dear, sweet Crystal. Oh, she'd put up a weak argument—*my ruby red dress will clash with my orange skin tone*—but she'd wanted to be here, finally putting forth the idea that, "Orange is the new pink." Crystal was willing to bite the bullet for Reese. And Tillie was proud of her for doing so.

"What's going on in that head of yours?" Keith asked, lips dangerously close to Tillie's cheek.

"I was thinking about Crystal. Turn."

"I like following your lead. But Crystal?" Keith pulled a face. "You're thinking about Crystal when it's me who's in front of you?"

"Exactly." Tillie pulled him off the dance floor, as everyone else left, too. "It's been a long week and I have a lot on my mind."

The bride and groom began a slow dance, having ditched the idea of tumbling and lifts.

"But you're not thinking…about me?" He frowned.

"Don't frown at the bride and groom." Tillie took her thumb and forefinger and pressed his cheeks upward until he gave her that easy-going smile she liked so much.

"I told you I was smitten," Keith said, taking her hand and pressing a kiss to her palm. "Smitten. Not a kitten. And I'm not talking about claws."

Carter and Reese were dancing together as if this entire disastrous week had never happened. They were looking into each other's eyes as if they couldn't believe how lucky they were to be married and in love with each other. And—

"Woman." Keith drew Tillie into the circle of

his arms. "I have been taking baby steps with you all day. Being sweet and amenable. And all you've done is treat me like I'm...*your friend*."

"You are my friend." But Tillie's heart went *ka-thump, ka-thump*. "You have to be my friend because tomorrow I head back to Clementine and you—"

"I'm going back to Clementine with you."

Ka-thump, ka-thump, ka-thump, ka-thump!

"Is it time?" Shay appeared at Tillie's side, shoving her glasses in a lopsided slant on her nose. She wore the sweetest ruby red dress with shiny red shoes, an outfit that Dorothy Gale from *The Wizard of Oz* would envy. Sophie Jean had put up her blond hair in a sweet French braid. And Reese had given Shay a single yellow and orange calla lily from her bouquet, which Shay kept clutched in one hand.

"It's not time to leave yet," Tillie told her daughter, fixing the set of her thick glasses. "We haven't had cake."

"Cake! Oh, yeah. I almost forgot." Shay clutched her flower and gave Keith a sly smile.

"Did I miss it?" Gran appeared next to them. She wore a simple black dress and had a black sequined pillbox hat perched at a stylish angle on her head.

"Miss what? The bouquet toss?" Tillie stopped looking at her family and stared up into the laughing eyes of the cowboy who'd won and lost and won her heart again. She was going to store her heart somewhere safe this time. But as she focused on Keith, suspicion gathered in her throat, along with fear. "Are you... Are you going to propose?"

"We all are." Keith gave Gran and Shay a nod.

Shay grinned and rushed forward.

As the music ended, all three dropped down on one knee.

Well, Keith helped Gran down to both knees.

"What's going on?" Tillie demanded, although in a lower voice than she might have normally used when things were out of her control.

"I thought you said you'd wait for us." Reese rushed over, tugging Carter with her.

Brad joined them. "Sorry I was late. Woodburn was trying to set me up with his granddaughter."

"Should I get down?" Tillie started to crouch but the group surrounding her all cried, *"No!"*

The DJ wasn't playing any music. People were starting to stare. The rest of the bridal party was closing ranks, smiling as if they were in on... whatever this was.

"Tillie Powell, I have loved you for most of my life." Keith stared up at Tillie with adoration shining in his blue eyes. "I loved you when we were friends. And I loved you from the moment your lips touched mine."

Okay, this is a proposal. Definitely a proposal.

"And if I've learned anything over the past few

days, it's that when you love someone, you need to gather them close and keep them in your circle."

This is NOT a marriage proposal.

Tillie didn't know whether to laugh or cry.

Shay lost her balance and stumbled into Keith, who righted her and asked her if she was all right. "You're taking too long" was Shay's answer.

Tillie decided to laugh-cry.

Keith's smile softened. "The boys and I have been talking and—"

No proposal of marriage involved consultations with brothers.

People were murmuring and shushing each other. Tillie was thankful they all had to drop their cell phones upon entry or she was certain someone would have been live streaming this...this...

What is this?

"We'd like to offer you a job," Keith finished.

"A job?" The world became a blur of red, white and black. Her vision swam. "This is...is a *job* proposal?"

"Yes," Keith answered calmly, smile never wavering. "We're moving Sunny Y'all to Clementine and we need a director of operations."

"Someone who sees the cracks in a plan," Brad said.

"Someone who keeps things running smoothly," Carter said.

"Someone who doesn't let others push her around," Reese said.

"They need a mama," Shay summarized.

"But what about the buy-out?" Tillie tried really hard to find her footing.

A hand closed around hers, steadying her. Keith's hand. "We realized that we're selling our intellectual property, patents and production schematics for the solar ear tags. But not the company name."

"Bully for you." The world was beginning to come back online. But Tillie's cheeks were hot, probably as red as her dress, and she wasn't able to field a smile.

He's not proposing marriage?

Oh, he could be so annoying!

Tillie drew a deep breath. "Thank you for the offer. When I receive a copy in writing, I'll review it and give you an answer in due course."

Gran scoffed. "Kids nowadays. I've never read the fine print on any job I've ever accepted."

"I'll give you time to consider the job offer, Tillie," Keith said, ignoring the elderly heckler next to him. "I know you don't want to just jump into something. I'll also be submitting a prospectus for your review."

"A…a what?"

"A summary of my financial standing." Keith smiled up at her with that mischievous grin.

Ka-thump. Ka-thump.

"I want you to know what you're getting when you marry me." He tucked Shay close to his side.

"When I marry you, Shay and Velma, I mean. Because you're a package deal. And I know where I stand in the pecking order."

"Just south of me," Gran teased.

"Are you through?" Tillie asked, knowing he wasn't, but she becoming overwhelmed with everything he was laying out on the table.

Keith shook his head. "Nope. I haven't asked you properly. But I wanted to present my case, not rush and put the cart before the horse."

"Smidge before Hercules," Shay said, looking thoughtful.

"That's right," Keith told Shay. And then he stared up at Tillie with all the love she'd ever hoped to see in those bright blue orbs. "Tillie Powell, I love you from the top of my head to the tips of my toes. Will you do the honor of becoming my fiancée with the intent of marrying me when you're good and ready?" Keith cleared his throat and for the first time since he'd taken to one knee, looked uncomfortable, unsure. "That is, if you love me the way I love you."

Tillie laughed. She grinned. She made eye contact with every person gathered around them.

These people… They were her family.

And Keith… He was the apple of her eye. The man that made her heart *ka-thump* and her head hurt trying to figure out how they could spend their lives together.

"Yes. Yes, I love you, Keith, from the top of my

head to the tips of my toes. And yes, I'll marry you. I'll marry you on our timeline, one we work through together."

Keith got to his feet and drew her into his arms. "Now this… This is the way the best man and the maid of honor make a love pact." And then he kissed her. He kissed her with the promise of many more, with the idea that their love would last through good times and bad, in sickness and in health, and forevermore.

Cheers went up all around them.

And finally, Tillie felt like she'd gotten to the end of the week the way she'd wanted to at the start: with a happy ending.

EPILOGUE

Monday, five days before Keith and Tillie's wedding

"WHAT DO YOU THINK?" Keith asked Tillie, showing her his computer screen.

Tillie studied the production schematics she'd learned how to read in the past two years of directing operations at Clementine-based Sunny Y'all. "It's ambitious."

Keith scoffed. "That's what everyone says about breakthrough innovations. Look again. This is important to me."

"To us," Tillie murmured, taking another look, this time resting her hand on Keith's shoulder as she peered at the computer screen. "It's not going to be affordable until we scale up production and we can't scale up production until—"

"We get approval from the government." Keith turned his head and kissed her cheek. "Shouldn't you be out relaxing? The wedding is in five days."

Tillie shook her head. "We have two products

launching soon. Brad's visiting our manufactoring partners this week and I told him I'd be available if we need anything." Authorizations for additional spending (she hoped not), delays in the timeline (also on her hope-not list), failed quality control tests (that would be a disaster). Tillie was truly a worst-case scenario thinker. Even Uncle Boone said so. He regretted not hiring her. "Carter's out at a trade show selling the equine cooling boots and I promised him I'd overnight any special orders he had. And then there's you. The company CEO. You've always got to throw a wrench in the works." Tillie kissed the top of his head and ran her fingers through the brown curls at his nape, straightening when she heard the sound of approaching footsteps.

"Mama!" Shay ran into their office. Her blond hair was a tangle beneath her pink cowboy hat. She wore a basketball jersey over her blue jeans and her glasses... She wore specially designed prototype lenses from Sunny Y'all that had a sports band to keep them in place. "I'm home. Let's celebrate our wedding to Keith with a ride."

"Why does everyone want me out of the office?" Tillie looked from Keith to Shay, then back again. "What are you two up to?"

"Nothing." Keith bent to examine Shay's lenses. "How were they in school today?"

Shay framed the glasses she'd only been wearing since Saturday with both hands. "They're so cool. Every sporty kid wants a pair 'cuz they don't slip. But Daddy-O, I can see." She touched her hand to his forehead. "I can see you, right here in front of me."

Tillie thought she might cry. She sniffed.

She'd already cried bucketloads. She'd cried when Keith told her at Reese's wedding that he wanted to create special lenses for people with Shay's condition. He had an idea to harness the power of artificial intelligence to take the images in front of Shay—the ones she couldn't see because of that black hole at the center of her eyesight—and project them through curved lenses to the sides of her retina where her brain processed her vision.

Tillie had cried with each failed prototype. And then finally, last weekend, Keith had emerged from his workshop with the pair Shay wore today. They looked like curved ski goggles. But they worked. They worked!

The primary problem was cost, per the schematics Keith had shown her just now. The secondary problem was entering a new market. They weren't versed in the medical field.

But like everything else, Tillie considered those short-term problems. The team at Sunny Y'all would solve them. Together. The same way they'd solved their differences two years ago to pull off Reese and Carter's wedding. They were all going on a work retreat at the Ambling Horse

Prairie Resort to strengthen those bonds, just as soon as they could coordinate everyone's schedule

A photograph of their friends and family from Reese and Carter's first anniversary caught her eye. Even Crystal had made the effort to attend. Tillie and Crystal had become fast friends. Tillie was going to serve as one of her bridesmaids next year.

"Come on, Mama. Let's go for a ride." With a conspiratorial look at Keith, Shay took Tillie's hand, not taking no for an answer. "Gran's having coffee in town with Grandma Mary." Keith's foster mother.

Keith followed them downstairs and out the door into the brisk February sunshine.

"I know you two are up to something." Tillie glanced at her two, dear troublemakers. "We're not getting baby goats, are we? They're too much trouble. Especially during wedding weeks."

Neither Shay nor Keith said a word. They kept walking with her toward the barn.

"You did not get me a new horse. Jam is a spring chicken at twelve. I'm having none of that."

Silence. Oh, those two were thick as thieves with a secret.

"I thought we were going for a ride. Are we not going for a ride?" Tillie tried to hide a smile when they didn't answer, resolving herself to taking the surprise whenever they decided to give it to her. Just like she had with Keith's wedding proposal.

They traipsed through the barn until they reached the last stall.

"Mama, you know how much I like cookie-selling season." Shay opened the stall door to reveal a large vending machine. "Daddy-O and me have an idea."

"I'm not sure the Holly Explorers council will approve of this," Tillie said slowly, hanging back. "Troopers are supposed to sell face-to-face."

"Did you know there's an engineering badge?" Keith wrapped an arm around Tillie and brought her closer to the stall.

"So… A cookie vending machine is for a badge, not to sell cookies?" Adorable as these two were, Tillie was still pragmatic when it came to rules.

The two inventors exchanged guilty glances.

"It's for a badge," Keith said in his compromising voice. "Maybe, someday, it'll be more."

"I want to sell more cookies and break the record," Shay said, staring right at Tillie. "But you said I can't go door-to-door."

"We put our heads together." Keith drew Tillie closer still. "And if we earn the badge and the attention of the council, maybe in the coming years, Shay can go for that sales record."

Tillie blew out a breath, feeling herself cave. "Where would you put a machine like that?"

"The feed store, the thrift store, bunkhouses at the larger ranches." Grinning, Shay ticked potential locations off on her little fingers. "Oh, and the teacher's lounge at school."

"We did our research," Keith said with pride. "Shay asked around while we were running errands."

Shay seemed to grin harder. "Daddy-O said you wouldn't let us try it if we didn't do our research."

How do they read me so well? I'm outnumbered here.

"Well… Maybe. If it's only for a badge…" Tillie allowed slowly. "I'm just trying to predict the council's reaction. Cookie sales in a machine would need to be divided amongst the troops. And some troops might consider it an unfair advantage."

Shay's grin fell.

"I'm just trying to think ahead, pumpkin." Tillie was always trying to think ahead nowadays. "And work out if Daddy-O has time to do this with you."

"You sound indecisive." Keith's grin was easygoing. "We could always decide with a round of rock, paper, scissors."

Tillie shook her head. "You've been beating me far too often at that game."

Keith and Shay shared another glance with a secret meeting. They'd become so very close, forging a relationship Tillie considered a blessing. Not every man could open his heart to a child that wasn't biologically his. And Shay… She'd come up with a nickname for Keith that honored his role in her life all on her own.

I'm so lucky.

"You two…" Tillie began in a tight voice as tears unexpectedly spilled over her cheeks. "You aren't supposed to make the bride cry during her wedding week."

They came together for a group hug, a family hug, a secure hug.

This is my life. These are my loves.

Tillie was supposed to be in control but whenever she thought she was, Keith and Shay threw her for a loop.

But she wouldn't have it any other way.

* * * * *

*For more great romances in
The Cowboy Academy miniseries,
visit www.Harlequin.com today!*